THE
BUTCHER

THE
BUTCHER

LAURA
KAT YOUNG

TITAN BOOKS

The Butcher
Print edition ISBN: 9781789099034
E-book edition ISBN: 9781789099041

Published by Titan Books
A division of Titan Publishing Group Ltd.
144 Southwark Street, London SE1 0UP
www.titanbooks.com

First Titan edition: September 2022

10 9 8 7 6 5 4 3 2 1

A CIP catalogue record for this title is available
from the British Library.

Printed and bound by CPI Group (UK) Ltd, Croydon CR0 4YY

For Violet, Ilsa, and James.
I love you always

PART ONE

BEQUEATH

1

When Lady Mae went into the kitchen to wash the dishes, she found that her mother had left her kit at home. It sat on her mother's side of the old, worn table, inches from where Lady Mae stood. Though she had been taught from as far back as she could remember that inside the kit were her mother's work tools—the ones for people in any case—lately, when Lady Mae found herself in the presence of the kit, there was a knocking at her breast and a speeding in her heart. The kit itself was small and ordinary, no bigger than the book containing Settlement Five's bylaws. Alone, there on the table, the tools inside the kit remained harmless. But in her mother's hands—and soon also her own—they commanded what Lady Mae had taken for respect. And that's what it was, right? The bowed heads, the quiet that fell on the square when she and her mother walked into town. It was absolution, a kind of credence. Her mother had explained it to her over and over. *It ain't always like it seems. Right now it's me, but soon it'll be you. They don't know no better.* Maybe they didn't, maybe they did. Maybe what they knew was so heavy and frightening, that to even look in the direction of it was impossible. And so when Lady Mae and her mother passed the other residents as they stood still on their porches with brooms in hand, their eyes stayed at the women's feet lest they let it show.

Lady Mae stood next to the table and looked down at the kit. Its forgotten presence in itself did not cause Lady Mae alarm—perhaps today her mother was only working on the livestock and the tools she needed, bigger and sharper, were hanging on hooks in the back of the depot by the livestock pen. But if her job that day was an atonement, and her kit was still there in the shack—Lady Mae resolved that she'd bring it to the depot. If her mother had to return to the shack and fetch them, the Deputies might come around. They'd been worse lately, too, or so it seemed. But then another thought crossed her mind. In the seventeen years she'd been alive, Lady Mae had never disobeyed her mother purposefully. Not once, not ever. But that morning as the hot wind blew up against the kitchen window, she pulled out her mother's rickety chair and sat down. She dragged the kit toward her, saw the cracked and shredded leather by the clasp. It looked like the skin of a fish salted and left to dry, and Lady

Mae ran her fingers along the spine. She would leave her shack shortly and make the walk to the depot, but first she wanted to see what was inside.

The clasp was cool on her fingertips. There was no lock and key, no numerical combination to open it up. She simply pressed down on the horseshoe-shaped latch, and it popped open. Lady Mae opened it slowly, and as she did, saw firsthand what she had long known was in there: small tools made of shiny metal and buck-horned handles each in their own sleeve. She lifted out the scalpel. It was heavier than she expected it to be, and though its blade was no bigger than her smallest finger, she was careful. Even without touching it, it was sharp enough to cut through skin and muscle with ease.

Lady Mae went from left to right picking up and examining each tool—the clamp, the saw, the tourniquet, the file, the bone cutter. Each had its own purpose, but there at the table in the midmorning light, they did not seem big or weighty enough to remove a finger or a hand or an entire leg—how could her mother adequately do her job with such rudimentary tools? How would Lady Mae be expected to do so as well in less than a year? She looked at her hands, and though they were dry and cracked they were young still: would they be strong enough when the time came? If she wasn't strong enough, where would it come from? Maybe she already had it. Maybe she was born with it, bequeathed from mother to daughter like everything else.

Lady Mae closed the kit and secured the clasp. She stood from the table, the chair creaking as it released her weight. It was nearly half past nine, and her lessons with Arbuckle started promptly after lunch. She'd have to be quick if she wished to make it back with enough time to ready herself for his arrival. Moving quickly, she took off her apron and pushed her dark curls up into her bonnet. Then she tucked the old kit underneath her arm and left the shack.

The day was already warm. The wind that blew from the west was hot and dry. Dust swirled around her, and the bottom of her skirts dragged along the dirt road. She couldn't remember the last time it had rained; the hills that were usually lush and verdant were the color of silt. If lightning struck, the flames would easily catch and quickly blanket the hills with their orange light. There was no water between the hills and Settlement Five, and there wasn't enough in the well to do anything besides put out a stove fire or two. The drought was unsettling, but Lady Mae and her mother had lived through worse. And their rations did not dwindle like that of the other residents' in times of duress, though Lady Mae wished they did; receiving anything from the Deputies—especially that which the other residents did not get—made her sick.

The first rock struck the small of her back. It didn't hurt, but she knew what it was and kept her eyes down to the ground. Her mother had told her: if the other children, especially the younger ones, saw how much their actions pained her, how it tormented her, they would never relent. And so she tried to ignore them as the pebbles and sticks soared through the air toward her. Instead, she focused on the tips of her boots and the way her fingernails felt on her palms, pressing into the skin until it was as though they would slice right through. The children called after her, their voices whirling together like a cyclone, trapping her in the middle of the road. A rock flew past her head. Another hit her in the shoulder. Laughter floated past her ears, and she looked to her right, catching a small body disappearing behind one of the shacks. It mattered not who it was—they were all the same: vile, unseemly beasts that had taunted and teased Lady Mae ever since she could remember.

She kept walking, digging her heels down in the dirt faster and faster until she was nearly running, tripping over laces that had become untied and kicking up the dust around her. She could see the depot down the road, its door open. Maybe her mother was watching and would come running out quick, throwing her body onto her daughter's to protect her as she always had, as she had always promised she would.

"Your mother's the devil!"

"You the devil!"

Lady Mae's pulse skipped. A sudden sweat appeared at her hairline. The sun shone down, and there was the flash of metal off the tin roofs to her right. The children were better when her mother was around, who had more than once grabbed one by the ears or the collar and dragged them back to their own shack kicking and screaming. Their parents behaved accordingly, whipping and haranguing their children in front of the butcher in hopes it might lessen their own sentence when it came time. But her mother was not there in the dust with Lady Mae, and any elder that stood behind the tattered curtains of their front window offered nothing but a quiet disappearance from view. *Did they hurt you too, Mama?*

"I'm gonna cut off your fingers one by one!"

"I'm gonna make you eat them!"

She should've started running toward the depot, but in that moment, there in the road not ten meters from her shack, she stopped walking. As the rocks continued to belt her back, she lifted her arms to protect her head. But it was of no use. Someone had thrown one high in the air, and as it fell from above it landed squarely upon the top of her skull. Her body went limp and collapsed to the ground, and the children around her cried out joyfully, hatefully, their disgust seething in their veins. They had gotten the butcher's daughter, maimed her as their parents had been. An eye for an eye, just as the Deputies preached.

"Scum!"

"You ain't wanted!"

The children crowded around her in a circle. They shouted at her, kicked rocks and dirt into her face. They pulled her long curls out from under her bonnet and stomped on her back. They thought they had won—the butcher's daughter lay prostrate on the ground—but as their taunting let up, as they turned to walk away, Lady Mae dragged herself up out of the dust. She crawled first to her hands and knees and spat. She put her hand to her skull, the warm blood stuck between strands of hair. The children stared at her, nudged each other with their elbows and walked back, silent and wondering, toward Lady Mae.

"I ain't afraid. You ain't nothing to me."

Her lips moved, and she heard her own voice as the words drifted in the still summer air. The children stopped moving and stood, hands hanging from their sides, their tiny fists clutching stones. They watched Lady Mae stand up and take a step forward, slowly, purposefully, dragging her back foot to meet her front. She took another step, and then another and another still. Closer and closer she got to the beasts, their eyes, their little bodies, their heads shifting toward one another, unsure of what to do, as though scared that they weren't as strong as they thought. She was Lady Mae, the butcher's daughter, after all. But what they couldn't know is that something had unmoored inside of her, and as the hot wind blew the dust up around her, she wiped the blood from her mouth, leaving a grotesque smear that went down the edge of her chin. The children, who thought themselves safe from any punishments—safe because Lady Mae had never told the Deputies of the treatment she endured—saw a flicker in her eyes, as if a wave of electricity had suddenly swelled up from deep down. She'd felt the rush before, many times in fact, but always it seemed too dangerous to embrace. When it bubbled up, she tried to push it back down for it went against her mother's words instilled in her so long ago. It ain't going to change nothing, her mother had said. You're better than that, Lady Mae, she'd said, those kids need forgiveness just like everyone else. But in that moment, Lady Mae wondered if she was any better than the savages and how hard she could throw a fist-sized rock and how much blood would pour from their small heads. They didn't deserve forgiveness, and Lady Mae was tired of blaming her injuries on chores, the woodpile, her own clumsiness. Her mother never believed her anyway. She was tired of running, and so as she squared her body toward the small group of children, she felt her fear unravel and make its way out of her.

"You better watch I don't tell my ma," she said. "Assault's against the law."

She'd never spoken to the children other than to yell *stop you can't no please*. She'd never threatened them, and because of that they thought themselves invincible. Maybe they were. But maybe she was, too. After all, she had come from her mother, had inherited her eyes and mouth and high cheekbones; might she also have gotten the same strength that allowed her mother to go to the depot day in and day out?

"You ain't gonna say nothing. We'll make sure of that," a boy called. It was the older Thompson boy, the meanest one, and he stood stuffed into an old shirt, dirt on his cheeks. He was ugly, and it wasn't just because he was cruel. The younger one—too young to understand just how awful his brother was—ran up to Lady Mae and pushed her hard back onto the ground. Edith Cummings, the only girl in the group, threw a handful of gravel at her face. But Lady Mae, whose ears still rang and with eyes still blurry, rose to her knees again, the tiny stones cutting through her skirts, and looked the awful girl in the eyes.

"I ain't afraid."

She brushed the dirt from her hands. But she was weak, and the children were losing interest, calling to one another to leave her, that she ain't nothing, nothing but a poor girl whose mother ought to be hanged. As quickly as it had churned through her, the strength vanished, and in its place she felt the familiar fear, the sticky panic underneath her fingernails.

"Come on," yelled Balthazar Jones. "Let's get out of here." Being the oldest he gave the orders and the others listened. They backed away slowly, keeping their eyes on the butcher's daughter. When they were far enough away, they turned and broke into a run.

"We'll get you, Lady Mae! Ain't nowhere to hide."

"Come and get me," she called after them too softly for them to hear. "Come and get me if you think you can."

And as they disappeared from her view she felt her body again, bloodied and bruised. She rose to her feet, each step like fire whipping around her bones. She turned in the direction of the depot and began walking, knowing that when her mother saw her she would take Lady Mae into her arms and press her head against her chest. There she would hear the rhythmic beating of her mother's heart, the life inside of her undeterred. But as Lady Mae approached the depot, she slowed. What would she say to her mother this time? How would she explain the blood, the bruises, the torn dress? Lady Mae didn't know how to hold the rage that had filled her—her mother hadn't taught her that—and she could not tell her mother of the burning resolve she'd felt to fight back, how though she'd felt it before, this time it was different. *You ain't give me words for it, Mama.*

She walked gingerly up the depot's porch steps, her feet heavy and hot. The door was open, but before Lady Mae called to her mother, she heard a man's voice, low and growly. Peering through the window, she saw her mother bent over the man. Her mother's back was to the window, and the man sat in the chair, a tourniquet around his forearm. Her mother held a saw in her left hand—the same kind of saw that was in her kit—and the sun, which had just lifted high in the sky, glinted off the blade. The man sat still. Lady Mae ducked down and leaned her back up against the splintered wood of the shack. She wasn't allowed in the depot, not ever, and most likely she'd be in trouble if she was found peering in through the window. So she crouched and listened to her mother's voice.

"You move the worse it'll be," her mother said.

"I ain't gonna move," the man said.

"That's what you said last time."

"Just do it already."

"On three, then. One, two—"

There was a choking scream, one that gurgled far back in the man's throat, and then Lady Mae heard a familiar sound, a grinding of metal to bone that was not unlike that which she heard when it was her turn to clean the chicken for a special meal. She listened: four, five, six, seven, eight, nine. And then her mother's voice humming softly. In the sky, a small murder of crows bent and rippled, but none cried out.

She looked down at her own fingers and wondered how many layers of skin and muscle and bone there were. Would hers be warm and sticky where the skin pulled back, the phalanges jagged and sharp? What if the blood wouldn't still and it flowed out of her until she was as dry as the earth? She felt a tightness in her jaw and the bubbling of spit in the back of her throat. Earlier that morning as she watched her mother ready herself for the day, she had wanted her mother's hands to cup her face as she used to and tell her it was nothing, that it was just part of her job, that the patients really did deserve their atonements. But instead, her mother had grabbed her daughter's wrists with each of her hands so tightly that Lady Mae saw the blood slowing as her mother's knuckles turned white. Their arms held there, heavy and alike, in the empty space between their bodies. Lady Mae did not dare pull away.

"You must believe," her mother had said. "You must trust. But above all, you must be careful of the questions you ask; the wrong one can lead you to the butcher, even if it's me."

Lady Mae lay the kit next to the door and crept away from the depot. The man in the chair—she hadn't expected that, though she couldn't be sure of what she expected. She knew what her mother did and that she was quick with it; whether it was an animal or a person, her hands were steady and precise. It was both exactly and completely unlike what Lady Mae had envisioned in her mind. Her mother had looked exquisitely barbaric standing over the man in the chair, her toes inches away from the blood on the floor. She knew there was blood—always there was blood; there wasn't a single dress of her mother's that didn't have faded stains on the sleeves. But that wasn't what had jarred Lady Mae—it had been her mother's singing, the song she then recognized as the one her mother sang her when she was hurt or tired or sad; it was her mother's job to maim, to console, and it would soon be Lady Mae's job, too.

Although she walked home from the depot quickly, Arbuckle was already waiting outside her door. As she crossed the road, she watched him fan himself with his hat. Even from far away, his straight nose, his shoulders that were broad and thick were familiar. She didn't want him to see her so ragged and maimed, and so she kept her head down. It was no use, though; he would certainly notice her injuries, as he was no stranger to mistreatment himself. He knew the difference between the mark of a hoof and that of a fist.

"Afternoon," Arbuckle called. "I was just wondering where—" He stopped short as she came into view. "Lady Mae!" he cried, straightening up quickly and putting his hat back on. "What happened?"

"It's no bother." She walked up the porch steps and past him to her door. "Just some kids. Ain't nothing I can't handle."

She avoided his eyes and swung the door wide so that she was not in his way when he walked over the threshold. She kept the left side of her face turned away from him and tilted down toward the ground. It made no difference for as he walked into the cool, dark shack he stopped and brought his hand to her cheek. The touch—kind and without motive—was electric on her skin. She looked up at him, at his worried brown eyes that she knew wished her a different life, and held his stare as best she could.

"Let me at least tend to it," he said. He had questions, questions he would never ask aloud. She knew what they were and had long practiced her answers to them, hoping that the right words would convince him that what her mother did—what she'd have to do in a year's time—was necessary. That's what the Deputies said. People needed to eat just as much as they needed to repent. Arbuckle's gentle hand slid down her face to her chin and held it gingerly. He stared at her for a moment and then brushed his soft thumb across the crusted blood that had dripped down from her head onto her cheek. She looked away to her left and pushed his hand from her face, but before she did her fingers felt his warm skin. She could not help but let her tears fall.

"Want me to go after them?" he asked as he stood before her. "Because I will. I ain't afraid of them. They nothing but kids."

"I wouldn't want you to risk it. Ain't no way my mama could give you atonements. Just as well be me." She wiped her eyes with the back of her hand.

"I wouldn't do nothing but talk."

"Talking's just as likely to get you in the chair as anything else."

"I ain't afraid, heck, someone ought to be saying something."

"And that someone shouldn't be you, Arbuckle. What would my ma think? Might not let you come around anymore."

"But Lady Mae, you know I don't believe—"

"I know, I know. But just leave it be. Won't always be like this."

Lady Mae could not remember a time in her life without Arbuckle, who was only two years older than her. He'd been coming around since he was small—four, five perhaps—and she was hard-pressed to conjure up a memory that he wasn't in. She saw him nearly every day, and the days that he did not come by seemed long and dreary. He helped her with arithmetic beyond what her mother could, and in return, he received a small payment that Lady Mae knew he used for rations. His father spent their allowance on mash, filling up bottles instead of cupboards. He was the only friend she had ever had, the only one who did not hate or fear her, did not spit and hurl when she came near. Perhaps it was because Arbuckle himself knew the scorn of others; after all, many were maimed at his father's cannery just as much as they were at the depot. His father had on many occasions failed to check the belt line before turning it on. Hands caught and fingers sliced off, falling to the factory's floor with a quiet thump. This angered the law-abiding workers who were often mistaken for criminals, their missing limbs and digits betraying their innocence.

"You go on and clean up in the kitchen. I'll fetch some bandages," Arbuckle said as he walked through the doorway and placed his hat on the small table that held an oil lamp and an empty egg basket.

"It's fine. I mean it. I ain't going to have you play medic."

"Go on."

Lady Mae did as he said and went into the kitchen. She ladled out several cups of water into a bowl, and as the sediment swirled she dipped a towel in it and brought it to her face She wiped first her cheek and then held it to her head. The rough linen stung, and she dabbed at her hair and scalp tenderly but quick.

"Here," Arbuckle said and came up behind her holding a piece of fabric and a small piece of adhesive.

"That won't stick," she said. "Just leave it."

"Sure you don't want me to do nothing?" Arbuckle

asked. He put his hands on her shoulders and squeezed them lightly.

"It'll just make it worse." She pulled away from him feeling not for the first time a tumbling deep inside.

"I don't know. Seems to me *this* is worse. They'd get atonements for sure."

"Says you who goes on and on about how those atonements are bad."

"This ain't what I meant. Situations like this—"

"They'll stop when it's my turn."

Arbuckle didn't respond, and Lady Mae knew that would end the conversation. He didn't like talking about when she'd take over at the depot. He thought atonements purposeless and cruel—wouldn't say it directly to her, not as such, but all that thinking had to go somewhere. Arbuckle wasn't wrong; after all, he'd seen his father go to the depot many times—small grievances over the use of a pasture, the stealing of another's livestock, drinking too much and fighting in the square. Arbuckle's father had not fingers, but ten stubs of differing lengths, and said as long as he could still open a jug of ale it was no matter to him. But his visits had not cured him of his meanness, and Arbuckle knew this well.

"Does it look that bad?"

His face softened, the stony disapproval vanishing. He took her chin into his fingers delicately. "Ain't no hiding it."

"I'll say I wasn't paying attention when I was cleaning the coop." She reached up and took his hand from her chin, holding his fingers between hers for a heartbeat, a breath, a blink. Then she let it fall to his side.

"She won't believe it," he told her and pulled out the chair at the kitchen table. "You know she can't do nothing if you don't report it."

"I ain't need any more reasons for something like this to happen."

Arbuckle sat down and breathed out slowly. His brow creased, his mouth twisting as if trying to keep inside the things they both knew not to talk about. "Up to you," he said.

She licked her lips and felt the dried crumbs of blood, tasted her coppery insides. Arbuckle didn't need to say anything for Lady Mae to hear him; the disapproval hung between his eyebrows. His jawbones rose and fell by his ears, the taste of worry fresh in his mouth. She tasted it, too; he was right as he always was.

He put his sack on the kitchen table and took out the book for the day. They were studying algebra, and he pulled out a small abacus as well, its wooden beads worn smooth from years of use. She was good at arithmetic, but what was in her mind was of little consequence; what would matter when she turned of age would be her hands, the steadiness of her long, slender fingers. Most important would be her constitution, and she knew this. If it were of salt like her mother's she might be able to saw down to the last fragment, but if it weren't, if it were mired—then what?

"You going to be able to do lessons today?" he asked, untying his kerchief. He blotted his forehead and his upper lip with it before opening the book to where they had left off the day before.

"Looks worse than it is. Come on."

"Alright. Don't say I didn't warn you."

"And don't say I didn't listen."

He traced his finger down the thin page of the book. "I've got one for you."

"Ain't no problem no matter which way you figure."

She'd been schooled at home—and always at home—since she could hold a pencil; she often found problems Arbuckle proclaimed difficult quite easy, and in her he'd met his match.

"At 1.62 ½ per cord, what would be the cost of a pile of wood 24 feet long, 4 feet wide, and 6 foot 3 inches high?" Arbuckle asked.

She took to her abacus then, sliding beads up and down and grabbing a pencil, wrote out an equation that Arbuckle had taught her a few months back. She quickly went back to the abacus to make a correction.

"Seven dollars, sixty-eight cents," said Lady Mae.

Arbuckle flipped to the back of his primer to check the answer and smiled. "Right you are," he said. And then, "That's a lot of wood."

"Like Willard's stack—always peeking out. Aren't you scared when you walk by?"

"No. It ain't nothing to me," he said and shook his head. "No such thing as ghosts."

"Says you."

Her eyes dropped back down to the abacus for a moment. *What if I can't, Mama.*

"Arbuckle, can I ask you something?"

"You know you can." He put the primer down and rested his elbows on the table, his hands clasped lightly together. Lady Mae felt young and foolish, the lump in her throat belying her demeanor.

"Your pa ever say anything to you after he sees her?"

"Like what?"

"Don't know. Just anything, I guess. How she acts or what she says, maybe, if she says anything at all." She twisted her fingers around one another as she spoke, tugging and pulling on her skin as if the answer she sought was just underneath.

Arbuckle leaned his head back and looked at the beamed ceiling, blackened from years of chimney smoke. "Well, I don't know. Not that I can think directly." He kept his dark eyes focused on the ceiling, and Lady Mae knew he was lying. Of course his father said things—they all said things. And of course he'd never tell her, never hurt or upset her knowingly. He'd grown up protecting her, putting both his mouth and body in between her and the rotten children that circled her.

"Will you tell me if he does?" she asked, hoping he'd never have anything to tell her.

"I sure will."

She sat there and stared at the abacus on the table while Arbuckle flipped through the pages of the primer trying to find a problem that would stand up to Lady Mae's mind. It was hot, and though the windows were open as far as they'd go, sweat dripped from both of them.

"I'll get us something to drink." She jumped up and went to the icebox, which was cool but not cold as they'd not had ice since the drought started, but at least the sweet tea would feel good on the throat. She poured out two glassfuls and set them on the table.

Arbuckle lifted the glass and brought it to his lips, sipping gingerly and with relief. "You and your ma sure do—"

"She was acting funny this morning." Lady Mae picked up her tea and pressed her hot palms against the sides of the glass.

"What you mean?"

"Don't know exactly. Quiet, I guess."

But what she wanted to tell him was that morning, as she had been helping her mother hook her corset to the hidden band of buttons on her skirt, she noticed something fall out of her mother's skirt and onto the floor. Lady Mae bent to pick the thing up off the floor—from where she stood it looked like a thimble—

but when she put it between her fingers it was smooth and hard. Since it was dim in her mother's room with the curtains drawn closed, she brought it close to her face. At first, she thought it was a dried piece of cheese from one of the traps, but as her eyes adjusted, she realized that she was holding a tip of a finger, its nail still on.

Lady Mae wanted to tell Arbuckle about it, but she tried not to talk about atonements or punishments with him. She certainly wasn't going to tell him that her mother had said she kept the discards regularly, as if any one of her pockets might be hiding a thumb or a middle toe. And though Lady Mae understood that the residents sometimes liked to take their discards home with them so that they could feel whole even if they weren't, she knew Arbuckle wouldn't. She was both angry and saddened about the gulf that remained no matter how much time they spent together. It sat there, floated behind them as they walked down the crescent road. She'd never get away from it, and so without a word she stood up and disappeared into the living room to fetch the telegram. She sifted through the papers that sat on the table beside the door and found it buried underneath as if hiding it would make it untrue. She walked back into the kitchen and thrust the telegram toward Arbuckle. "Here. Came a few weeks ago."

"What's this?" His strong hands unfolded the piece of paper. As his eyes fell on the words, Lady Mae stood next to him, her hands crossed over her chest, her fists balled, and read the words again herself.

Miss Lady Mae Hilvers
Old Mill Pass
Number One

THIS IS TO CONFIRM APPRENTICESHIP UNDER SECTION 194 FOR FUTURE APPOINTMENT AS BUTCHER STOP PLEASE REPORT FOR REGISTRATION NO LATER THAN 6TH OF AUGUST STOP DIRECTIVES TO FOLLOW STOP THE DEPUTIES

Arbuckle turned it over and folded it closed.

"Lady Mae, I—" He held his hand out to her, offering her the comfort she sought but would not ask for. She took it instinctively and without trepidation, and when Arbuckle opened his mouth to say the words that would carry no weight, she held up her other hand.

"Don't say nothing about it. It's time is all." She looked down at the primer and the abacus on the table and nodded toward it. "Guess that don't much matter."

"You never know. Things could change." But there was worry in his voice. She knew him well enough.

"Ain't nothing going to change."

Lady Mae sat back down at the table. The telegram lay before them. Even if she tore it up, even if her mother kept her home, even if she hid, it wouldn't matter. *When did you stop being scared, Mama?* The Deputies would come at dawn on her eighteenth birthday, carrying with them a wagon filled with books, a smock, and a satchel of cursory tools. It wasn't the butchering of livestock she needed to learn; that was easy—just a quick slit of the throat and leave it to bleed out. It was the atonements she'd need to practice. Most likely there would be a case of specimen jars filled with frogs and skinned rabbits, and when she had mastered the rudimentary incisions she'd begin at the depot beside her mother, watching as she electrocuted and boiled for the lesser crimes, sawed and stitched for the worst.

"At least you'll be with your mama. She won't let nothing happen to you."

"This morning I asked her about it. She wouldn't answer really."

She kept her eyes fixed on her hands on the table. She didn't want to cry again in front of Arbuckle, though she could, and he would no doubt comfort her; even with a bastardly father he always knew how to soothe Lady Mae.

"Did she tell you?"

She shook her head, unable to describe how her mother had grabbed her wrists and told her to never question. The words licked like flames in her mind, but try as she might she couldn't figure how to explain to

Arbuckle the desperation in her mother's voice—the warning call hidden beneath her mother's trembling mouth. Lady Mae tried hard to control herself: she clenched her jaw and balled her fists. She pressed her tongue to the roof of her mouth, bit down on her cheek's fleshy meat. And though she was sure Arbuckle knew already, she didn't want him to see that she was scared. She did not—could not—know the dangers of her appointment; anything her mother had told her had most certainly been censored. What she had seen that day at the depot, what she had heard, was both exactly and not at all what she had expected. Her mother had tried to protect Lady Mae from the worst of it, but she noticed when her mother came home in a different dress than the one she had left the house in. She heard the metal edge of the knife on the stone wheel they kept in the kitchen late in the night when her mother was supposed to be sleeping. But most of all she had watched her mother in the early morning as she sat at the table, her head in her hands and her shoulders shaking.

"I'll find out soon enough."

2

When her mother came home that evening, Lady Mae was at the stove. The front door slammed shut, and she stayed where she was, stirring the ham hock and peas. There was no way that she could avoid her mother's gaze, but she didn't want her battered face to be the first thing she saw after a day spent at the depot. It pained her mother to see her so, and though the attack had been bad, it certainly hadn't been the worst one. Still, she hoped the low light of the stove fire would mask her injuries. It wasn't so much the bruises and the cut on her face, though they did sting and throb. No, what hurt the most was how no matter what her mother or Arbuckle said, she was a leper, infectious and poisonous.

"Evening," her mother said.

"Evening, Mama."

She heard her mother pull the chair out from under

the table and set her tired body down. The fire crackled and the stew boiled.

"Supper's almost ready."

"Smells it," she said. And then, "You ain't allowed at the depot. Not yet."

"But your kit was here and I—"

"You think I ain't got tools there, too? Law says you ain't allowed. Not yet."

"I was just trying to help."

"And what did that get you?"

She heard the chair creak and her mother stand. Then there were hands upon her shoulders, soft and knowing, and Lady Mae turned around. She was taller than her mother, but as her mother inspected her face, her eyes flitting from one injury to the other, she felt small. No doubt, her mother saw the scrapes from the rocky dust on Lady Mae's forehead and cheek.

"I was cleaning the coop. One of the hens got spooked, and I fell into the—"

"You go on and tell truthfully now, Lady Mae."

She pulled her daughter close and hugged her tight. Her mother was small and strong, her surprisingly gentle touch known throughout Settlement Five. "My girl," she whispered. "What did they do to you?"

Arbuckle. He'd gone and went to the depot after lessons, told her mother everything, she was sure. This weren't the first time. Wasn't going to be the last, either.

The kids were just getting worse and worse. She felt a sudden flash of anger; it wasn't his to tell. But there Lady Mae was in the kitchen, spoon in hand, lying to her mother again. He was right—they weren't going to let up. Truth was she was grateful that someone besides her mother cared about what happened to her, and she did not wish to begrudge him that.

"I was bringing your kit, and they were out. Started throwing things at me."

"That all?"

Lady Mae dropped her eyes. "They pushed me. Kicked me here." She brought her hand to her rib, the spot tender and painful.

"Anything broke?"

"Don't think so. Hurts, though."

Her mother brought her hands to Lady Mae, touching lightly her cheek and then her side. Then she pursed her lips and let out a slow breath through her nose. Lady Mae's eyes fell to the floor, and her ears went hot and itchy. She was embarrassed, and doubly ashamed as such. Her mother did not chide her daughter for trying to keep it all a secret, but still the guilt remained. Her mother went back to her chair and sat back down, leaning over to untie her boots. "Did you fight back?" she asked.

Her mother had never suggested fighting—walk away, she'd said. Run if you have to. Call for help. And so at the mention of retaliation Lady Mae's stomach turned, and her throat tightened. She wanted to tell her mother what she'd felt, how when she was in the dust something had burst and bled through her. She'd wanted to lash out at the tyrants, mark them as they'd marked her. It had been there, just at the edge of her fingertips, but then it had vanished. She looked at her mother's bent head and hunched shoulders. *Don't know how to fight, Mama.*

"They just won't quit."

"No, they won't. Not if you don't do nothing. You're of age—I can't step in for you like I used to."

"Don't need you to step in."

From where Lady Mae stood, even in the dim light of the kitchen, she could see the weariness. Her mother was tired, and it wasn't just because of her work. "Well," she said. "They should be punished. That's what the laws are for—what good are they if no one uses them when they ought to?"

Lady Mae stared at her hands, felt the sick in her throat. "They hate me, Mama."

"They don't hate you. They just don't understand yet. They will. Here, take these," she said, and Lady Mae reached down for her mother's boots, the tips of which were long-stained red. Her mother stroked her daughter's hair, tucked pieces behind her ears.

"My child. Remember: everyone's got their lot. And there ain't no changing it for no one. That's the way it is, the way it's been for—for as long as anyone can remember I reckon. Me, my own mama, my grandmother, and her mother before. Before that, well, they say there was nothing but chaos—all them people running around ain't having to answer to nobody. Doing whatever they felt, no matter which way it went. But now, well, they figured it out, I suppose. Someone's got to mind the animals, and someone's got to mind the shops, and someone's got to mind the guilty. We all got a job to do. Yours—what yours will be, anyway— ain't any worse or better than anyone else's."

"But—"

"But nothing. I'm done coming home to you like this. I ain't going to have it no more. You're reporting them and that's that."

"No, Ma, just please, just let it pass, I promise—"

"Got no need for your promises. Just following the law is all. Did they strike you?"

"Aye."

"Did they say blasphemous things?"

"Aye."

"It's done, then. I don't want to hear nothing more about it. Go on and wash up. I'll finish up supper."

Her mother kissed Lady Mae on the forehead, pressing her dry lips softly onto the smooth skin of her daughter. She couldn't be sure, but Lady Mae thought her mother held the kiss for longer than usual, that she had gripped her shoulders tighter as though if she didn't, Lady Mae would slip from her grasp and float away. She hadn't imagined it earlier: her mother was worried.

The courthouse tolled at nine o'clock and her mother aimed to be waiting on the steps at that time. They had risen and dressed and breakfasted. They had cleaned the coop and hung the wash out to dry in the hot summer air. And they had done all of it in a comfortable, quiet silence, moving slowly in the early heat of the day. The drought was nearing the fortieth day, and the bright blue skies promised nothing but another one, the sun beating and blazing down onto the dusty earth.

There were three other residents waiting for court to open. Mr. Wilson, a shopkeeper, was first in line; his face slacked on the right side, his mouth turned down severely. She watched him as they waited, wondering whom his assailants were and what they'd beaten him for. He was a kind, old man, if not terse, but Lady Mae's mother had on more than one occasion said how he was one of the only shopkeepers that would talk to her. Lady Mae watched her mother smile at him, and even though his mouth was injured, he tried to smile back. He had all his parts it seemed—no missing fingers or limbs—and it was possible he'd never done anything wrong. Not all disobeyed the law. But though everyone knew the punishments for wrongdoings—up to twenty atonements—there were crimes still. For as long as Lady Mae could remember there were brawls and murders, cheating and thievery. Certain times were worse than others—usually toward the end of the month when the residents had used up their allowance and resorted to unseemly behavior to get what they wanted and needed. Some thought the atonements were worth it and plotted and planned their transgressions. Others were simply swept up in the moment, lashing out at those in nearest proximity. Whatever the case, the victims could show at the courthouse during inquest hours and request that their perpetrators be charged with what they felt fair and just. Until the day before, Lady Mae couldn't understand why anyone could do anything wrong knowing the consequences. But when she was there in the dust, her heart beating wildly, sweat dripping into her eyes, she wanted the children to pay, wanted them to hurt as she hurt. She remembered then as she stood outside of the courthouse how the vengeance had stuck under her skin.

The courthouse opened, and Lady Mae followed those who had also come to seek justice up the steps and through the large, iron doors. No one spoke; she heard only the clicking of boots on the wooden floors and the rustling of stiff fabrics as they lined up outside of the courtroom. Mr. Wilson had tied a cloth around his arm to staunch the bleeding. It was dark and dirty;

underneath was the muscle, a white fleck of bone where she couldn't see. *What does it feel like, Mama?* He breathed hard and quick, sweat on his brow and a darkness just below his eyes.

When it was their turn, Lady Mae and her mother entered the courtroom. They walked up the aisle past pews that would be filled when the hearings began that day. The highest ranked Deputy sat up on the bench. He oversaw the other three Deputies that had worked Settlement Five since before Lady Mae was born. Her mother had said that there was talk of an uptick in crime and the need for a fifth Deputy. Supposedly, one was on his way from Settlement Six, but it was on the other side of the mountains that stretched to the east. They'd been waiting for months, and her mother didn't see the point, as they were able to make do with what they had.

"Morning, Winona," the Deputy said. He leaned forward on his elbows, his thick, dark beard reaching nearly to the bench.

"Morning, Deputy Daniels," her mother said.

"What have we got here?" He looked Lady Mae in the eyes, and though she wanted to, she didn't look away. She knew who he was—knew all the Deputies by name and reputation. Deputy Daniels, though, had the strongest taste for justice of the four Deputies in Settlement Five.

"My daughter. She's putting in."

"That so?" He held his stare to Lady Mae, even when her mother was speaking.

Her mother nudged Lady Mae with her elbow. "Go on, now."

"Yes, sir," said Lady Mae.

"And what's the charge?"

"They did this." She pointed to her face. "Pushed me down. Kicked me in the head. And in the back."

"Who's 'they'?"

"The Thompson boys, Edith Cummings—she was there. Balthazar Jones. Those were the worst."

"That all?"

"There were others, but they stayed up by the shacks."

"And no one sought to help you?"

"No."

"Were they provoked?"

"No."

Deputy Daniels raised his eyebrows at this, and though Lady Mae was young, she was old enough to know that the provocation had been happening for years. Every single time one of their parents came home with just a little less than they had left with, the children took one step closer to the loathing that would soon, if not already so, engulf their small bodies. The mutilations of their parents or other townsfolk were most children's first memories, and so although she did not provoke them—had never provoked anyone in any way—she did not need to. Their desire to descend on her like monsters was nearly innate.

"Were you able to defend yourself in any way?"

The strength, the power had unfurled like silk inside of her when she was down on the ground the day before. The seething in her bones had felt good, comfortable and strong, as though it had been there her entire life, and she was only just now realizing what she could do with it. But she hadn't been able to hold on to it. There in the courtroom she felt not bold nor brave, but a shame that burned hotter than the sun. It had been just a flash—that strength in the dust. And now it was gone.

"I told them to stop, but there were too many I reckon."

"And you swear by this testimony?"

"Aye, sir."

"Very well. How many atonements do you ask for?"

Lady Mae had thought about it as she lay in the darkness the night before, her face throbbing and her body sore. Whatever she asked for they'd get—all of them, each one she named. After all, who was it besides the victim to measure the extent of the crime? And guilty looked all kind of ways. Still, rarely was the full allotment of twenty atonements assigned; residents feared retribution, as if they knew someday they, too, would do harm. Everyone wanted a sympathetic reputation, so when the time came that they were themselves charged with a crime, their victims would show mercy. It was unspoken, but was just as good as law. Part of her had wanted to give the children twenty each—thirty, forty if she could. That would keep them from hurting her physically. But there were other ways to harm, and she knew them well.

"One."

Her mother had wanted more, but Lady Mae pleaded. If she gave any more, it'd just be worse next time. And while her mother insisted that there might not be a next time, not after charging them, Lady Mae doubted that. For as long as there were butchers, there'd be residents to hate them. And as long as people lived, there'd be lawbreaking and retribution. Her mother spoke of it, her mother's mother had, too.

"Sentencing will proceed at eleven o'clock tomorrow. Dismissed."

Lady Mae's mother shuffled her out of the room and down the long hall toward the exit. By this time, other residents had lined up and were waiting to be called into the courtroom. They stared out of the corners of their eyes as Lady Mae and her mother walked by, curled their lips and showed their teeth. But none spoke. The butcher and her daughter had attended an inquest, and it was anyone's guess who the perpetrator was. Though many despised and insulted them, most stayed away. But it was that berth, that purposeful distance, that stung the most.

They descended the courthouse steps, and Lady Mae saw that the square was dotted with residents doing their morning chores. Some scrubbed the scaffold, others carried parcels and crates of goods. It was just another day. As Lady Mae and her mother walked along the cracked crescent road, her mother, congenial and forthright, said good morning to each resident. Each one replied, a methodical greeting empty of conviction. The residents spoke only when spoken to; there were no other offertory gestures or words of goodwill. The shopkeepers had their doors propped open and stood on their porches, talking. But as Lady Mae and her mother passed by, they would hush and still. Lady Mae heard the ends of what they said, though, saw them avert their eyes as she and her mother approached.

Once they were beyond the square, Lady Mae hooked her arm around her mother's.

"Ma?"

"Yes?"

"What'll the sentencing be like?"

Her mother squeezed her daughter's arm. "The other children will be there. They'll take the stand, speak for themselves just like anyone else."

"What if they lie?"

"My girl. You've been hurt badly, and I do not believe Deputy Daniels thinks you are telling lies." Her mother pulled Lady Mae's hand up toward her chest and held it there as they walked, bending her head down and kissing her daughter's knuckles.

"What if it gets worse?"

"It ain't going to get any worse than this."

But that did not soothe Lady Mae, whose fears were inexplicable and deep. She wanted to tell her mother that it could be worse—it could always be worse—but she did not wish to worry her, and so instead she looked at her mother and gave a small smile, one that she knew would not fool her. *They hate me, Mama.*

As they walked, Lady Mae looked up at the wisps of clouds, at the birds that were circling high above. They dipped and dove and called to one another across the hot summer sky. Her mother took out a handkerchief and blotted her forehead and the back of her neck. Their skirts dragged in the dust.

"Ma?"

"What is it?"

"You ever think something different than the rest?"

"Such as what?"

"Don't know. Just different. Being in there—back in the courthouse—there always that many residents waiting?"

"Not sure. Never been to an inquest. But I suppose so. Seems I've seen most everyone in the settlement at one time or another." She sighed as she said it, shook her head just enough for Lady Mae to notice.

"Stands to reason if everyone knew what was in store they wouldn't do nothing."

"Reason ain't got nothing to do with it."

"What does, then?"

"Rage, jealousy. Sometimes love."

"People do things for love?"

"Yes, I suppose they do. I'd do for you, Lady Mae."

She looked at her mother with wide eyes. "You'd hurt someone for me?"

Her mother's lips thinned, but she nodded. "In a heartbeat."

"But you're my ma. You got to say that."

"Even still. I reckon most I see gone and done things either because they love too much or too little, or maybe 'cause they ain't got no love themselves." Her voice lowered and slowed as she spoke as if she, too, were realizing it for the first time.

"Can you tell when they're in the chair which it is?"

Her mother looked over her shoulder. Speculation was against the law. It was written right there in the declaration all residents had hanging on a wall in their shacks. The Deputies said assumption led to nothing but hearsay and bedlam, though in Lady Mae's experience the rumors were almost always true in the end.

The road was empty, though, and so her mother said in a low whisper to her daughter, "Sometimes. Sometimes the residents tell me. They ain't supposed to, but they do."

"What do they say?"

"What they done, how it made them feel. Most just want to be heard, want to feel justified."

"What do you say?"

"It's not always—" she began and then stopped and cleared her throat. Up ahead a woman stepped off her porch and walked toward them. Her mother remained silent until the woman passed and was well out of earshot.

"I listen. Then I tell them what I think they need to hear. Sometimes they just need someone on their side."

"And you're allowed to do that?" Lady Mae could not believe what her mother was telling her, and she assumed it was because of the telegram. Perhaps her mother figured there was no use keeping anything from her daughter anymore. But still, the thought of the residents searching for consolation from the very person tasked with punishing them seemed to Lady Mae unfathomable.

"Sure. I aim to give just as much as I take away."

"So what they really need is a friend? Someone to listen to them?"

"I guess you could see it that way."

"What if the Deputies got it backward? Maybe they ought to—"

"Be mindful, girl," interrupted her mother, and Lady Mae fell silent. The two of them looked up and down the crescent road, but they were far from any other residents. "You know you ain't allowed to question. Even if I'm the one you're asking."

"I know I ain't the only one that wonders," Lady Mae said defiantly.

"Arbuckle been saying things to you, hasn't he?"

"You know how he is."

Her mother sighed loudly, but there was concern in the edges of her eyes. "What's he been saying now?"

"Nothing in particular." Lady Mae looked at the ground, tucking her bottom lip underneath her teeth.

"Lady Mae, you go on and tell me directly."

"I reckon he thinks atonements aren't always the right way to do things."

"And he's said as much?"

"Aye."

"Lady Mae," her mother said slowly. "You best be careful. Arbuckle is a good boy, especially considering his sorry excuse for a pa, but them Deputies abide by the law and, specifically, *that* law. They lay down the terms and we accept them, simple as that. And if they hear of anyone—even Arbuckle—suggesting that they got it all backward, he'll be strung up on the scaffold like anyone else. Won't matter what lot he's got here. The Deputies will just go and find someone else to take his place."

"But they can't do that. It's an inheritance."

"And who's going to stop them?"

Lady Mae did not have an answer, and so she looked straight ahead at the horizon, wishing for the rain to come and wash them all away.

Later that evening after they had supped and cleaned and readied themselves for sleep, Lady Mae and her mother sat in the living room, each with a settlement-approved book in hand. Lady Mae was reading one that Arbuckle had given her; though he was older he often loaned Lady Mae books he thought she might be interested in. Something new for you to think about, he'd say. Sometimes the books were thin stories of children on adventures beyond the settlements that dotted their region, in imaginary places full of life and wonder. Other times they were philosophical in nature, ruminating on some kind of long-held belief or law. And though she was not interested in all the books he gave her, she devoured those as well because they were from him, read by his eyes, given to her by his hands.

"Lady Mae," her mother said. She lowered her book to her lap, but did not take her eyes from it.

"Yes?"

"What else Arbuckle been saying about atonements?"

Lady Mae closed her book, keeping one finger on the page. She looked up to the ceiling as she thought of the words Arbuckle had whispered over her kitchen table during lessons. She could tell her mother anything, had always told her everything. But he'd been heretical, and she didn't want her mother to put an end to the lessons.

"Just says things like they don't work—says it ain't never stopped his pa."

"Well, that's true. But he's just one resident."

"Says maybe residents ought to learn how to forgive and forget to begin with, that them Deputies need to help more. Maybe then residents wouldn't get so desperate and go and do things they'll regret."

"Not all regret it, Lady Mae. And those," she said, pausing, "are the ones the Deputies want punished. Everyone else—well, they know how it is from the moment they can walk and talk. Just the way it is."

"I know. It's just that—"

"Just what?"

Lady Mae faltered, trying to figure out how to piece the words together that were there in the sides of her mouth. She'd heard what Arbuckle had been saying all these years, knew its weight. He was onto something— she felt it deep in her bones—but to say it, even to her mother, would be blasphemous. Still, she could not help herself; it came bubbling up and out there in the dim light of the room.

"What if he's right?" Lady Mae asked. "What if everybody's missing something? You taught me what's right and wrong, but do you reckon everyone knows it as well?"

"No, Lady Mae. Lots don't know right from wrong, and even those that do can easily lose their way."

"But you haven't. I haven't. Arbuckle hasn't."

Her mother rose from her chair and placed her book on a side table. She went over to Lady Mae and gently lifted her grandmother's quilt—Lady Mae's great-grandmother's—from the back of the sofa and began to fold it. It was old and worn, the edges frayed. The soft patchwork had been repaired over and over again by each woman in the family; her own mother had recently redone the border using the faded fabric of a dress Lady Mae had outgrown.

Her mother knelt then, taking her daughter's hands into both of her own. "We're different, the three of us," she said to her worried daughter.

"How?" asked Lady Mae.

"We've all been victims, pure and simple. For you and me our lineage is to blame, for Arbuckle it's his pa. We know what hurts. You felt it yesterday with those children no doubt. And I'd bet that you might've felt something else, too—anger, maybe. Rage."

"I did."

"You can't let that take over—that's what gets residents in the chair. You got to try to turn it into something else. Pity, maybe. Some kind of understanding."

"You sound like Arbuckle."

"I ain't never said he was wrong."

"But I don't know if I can, Mama. I wanted to hurt them kids." Lady Mae pulled her hands out from her mother's and grabbed the edge of the quilt, balling the beautiful squares up into her fists.

"I know you did."

"And that weren't the first time I felt it."

"I know it, Lady Mae. I've felt it, too," her mother said softly.

"What'd you do about it?"

"There weren't nothing to do. I kept it in here." She brought her hand to her chest. "Anything else would've spelled trouble. Listen to me carefully, Lady Mae. You're going to feel what you feel—ain't no stopping that. But what you do with it is something else."

"How you mean?"

"Them kids behaving the way they do—it ain't their fault. Not really."

"Whose fault is it?"

Her mother did not respond. She instead wrung her hands, spinning the ring that she wore on her middle finger. Her eyes searched the empty space in front of her, and she twisted her lips, pursing them, narrowing her eyes as though she was making up her mind something good.

"Sometimes it ain't the people that are the problem. I want you to try to see that—it ain't any one boy or girl. It ain't even ten boys and girls. The problem— the trouble—goes deeper than that. And it's up to you whether you can see that or not. I can't always do it for you, and I ain't in a habit of telling you what to think. You've got to make your own way, decide for yourself. You hear me?"

"Yes, Ma."

"We're all capable of doing something great, Lady Mae. I don't ever want you to forget that."

"Okay."

"And you'll know when it's time to do it. You'll feel it growing inside of you long before you even know what it is. And when it finally surfaces you'll be surefooted and clear. Remember my words always, Lady Mae."

"I will, Ma."

As Lady Mae fell asleep that night, she thought of the fingertip and of what her mother had said. She'd been trying to tell her something without speaking directly, and the only sense that Lady Mae could make of it was that it had not been just a warning. There was more behind the *I reckon* and *you hear* and *remember my words*. And though Lady Mae could not understand why, a worry pressed upon her. She leaned over to blow out the candle and watched the flame flicker, thinking of how the children had also bent and twisted around her body the day before. But just as she was about to extinguish it, a gust of wind came through the open window, and the candle went out.

3

During the walk into town the next morning, Lady Mae noticed the shops along the way were shuttered, the crescent road quiet and still. As she and her mother came around the corner of the square she saw why: a throng of residents nearly ten deep waited by the entrance to the courthouse. Word had spread quickly; they had woken early and readied themselves, made breakfasts large enough to keep them full through the testimonies and verdict. Their attendance at trials was expected at least a few times a year, but this was different, and their heads and shoulders shifted and moved with excitement. They were going to hear Lady Mae and watch her small mouth and bright eyes for any kind of tell. She'd speak through her still swollen lips and she'd name the children—one, two, three, four—pointing at them from the stand as she told Deputy Daniels what they had done to her. *Don't know if I got it in me, Mama.*

To the left of the crowd, over by the old well, stood Arbuckle. That he was there was both shameful and comforting to Lady Mae. She had not told him of the trial, of the way she had felt in the dust, and seeing him felt like a lie undone. She hoped he would understand; when he'd told her to charge the children, he meant it. But though he'd not said to think twice or go easy, she had on account of him. One atonement each, the least she could ask for. The humiliation shot through her, and it wasn't just that she hadn't defended herself. It was that there was a need at all, that simply existing required such self-preservation. Her mother was right—Arbuckle wasn't wrong. She wanted to call to him, to put her hand in his and squeeze it three times like they used to when they were scared. He'd hold her close, and she would burrow her face into his chest. But she did not want to draw any more attention to herself than there was already, and so she followed her mother and pushed through the mass of residents to get to the courthouse doors.

"Lady Mae!" Arbuckle called as they passed by him. "Lady Mae!"

The residents turned their bodies toward him, their disdain for him—for his father—second only to the butcher and her daughter.

"Don't let them scare you. You say what happened, now, just like you done yesterday."

The residents, who had been staring at Arbuckle as

he spoke, now craned their heads toward Lady Mae, eager for her response. They stood silently and still as if the words that fell from her mouth would be revelatory and full of weight. But she did not speak. Instead, she broke from her mother and quickly went to him.

"Arbuckle, I, I—Ma. She said I had to."

He nodded slowly, his eyes down toward his feet. "I don't disagree."

"You don't?"

"Seems it won't stop—them getting at you—unless you do."

Lady Mae looked behind her. "You ain't cross?"

"Cross? Why'd I be cross with you?"

"Just I know what you think and even my ma says you ain't wrong and I—"

"Listen, Lady Mae," Arbuckle said and put his hands gently underneath her elbows. "What you got is worse than anything that'll happen to me. You're right. I do think things. And I thought long and hard about this, too. Can't figure another way. Them kids could've killed you."

"But they didn't."

"Not this time," he said quietly.

"You going in?"

Arbuckle tucked his bottom lip under his teeth and put his hands in his pocket. "I will if you want me to. Supposed to go to these things anyway, right?"

What Arbuckle was doing, and no doubt doing for her, was something she'd not ever have asked of him. But she knew him well enough, and so before turning and rejoining her mother, she held her hand to his chest. "Thank you," she said, and turned to go.

"But Lady Mae," he said. "They's just kids."

She nodded, but right underneath was her dreaming in the night of killing the children who accosted her one by one, taking first their fingers and then their toes and then chiseling away at their flesh little by little until it scattered and floated around her like ash. She did not know how to say that to Arbuckle who, though condemned himself, felt not anger nor wrath.

"I know," she said.

Lady Mae and her mother walked down the long hall past the inquest chamber, the wash closet, the framed portraits of all four Deputies assigned to Settlement Five. There was silence and the sound of crying, a cough, and then nothing. Her mother stopped in front of another windowless door, above which was a sign that said Hearings and Sentencing. Her mother pushed the door open, and they stepped into the courtroom, already warm and thick with the heat of the day.

They were the first ones to arrive and took their seats on the north side of the room where the victims sat. The perpetrators, the assailants, and offenders, would be led to the south side. There were no bars or shackles, no locked cages to put them in; each resident knew the punishment for courtroom crimes.

"Lady Mae," she said, lifting her daughter's chin with one hand and sweeping back her hair with the other. "This is a sentencing, and you have every right to say exactly what you told me last night. Don't hold nothing back."

"I don't feel so good."

"I reckon you don't." Her mother gently rubbed Lady Mae's arm. "Ain't nothing good about this situation, but it's got to be done. Ain't nobody can do it but you."

"But what if it don't work? What if it happens again?"

"Then we do this again. And again and again until it's done no more." Her mother reached over and grabbed her daughter's hand with both of hers. "I ain't ever going to let anything happen to you again, you hear?" She shook as she said it, as if speaking such a conviction aloud made her nervous. It was not like her mother—nor any other parent—to intervene and defend. The children, especially that of Lady Mae's age, could think and speak for themselves and were expected to do as much. That her mother was so insistent made Lady Mae uneasy.

"Aye, Ma."

The courtroom doors opened, and the four children that Lady Mae had accused appeared. Deputy Parson followed behind them all. At first glance, the Deputies all appeared the same: black suits, tall, pointy hats, chains hanging from their hips. But Lady Mae could tell them apart because she'd been looking at them all her life. In the end, Deputy Parson was no different than any of the others. They all followed orders— from whom, Lady Mae did not know, not really. Like all children, she learned from an early age that there were other settlements, nine to be exact. And that in each was a handful of Deputies who were born of other Deputies, a butcher born of another butcher, shopkeepers, workers, and so on, each resident taking the place of their parent when they came of age. But who decided that? Maybe no one was giving the orders. Maybe the four Deputies in Settlement Five sat behind closed doors and simply decided for themselves.

Lady Mae watched as the children took their seats. The boys hung their heads low and kept their eyes down. But Edith, the only girl, stared at Lady Mae the way Arbuckle's father had stared at her mother. Edith had never been accused before and was clearly unafraid. There was speculation, though in itself against the law, that her parents were informants. That's why she always got away with it. But whether or not the rumors were true, Lady Mae had publicly called her by name, and as the girl sat in her chair, she kept her unblinking eyes on Lady Mae.

The residents came into the courtroom next. They filled the front first—they wanted a good look at the butcher and her daughter, wanted to stare at them without having to look away. Lady Mae did not turn around, not even to search the room for Arbuckle, whose kind eyes and small smile would no doubt comfort her. They filed in quietly, and all Lady Mae heard was the creaking of the benches as they sat and tried to get comfortable. She could feel the energy in the room, a low simmering of excitement and anticipation, but it did not rise above a few murmurs. No one wanted to be too eager lest they found themselves up on the stand having to answer questions for their own crimes. People always remember, her mother had said, and ain't no one want to be at the wrong end of revenge.

"All rise," called Deputy Parson from the corner of the room near the chambers. Acting as bailiff, he was the smallest of the Deputies, a skinny whiff of a man whose hat was as nearly as tall as he was. His moustache hung down the sides of his mouth like dripping tar, the ends waxed to a point. He was younger than the other Deputies and had not yet earned the right to patrol outside of the courtroom.

Lady Mae and her mother stood up from their chairs as Deputy Daniels came out of a small door and went to his seat at the bench. He did not look up at Lady Mae or her mother, did not glance at the accused or the other residents that he knew were there. He instead looked down at the stack of papers he held in his hands and read from the one on top.

"Lady Mae Hilvers?" he asked.

"Yes," she replied. Her voice was quiet but clear.

"You have accused these residents of assault, is that correct?"

"Yes, sir."

He looked up, squinted, and adjusted his glasses, straining to see Lady Mae from across the room.

"Please approach the witness stand," he ordered.

Deputy Parson walked over to her and waited as she rose from her chair, smoothed her skirts, and came out from behind the table. She tried not to limp, but each step pained her and so though she walked steadily, she did so slowly. The courtroom was sweltering and quiet, and the residents watched Lady Mae as she climbed three steps and took her seat next to the Deputy on the witness stand. She looked directly at him and did not turn her head to look at the residents, though she sensed them in her periphery; if she didn't look at them, then maybe she wouldn't break. Maybe she'd keep it inside of her scraped cheeks and cut lips, still her voice from wavering. But whether she looked at the other residents or not mattered little as she heard clearly the whispers, the *girl*, *butcher*, *penance* that floated across the sunny room to land on her pounding heart.

Deputy Daniels leaned toward Lady Mae, putting his weight onto his elbow. He licked his fat lips and combed through his beard with swollen fingers.

"You have asked for one atonement for each of the accused, is that correct?"

"Yes, sir."

He took a good look at Lady Mae, shifting his eyes from one side of her face to the other. Her bruises were fully formed now, dark splotches underneath her skin. His eyes lingered on the scratch across her face, and she brought her hand up to it instinctively. Her fingers felt the gauze, felt how it stuck to her skin and itched.

"They did this to you?" he asked.

"Aye."

He took in a deep breath and glanced toward the four children that sat across from Lady Mae. Her eyes followed his, and she saw that only Edith was looking at her. The boys had their heads bowed still, their hands in their laps.

"And you say you did not provoke them?" he asked.

"I did not," she replied.

"Thank you. You may sit."

As she walked slowly back to her seat, she felt on her flesh the stares of what seemed nearly the entire settlement. It burned, churning like lava deep inside of her, bubbling and seeping down into her fingertips and toes. Each step echoed, the wood floor cracked and snapped, and she thought she heard Arbuckle call her name. She looked up then, quickly and without thinking, and saw hundreds of eyes upon her. There they were, knitted together in the stifling heat, their hot skin shiny, their eyes weary but wide. They nudged each other, pointing low toward Lady Mae, whispering out of the corners of their mouths. The panic rose fast—the lump in her throat and the pressure on her chest—and try as she might she could not find Arbuckle in the crowd, though she was certain he was there. She took her seat next to her mother, who reached over and patted her daughter's hand. Lady Mae felt the clammy palm and cold fingers on her own skin, her own tell safely hidden inside.

"We will hear from the defendants," said Deputy Daniels. "Edith Cummings, approach the witness stand."

Deputy Parson neared the girl to bring her to the front of the room, but as he did she jumped up and pushed her chair back with such force that it toppled over, its crash bouncing off the walls of the scorching courtroom.

"I don't need no help."

Leaving the chair on the ground, she walked up to the stand, her eyes on Lady Mae the entire time. She mumbled something under her breath as she passed Lady Mae and her mother, but it was unclear. As the girl took her seat on the witness stand, the alarm in Lady Mae boiled up like milk sugar. Just because they were there in court didn't mean they'd leave Lady Mae alone—the potential consequence hadn't deterred them. Maybe they'd lose a finger or a toe and think it was worth it and go after her again and again until she was nothing but a pulpy mass left to die in the dust. Maybe little Edith Cummings would not raise a fist to her again, but there were others—plenty of others—that would. Perhaps there were children and adults alike that lay in the darkness of night, unable to sleep in the hot, sticky air. They might rub their fingertips together, trying to decide which one would be worth getting their hands on the butcher's daughter.

"Edith Cummings?" asked Deputy Daniels.

"Yes."

"You have been charged with assault. What is your plea?"

"I ain't done nothing wrong."

"Says here you were one of four accused of throwing stones at Lady Mae Hilvers. In addition, you lay your hands to her body. What say you?"

"It weren't me." She flipped her hair back behind her shoulders and sighed loudly.

"Are you saying you were not there?"

"I was—no, I mean—I was just passing by."

"And you did not raise a hand to her?"

"No. I just watched is all." But as soon as she spoke her hand flew up to her mouth to cover it as if the words that escaped her were not her own.

There was a collective gasp from the courtroom, a hushed rustling of bodies, whispers that floated up into the air. Edith Cummings had unknowingly admitted enough to get her in the chair; watching a crime was disallowed. They weren't to report it—only the victim or the victim's family could—but they were to turn their backs, their eyes, their ears. Unless of course it was on the scaffold during an outcry. Then they were expected to jeer and chant, to gather gravel in their fists and throw it as far as they could. Only then was a mob welcome, egged on by the Deputies and embraced by the residents.

"You watched?"

"No—" she stammered. "That ain't what I meant. I was there, walking into town. It was them Thompson boys. They started it."

"Now you know as well as I that it ain't of import who started what. Did you or did you not lay hands to Lady Mae Hilvers?"

Realizing the predicament she was in, the girl nodded, as she knew enough, and she knew not to lie in court twice.

"She has asked for one atonement and shall be granted such," said Deputy Daniels. "You may step down."

The girl stood. She held on to the balustrade with one hand, jumped down over the two steps and landed hard on the floor. She walked back to her seat slowly, purposefully, sucking her teeth and drumming her hands on her hips. The girl was trying to make Lady

Mae look up, who, though wanting to meet the gaze of her assailant and show her she wasn't afraid, kept her eyes focused on Deputy Daniels.

The Thompson boys were next. Rarely were they seen without each other, acting as one monstrous body in mind and voice. The younger one called the shots—the older one did the work; they were a gang of two, born into a family of nine, and cared not for any consequence they might suffer for their actions. They took the stand together, shuffling their large and small bodies up toward the front of the room, muttering and snarling as they passed Lady Mae. They shouldered one another into the witness stand and tried at first to share the seat, but when they couldn't fit, the older one stood behind the younger one, his arms crossed and his lips thin.

"Jonathan, Josiah," Deputy Daniels said.

"Aye," they replied.

"You have been named perpetrators. What is your plea?"

"Not guilty."

"Not guilty."

"State your case."

"We was just walking home when we saw her." Josiah pointed to Edith Cummings, whose parents sat behind her in the first row. "She was already throwing stones."

"That's not true!" cried the girl.

"Is so true," said Jonathan. "She was hiding behind Wilson's place, and she called to us when she saw us. Said Lady Mae was on her way to town and—"

"They nothing but a bunch of liars! They threw 'em first!" Edith yelled and stood up. Her parents tried to pull her back down, tried to wrestle her into her seat, but she escaped their grasp.

"And you," she screamed, rising up and leaping across the aisle. She grabbed Lady Mae's hair and yanked it back as hard as she could. "Good for nothing, horrible—"

"Order, I say! Order!" Deputy Daniels yelled and stood, his gavel in hand.

Lady Mae reached around her head and tried to grab the girl by her forearms, but could not get Edith off her. "Mama!" she cried. "Mama!"

Her mother stood up, and with the palm of her hand shoved the girl on her forehead, pushing her off Lady Mae. Edith went sprawling to the floor where she crumpled and whimpered and clutched her own mother's arm desperately.

"Deputy Parson!" cried Deputy Daniels. "Remove Miss Cummings from the courtroom immediately!"

Edith's parents, who under law could not intervene, watched horrifically as Deputy Parson yanked the girl by the wrists and flipped her over onto her stomach. He put his knee into her back and his elbow around her throat. But he would not kill her. Having committed a crime in court, she would instead face persecution on the scaffold in the square. The outcry would be announced, the shops would close, and the town would fall silent as the residents gathered below the wooden platform to watch the girl burn.

Lady Mae heard the girl's mother cry out once before she suppressed it. *Could you have held your tongue, Mama?* She stared, holding her hand to the back of her head, at the woman whose daughter was being dragged away flailing, screaming, clawing at the benches and the ankles of the residents who shook and kicked their feet as she grabbed at them, who looked away in disgust and fear as if an acknowledgment might also cost them their lives; she stared, without blinking, until her eyes dried and the cries ceased and the door slammed.

That evening as they supped, Lady Mae tried to build up the courage to ask what would happen to her mother. She had laid hands on Edith Cummings, and even the butcher wasn't above punishment. She worried, and her mother saw the concern on her daughter's face.

"Go on and eat up, Lady Mae."

"I ain't hungry."

"I suppose you ain't, but sitting there worrying ain't gonna do you any good."

Lady Mae pushed her plate away and crossed her arms. Underneath them she balled her fists, felt the knot below her ribs. If anything happened to her mother—she couldn't think that way. But still the thoughts knocked between her ears: *never leave* and *what would become* and *how would I.* The voice was her own, the anxiety bottomless.

"But what's gonna happen to you?"

"What do you mean?"

"What you did to Edith. You ain't allowed to do that."

"No, I ain't. But that ain't no concern for you. I'll be fine."

"How's that?"

Her mother took in a deep breath and smiled at her daughter. There was something she wasn't saying, and it was the same thing that had been there the morning of the day before. Lady Mae read it in her eyes that did not crease at the corners, but instead studied her daughter's face. She reached her hand out across the table, wiggling her fingers at Lady Mae. But she did not take her mother's hand.

"I'll go talk to Daniels tomorrow," her mother said. "Course I'm going to protect you—you think the Deputies wouldn't do the same for their own kin? If there were any here? Besides, since Edith's accused, she ain't got no right to press charges. Just made it worse for herself is all."

"What'll happen to her?" Lady Mae's voice was small.

"Come Saturday she'll be up on the scaffold."

"But she ain't nothing but a child. Only a couple years younger than me."

"Makes no difference to the Deputies."

"What'll they do to her?"

Her mother did not answer, her eyes upon her fork that poked at the potatoes on her plate. Lady Mae did not ask again.

4

When Lady Mae came into the kitchen the next morning, her mother was at the stove frying beans and eggs; they would not have meat until the next allocation day and even then, they would receive little. Though there were many animals dead from the drought, their muscles stiff from the final throes of starvation, in the heat the meat turned rancid within hours and was not fit for butchering. The animals couldn't be burned either—not without risking the entire settlement—and so the bodies and offal, dumped behind the depot and left to rot, piled up. It mattered not to her mother, who was long immune to the bodies, the flies that swarmed in the sticky air, the sour stench of rotting flesh, but even in her sleep on the other side of the settlement, Lady Mae gagged when the winds blew right.

"Good morning," her mother said.

She lingered in the space between the doorway and

her mother. She had heard her mother in the night; the cries started low and sounded as if one of the neighboring animals was birthing a calf, bellows escaping its throat and mouth, choking and sudden. With each mournful swell, Lady Mae rose in her bed and tossed her legs over the side. But just when she had resolved to check on her mother, the cries would stop, and Lady Mae would lie back down on the bed, listening in the silence for them to start again.

"Don't forget to do the coop first," her mother said. "One of them ain't been laying right—best we sort that and make sure ain't nothing wrong with the others. Found one without a yolk this morning."

"Maybe something spooked them," said Lady Mae as she sat down at the table.

"Maybe."

Her mother scraped the bottom of the iron pan, loosening the blackened bits that were her daughter's favorite. The eggs popped and sizzled in the fat.

Lady Mae felt her stomach turn and twist. The nervousness crept up her legs and arms until her head was hot, until her throat tightened and her palms sweat. She knew her mother had worries, but she never spoke of them, and there she was in the smoky kitchen, her back to her daughter, letting the words tumble from her mouth. It was one thing to worry aloud when her daughter came home beaten and tormented; it was another to do so in the stillness of the morning when they were safe behind the walls of their shack.

"You think someone could've gotten in?" Lady Mae chose her words wisely. It was not all that she wished to ask her mother, but she did not know how to ask otherwise. *You didn't want this neither did you, Mama?*

"Maybe tried to, maybe not. You just keep a watchful eye; you hear?"

"Aye," she said softly.

Her mother wanted to say more. Lady Mae could see it in her small shoulders, in how her hair was not pinned up neatly, the frizzy curls peeking out from under her handkerchief. Maybe her mother knew Lady Mae was staring at her. Perhaps she felt her daughter's eyes on the back of her sweaty neck.

"Mama, is there something else that—"

"Look at you!" She quickly turned around, dripping spoon in hand. She thrust her hands toward her daughter's bruised face, splattering the floor and the cupboards with the red juice. "What more has got to happen? They could've killed you."

"But they didn't."

"Not this time. But each time I leave you—it's in my mind to—"

She took a deep breath and put the spoon back in the pot. She began ladling the beans hurriedly, dumping them onto the metal plates before going back and scooping out the fried eggs, slapping them on top of the beans. When the plates were filled, she lifted her arm and put her forehead in the crook of it; the day was nearly unbearable already.

"Lady Mae." She put her arm down and blotted her forehead with a rag. "You're getting older, getting ready to take over for me. Whole town knows it. Seems to always go this way—did for me as well. The residents, well, they get to thinking that the eve of an inheritance be the best time to make a fuss, try to change things. I don't know—maybe some think if they stood in the way they could stop atonements once and for all."

"What do they think would happen then? If there were no atonements?"

"Your guess is as good as mine. I suppose," she said quietly as she put the lid back on the bean pot, "that some think we'd all learn a little forgiveness. So I've heard, anyways. I don't know. Maybe they're right."

Lady Mae had never witnessed her mother conceding to the residents of whom she stood over and severed and electrocuted and cut. As she sat there watching her mother make a modest breakfast, Lady Mae wondered how much forgiveness her mother had demonstrated throughout her life. After all, she hadn't ever accused anyone of anything that Lady Mae knew of—not even those that caused her mother's limp, the scar on her upper lip, the permanent fear that held fast behind her eyes; she had taught her daughter that the world was out of her control but that which was in her heart was not.

"After all, weren't always like this, now was it?"

Lady Mae had not ever heard her mother speak in that way; though she intellectually understood that life in Settlement Five and the Deputies and inheritances couldn't have *always* been, she had no proof otherwise. Neither did her mother, who, just speaking the words *weren't always* had committed blasphemy. Her mother was trying to warn her, and said, "I want you to be careful, Lady Mae. You've got to be watchful." And so Lady Mae watched as she brought the two plates over to the table. As she sat down, her mother kept her eyes focused on her food, on her hands, on the napkin she had sewn herself— focused on everything but her daughter's questioning eyes. Her mother's suspicious words frightened Lady Mae, and the gray that followed pulled on her like quicksand.

"What do you mean?"

"Never mind what I mean. What I'm saying is that I want Arbuckle to stick near you when I'm not around. Just until the inheritance has passed."

"But ain't nobody likes Arbuckle, neither." She picked up her spoon and pushed the beans around her plate to cool them. "What's he going to do?"

"Well, for starters he's nearly six and a half feet tall. That'll keep some away. And he's had his own share of run-ins. I reckon he knows a thing or two that you don't."

"But I don't want—"

"You don't leave this house without one of us. Not until the inheritance has passed. Understand?"

Her mother picked up her own spoon and began to eat. But Lady Mae was not satisfied. "Ma?"

"Yes?" she asked as she brought a spoonful of the red beans to her mouth.

"Are they really—what will happen to Edith?" she asked and began to eat her own simple meal. "They ain't really going to kill her, are they?" The beans were hot and meaty and burned her tongue.

Her mother scooped up more beans, and she held the spoon close to her lips and blew on them. Lady Mae had thought about the girl long into the night, seeing in the darkness over and over again the Deputies dragging her away. She had heard but had not seen anything other than the face of the girl's mother and how it had twisted and caved in on itself as if it, too, were melting under flames.

"The law is the law." She spoke quietly, tempering the anger behind her eyes. She still would not look at her daughter. Her mother had a tell, too, and it was palpable, thick like mud. "And everyone is taught what those laws look like. The courtroom is sacred, and anyone who demeans it must be punished. That is what the law says."

"But she was upset. I get upset, too."

"And you control it, don't you? Don't let it get out of hand, don't let it get away from you. Someone like Edith—well, best to take care of it now."

"But what if that were me?"

"That weren't you and it'd never be you."

"But what if it was?"

Her mother did not reply; instead she took another mouthful of beans and eggs and glanced up at her daughter, who was listening closely for what she knew lay just beneath her mother's surface, the thing that neither could speak of.

"I want you to come with me when I set out this morning. We'll stop by Arbuckle's. Want to tell him myself what I expect."

"He's coming here this afternoon. I'll tell him."

Her mother raised her eyebrows. "I know you're embarrassed. Thinking I treat you like a child, no doubt."

"I don't need no escort." Lady Mae pushed her plate away and crossed her arms.

"Yes, you do. You want a limp like mine?" Her mother stuck her leg out from underneath the table. "Or worse?"

"But now they know that they'll get in trouble."

"Don't mean it'll stop them. All it takes is one." She patted her thigh through her skirt. "Took two years before I could walk on my own again."

"But Ma, I don't—"

"Enough, Lady Mae. We're setting out for Arbuckle's together and that's that."

Arbuckle's shack was the same as Lady Mae's as all shacks were built from a rudimentary design aimed to give the residents shelter but not comfort. She and her mother had done what they might to make their own as cozy as they could, but beyond the old sofa and her great-grandmother's quilt, there was nothing much to distinguish their home from anyone else's. Arbuckle's porch was clean, but that was only because he took great pains to keep it that way. His father embarrassed him, but the drunkard was his father nonetheless, and Arbuckle spent a good deal of his life trying to please him.

Her mother knocked. There was a holler and a slamming of a door, footsteps, and the door opened. Arbuckle's father appeared, and from where Lady Mae stood behind her mother, she could see his unshaven face and dark circles under his eyes. His hair, matted and greasy, stuck to his forehead. He brought his hand to his face, his fingers healed at the knuckles, and rubbed his chin.

"What'd you want?" His voice was hoarse from the homemade cigars, the tobacco of which he grew along the side of their shack.

"Want to talk with your son."

"He ain't here." He leaned his shoulder against the doorframe.

"Well, where is he? I'll go to him, then." Her mother did not back away but instead leaned in toward the hulking man.

"Don't much know."

He cleared his throat and spat to his left. The phlegm landed next to her mother's feet, but her mother did not turn her head. She stared at Arbuckle's father and whether or not she was unnerved or intimidated, she gave no indication.

"Well, you tell him that I aim to speak with him. Send him to the depot if he returns. That's where I'll be."

"I ain't gonna send that boy nowhere. You go find him if you want him."

"You ain't making things any easier for yourself, Harland."

"And I ain't gonna make things easy for you, Winona."

"Very well." Her mother turned as if to leave, then paused. She turned her head and lowered her chin; she spoke over her shoulder. "But just so you know: you'd be right to leave that boy alone. You ain't above the law just 'cause you're his pa."

"He ain't gonna do nothing about nothing."

"So you say. But everyone's got their limit."

"I'm sure they do."

"Come along, Lady Mae," her mother said as she stepped off the porch.

"You go on with your mama now, little girl. Hate to see something happen to you out here on the road."

Her mother took Lady Mae by the arm and held it tight. She did not let go.

By the time Arbuckle arrived at Lady Mae's house that afternoon, the winds that had begun in the night blew fierce. Lady Mae felt them from the stack when she was cleaning out the stove, heard the soft howl when she closed the flue. It kicked up the dust and dropped it down onto the tin roof, an earthy patter that came and went. But the winds were good; soon there would be rain for the animals and residents alike. The water would rush down from the hills and into the valley fast, flooding the square and the crescent road, sloshing up to the wooden porches where the men and women would watch it. They'd grimace and grip the railing knowing there wasn't enough hay in the entire settlement to dam the flow.

Arbuckle knocked at the door one two three times even though he didn't need to, and when Lady Mae opened it, he immediately took off his hat and dipped his head toward her. Though it was only midafternoon the dust clouded the sun, and she could barely see past the third shack down. She felt the sandy air on her skin and in her eyes, tasted the pungent dirt far down her throat. Reaching for his arm, she pulled him inside before he could greet her and slammed the door shut.

"Storm's coming," she said.

"Sure is," he said and hung his hat on the rack next to the door. He bent and undid his frayed laces. Then he slipped his boots off and lined them up next to Lady Mae's, one pair large, one pair small, both scuffed and worn and filthy.

"Ain't much we can do but wait," she said.

"Suppose you're right."

"Be thankful for it, though."

"As we all should be."

They stood close to each other in front of the closed door as they spoke; it was not the first time Lady Mae had noticed his hair, or his hands, or the way his jawbone moved when he was trying to watch his words. He'd answer her questions if she asked them, but she didn't often know how to ask them, how to whisper the *what now* and *what then* and *will you always*. Sometimes Arbuckle would lose himself; his words flowed free, and Lady Mae found herself in the books he read, in what he imagined, in what he wished for. She, too, had imagined. Had they wanted the same thing? Or did he still see her as the child he taught all these years?

"You okay?" he asked and brought his hand up to her temple, brushing her skin with his thumb from the corner of her eye to her hairline. His eyes never left hers, and he looked at her like he always had. But this time his hand lingered by her ear, and he gently tucked her hair behind it before taking his hand away. It was a simple gesture, one of kindness and concern, but whatever the meaning behind it made no difference, for Lady Mae felt not for the first time a fluttering against her chest and a heat between her legs. "Seems a little better," he said.

"It's fine."

"Your mama's worried about you—we working in here or the kitchen?" He slung his satchel from one shoulder to the other.

"Here, I suppose," she said and pointed at the sofa. "What'd she say?"

"Says it weren't never like this for her—not this bad. Reckons things are getting worse over time. Residents acting up more than usual."

He put his satchel on the table in front of the sofa and opened it, taking out a notebook, a case of pencils, and two small books. Lady Mae made sure the door was latched and joined him, sinking down into the cushions and letting her leg lean up against his.

"She was quiet over breakfast. Think there's something she ain't telling me."

"Sure there's lots of things she ain't telling you," he said as he straightened the items neatly in row.

"That ain't what I mean—it seemed like, I don't know—"

"I can tell you she's worried," he interrupted. "Says she wants me to watch over you."

"She asked you?"

"Aye. I obliged, of course."

Lady Mae slapped her hands upon her knees hard enough to make Arbuckle's eyes go wide. "Don't need no minder. I ain't no baby."

"No, you ain't," he said, shaking his head. "But you're just as much my family as my pa, and so is your ma. I'd be right to oblige."

There was thickness in her throat. Though she could cry in front of him, she did not wish to and thought of the rain, of what was for dinner, of the way the wind sounded at the windows. She bit her lip and swallowed quickly and asked, "She seem different to you today?"

"Sure she's worried is all."

"Not sure. Seems more than that."

"She just asked I watch out for you is all. I promise I'd tell you if there were more, but there ain't. Now come on, I got another one for you."

She thought that he had more arithmetic for her and reached for one of the books on the table. But he put his hand out to stop her, producing instead another book from his jacket pocket. It was small and dark, no bigger than his hand and no thicker than a clothespin.

"What you got there?" Lady Mae asked.

"Something I think you'll like."

She held out her hand, and he gave it to her. The words that had once been on the cover were worn away and the binding stiches were loose; small threads hung out of the top and bottom of the book. It felt smooth and soft, as though held by many. She opened it, and the binding cracked and snapped, the smell of the yellowed pages homelike and warm. Her eyes saw the title then, and she closed the book quickly and looked up at Arbuckle.

"Now I know you've been talking to my ma more than you're letting on, Arbuckle. Come out with it now."

He exhaled slowly and looked over sheepishly at Lady Mae. "Listen—your ma, she knows a thing or two. And if she says we all ought to work on forgiveness then forgive is what we should try to do."

"But she's the one that wanted me to take them kids to court."

"Don't reckon that's what she's saying exactly."

"Well what else you think she's saying?"

"That maybe we got it all wrong."

"I don't think you ought to be saying such things," she said, and turned to look out of the window. She pulled the curtains tight. "I know where you're going with this."

"Maybe she's right—maybe we're both right. Maybe we can do things differently. Think: if there weren't no butchers, them kids wouldn't be reared to hate you."

It was the first time that Arbuckle had acknowledged what Lady Mae knew to be true; she was hated and hated by many. It was a hatred born the day she was, inescapable and profound. No matter how kind she had been to others, how submissive or defiant, it was always the same. She had only Arbuckle and her mother, an existence lonelier than she'd let herself grasp.

"I didn't mean—I don't mean to upset you, it's only—"

"I ain't upset—just that—"

But the words failed Lady Mae just as they had earlier; she knew then in that moment the feeling that had been with her all day long. At first, when she breakfasted in broken silence with her mother, she had thought it alarm, hot and unyielding. Her mother had weighed her words, intent on keeping something from Lady Mae. And though Lady Mae told herself that had there been anything terribly wrong her mother would've said so, there had been her mother's tight grasp, the concern behind her smile. Lady Mae was right to feel alarm, to feel the bubbling of worry. That wasn't all, though. Something else was there just beneath the surface and neither her mother nor Arbuckle were telling her straight. So in that moment as she sat there next to Arbuckle, the only friend she had in the world, it came upon her like a flood, the waters of which would drown her for what she felt all day, the tangled mass that sat inside of her, had been loss, a choking, unfathomable loss that had slowly taken her breath away.

"I think something bad is going to happen," she said, her eyes hot and blurry.

"Bad like what?"

"Don't know. Just a feeling I got down here." She put her arms across her stomach. "Ever since I got the telegram I been thinking—"

"I'm here." He put his arm around her shoulders, his grasp strong and protective. She rested her head on his shoulder.

She had the words in her mouth. All she had to do was open her lips, and out would tumble her heart, her shame—all of it, and quick as rain. There was the telegram, the attack. Her mother's quiet.

"I know. You've always been."

"And I always will be."

"Shouldn't say always. It's rotten luck."

"No such thing as luck."

"Then how do you explain the two of us?"

"Simple. Ain't no one else likes us. I know your ma hired me and all, but after all this time? You're more than just my pupil."

Lady Mae's breath caught. Ever since she received the telegram, she'd thought of telling him—what? That she was a child no more? That she spent the time without him thinking of the time with? She felt it there behind her breastbone, a deep urge to lean into him. "That so?" she asked. "How you mean?"

He pulled his arm off of Lady Mae's shoulders and

leaned forward, resting his elbows on his knees. He clasped his hands and tapped the tips of his thumbs together. "Well," he said. "First off, you're like kin to me."

"Kin?"

"Aye. Always thought what it would be like to have a brother, a sister. You the closest thing I got to it." He nudged her knee. "Hear me? The closest thing I got. Now go on," and he nodded to the small book on the table. "Go on."

She picked it up gingerly as if it would hurt her, as though the book itself held in it a power to destroy. She opened the cover and skimmed the title on the thin first page: *On Reason and Forgiveness*. Arbuckle reached over and turned the page for her, tapping the first sentence with his long finger. And so to please him as she liked to do, she read the opening line.

Forgiveness is only decreed when met with the removal of opinion and blame; such a decree can only occur with the suspension of simultaneous judgment.

"I ain't allowed to blame them? Edith and those boys?" Lady Mae raised her eyebrows at Arbuckle.

"That ain't it exactly. They did do something, and should be held accountable. It's what comes after. Here, see?" he asked and pointed to the phrase *suspension of simultaneous judgment*. "You can hold them accountable, but after—here," he said and flipped forward several pages. "Read this."

Forgiveness, in its simplest form, is to pardon, to let go, to release the burden of hurt. It is not condoning a wrong, or forgetting an offense; the purpose of forgiveness is to create hope for the future.

Lady Mae looked up from the book. "I don't see much hope coming. You and me, our lots," she said quietly. "All of it's written out for us—been so for a long time."

"But maybe that's the point."

"I don't follow," Lady Mae said and went to turn the page.

"Maybe them Deputies are trying to keep us from hoping," Arbuckle said, placing his hand on hers. "Maybe that's why they came up with the inheritance to begin with."

"Why'd they do that?"

"Well, what comes after hope?"

Lady Mae shrugged and pulled her hand out from underneath his. She was growing tired of the riddles, of always having to be the one to steer him straight again. He wouldn't come right out and say it, not ever. When pressed to reason why, he'd said telling someone something weren't the same as them getting there themselves.

"Let me say it this way: if you wanted something and thought it could be, wouldn't you try to do it?"

"I suppose so."

"And if all of us tried, who'd stop us?"

"Tried to what?"

"I don't know. Do what we want, live how we choose. Forgive each other."

"Them Deputies would never allow it. Anyone who tried would be up on the scaffold come Saturday."

"But there's only four of them. There's hundreds of us."

"What are you saying?"

Arbuckle brought his hand up to his head. He held his thumb and forefinger to the bridge of his nose and closed his eyes. "I'm just saying maybe there's something none of us have thought of yet."

"Can't reckon what that'd be."

He fell quiet then. Lady Mae thought she had angered him, disappointed him in her inability to believe that what he was saying was possible. "Besides," she said, "you know as well as I what happens when residents go and try something. When Settlement Three—"

"I ain't talking about Settlement Three."

"Well it's something to think about, now ain't it?" asked Lady Mae. She was suddenly angry at him—did he not remember how the only surviving man tore through the brush, naked and lashed, as they played behind her shack? How when he opened his mouth to speak, they saw that his tongue had been cut out? Mama, she had called, Mama! And her mother came running out of the shack, knife in hand, and approached the man. Lady Mae could not understand what the man said, but her mother, who leaned over him as he collapsed in the dust, nodded and placed a hand on his shoulder. She said something to him that Lady Mae did not catch, then told her young daughter to get inside, lock the door, and not come out until daybreak. But it had not rained, and though her mother had thrown the washwater into the dust, a dark red spot remained.

"It's just," he said. "It's—I don't know, Lady Mae. I guess just gets at me here, seeing you go through all this." He brought his closed fist to his chest. "There's got to be another way."

"There ain't. And even if there was, there's no point—nobody's ever going to forgive me. Or my ma."

"Well they sure can't if they ain't never been taught how."

Arbuckle took the book that Lady Mae held in her hand and flipped through it quickly, searching the print for the thing for which he had brought the book in the first place. There was something there—there was always something there—and he seemingly wanted to share it with her as he had shared so many things.

"Here." He pointed to a passage nearly halfway through the tiny book. "Go on, read it."

Lady Mae took the book back and focused on the

typed pages. The letters bent into each other, pressed close and blurred. She swallowed and read the sentence.

If there are those that do not wish to forgive, then surely the larger group cannot move forward until they have overcome their reliance on resentment as a tool to control.

"But I ain't got no resentment." Lady Mae handed the book back to Arbuckle, who kept the page marked with the tip of his finger. She was lying, of course, as the resentment burned deep inside her bones, but she did not know how to twist her tongue to say *felt it my whole life*.

"I ain't talking about you."

"And Ma only just started acting angry," she said, trying to convince herself. "And it was toward them kids is all."

"I ain't talking about your mama, neither."

"Who you talking about, then?"

He did not say, but instead widened his eyes and raised his brows at her. He did not say because he couldn't say, because to say it aloud was blasphemous and dangerous, even there in the safety of Lady Mae's front room. As she waited for him to respond, she felt the churning deep inside. It bubbled up, felt like blistering fire. If anyone heard them, they'd call treason and both would find themselves on the scaffold under the hot sun of midday, hundreds of eyes waiting patiently for the outcry to begin. They'd stand side by side, bodies inches away from each other. The residents would hurl words at them, spit at their feet, raise their butchered fists in the air, joyous to be witnessing the fall of the butcher's daughter and the only boy that loved her.

"You talking about them—"

"I am."

"Arbuckle, hush! Ought to know better than to go around saying things like that." Lady Mae twisted her body around, parted the curtains ever so slightly, and looked out of the window. The sky, now a dark brown, was thick with dust. Tall grasses in front of the shack bent and whipped in the strong wind.

Arbuckle looked out the window, too. They sat there silently listening to the whistling cracks and creaking roof, to the hatch door banging against the side of the coop.

"Lady Mae... what if it could be different?"

"Different how?" she asked and turned from the window to look him squarely in the eyes.

"What if there weren't no laws that said how you had to go about things?" he asked her.

"You talking about atonements?"

"Not just. What if," he said and stood up. He rubbed his hands together and then put them on his hips. "What if instead of coming up with how many atonements to give, the residents thought of the reasons why they should forgive someone?"

"Arbuckle!"

"Just a question is all." He paced back and forth as he did when he was onto something. "Ain't nothing wrong with wanting to forgive someone."

"Sure is when doing so undoes a law." But the words felt strange rolling off her tongue.

Arbuckle stopped in front of her and grabbed her by the shoulders softly. She could see him grinding his teeth, working his jaw in a fit of restraint, but try as he would he could not contain such treacherous thoughts. "What's to say the law's the right thing?"

"The Deputies say is what." She lifted up her hands and slowly took his off her shoulders, but she did not let go of them. She held them fast, desperately. What Arbuckle was saying wasn't allowed; that much she understood. But it weren't wrong, neither, and with that she knew not what to do.

"What's to say they're right?" he asked her, taking her hand and rubbing the skin between her thumb and forefinger. He pressed it softly, and she felt a pinch, a sting at her temple.

"You want to say they're wrong?" she asked, pulling her hands away. "Get you skinned for sure."

Arbuckle crossed his arms. He looked down at her from above, and she searched his eyes for the intention that she knew was inside. He couldn't help himself no more than his father, no more than her mother or herself. It was in him and she knew it and it was all she could do to not let the anger burn her up. *You could've steered him, Mama.*

"Can't skin us all," he said.

5

That evening Lady Mae sat on the sofa and waited for her mother to return home from the depot. After Arbuckle had left, she'd put up the chickens; the storm was nearly upon them, and the muddy sky sagged thick with wet. The rains would be swift and dangerous, and they couldn't afford to lose any more hens. Lady Mae closed up the coop, and as she did she thought of her mother's meddling, of Arbuckle's honesty, of the way her own hands felt in his. *I ain't no child no more, Mama.*

Her mother did not often anger her. Her voice was honey, her firm hand cradling. Perhaps what Lady Mae felt was not anger at all, but in any case she aimed to say something when her mother came home. She thought suddenly of her mother's dress, of what might be lurking in other pockets. She looked down at her own hands, curling her fingers one at a time inside of her palm; would she miss them if they were gone?

When her mother saw what Lady Mae had found on the ground—the fingertip—she had told her daughter that some residents wished to keep what they'd lost. True, some took their amputations home with them in a small glass case or even a satchel; did it help them to still have the tips and toes near, to be able to glance at them now and then? Maybe those residents kept their parts in a jar or bucket, tucked away behind their medicine cabinet or in their cellar. Or maybe they tied them to a string and brought them out once a year on the anniversary of their atonement to remind themselves that they survived. Others tore out of the chair without thinking—her mother had said it were the toughest of the settlement that ran the fastest.

But why had the fingertip been in her mother's pocket and not with the offal behind the depot? Her mother had patted her pocket as she said it, as though there were more bits and pieces than the one Lady Mae found. It wasn't like her to forget, though Lady Mae did see the distraction that hovered behind her mother's worried eyes. And while she had received the telegram weeks before regarding her upcoming obligations, that morning had been the first time her mother had mentioned the inheritance aloud. Lady Mae relaxed her fingers and felt something swirl inside of her.

The oil in the lamp next to her burned steadily in the falling light. She stared out the window, stared until her eyes went foggy and dry and thought of how she should've told Arbuckle her misgivings. Then, there, something moved in the distance, far down the road.

Squinting, she saw the shadowy shape of her mother grow as she came up the road. She was walking quickly, her arms swinging long as if scooping the air would get her home faster. The back edge of her dress billowed behind her, and Lady Mae saw the dust still sparkling in the twilight. She got up to fold the quilt that had fallen off the back of the sofa and saw then her mother break into a run, holding her kit of tools close to her chest. Lady Mae watched, confused, as her mother twisted her head to look behind her, stumbling and falling to the gravel road, her arms spread wide and her kit spilling open in front of her. Scrambling to collect her instruments, she climbed to her knees and shoved them back into her kit. She ran again, faster than before, and Lady Mae heard through the open window her mother shouting, her voice rising above the call of the cicadas. But she was too far away to make out clearly what she was saying.

Lady Mae had planned on demanding answers in regards to her conversation with Arbuckle, but a sickly feeling gave rise in her throat, and she found herself stepping backward into the dark corner of the room holding her great-grandmother's quilt in her arms. *What's gonna happen, Mama?* The clock ticked and her mother's voice grew louder and louder until the door burst open and the flame on the lamp went out from the gust of wind. Leaves scattered, their dried stems and tips scraping the wood floor as they tumbled inside.

Her mother slammed the door behind her and stood facing it, her head down and her hands on the latch. She hadn't seen Lady Mae, and though she stood like that for only a moment, she was rock still, her breathing rapid.

"Mama?"

Her mother spun around and backed up against the door, leaving one hand on the latch. "Go on. Get supper on," she ordered.

"What is it? What's wrong?"

"Go on now, in the kitchen."

Lady Mae did as she was told and turned to rush into the kitchen. But as she neared the doorframe she heard her mother's voice call after her.

"He was a child. Just a child. Six years old. When I tied the tourniquet, I had to wrap it four times around."

Lady Mae stood in the space between the living room and kitchen. She could not figure what her mother was saying, not exactly. But her mother's voice had trembled, and there even in the falling light of the day, her mother's sorrowful shoulders sagged and shook, her body engulfed in sadness.

"What'd he done?"

"Don't know. I just read the statement."

"Didn't it say nothing? Didn't it give an explanation?"

She wanted badly for her mother to say the boy deserved it; that he had murdered or destroyed or tormented. Instead, all her mother said was, "It don't work like that. Statement just gives directives, that's all."

"And what were they?"

"Four atonements."

"For a child?"

"Don't matter big or small."

"What'd he chose?"

Her mother didn't reply right away. Instead she leaned toward the window, quickly looked out, her eyes scanning the road and then the room before turning back to Lady Mae. She kept her hand on the latch.

"I couldn't do it."

"What do you mean you couldn't do it?"

"I couldn't do it. Didn't do it. Sent him home, packed up my things, and came back here."

They spoke back and forth in the dark now. Just the other day they had talked about her inheritance, but Lady Mae had not asked what would happen if the resident committing the crime was the butcher. It had occurred to her, though, and she had often wondered in the thick, black night if she could just say no. But she never broached the subject as doing so would tell her mother all she needed to know. Lady Mae didn't want to add to her mother's worry that she carried inside, and so she said nothing. She had kept it hidden and secret all this time, a burning, torturous question to which her mother held the answer. Now, in the living room, Lady Mae held her great-grandmother's quilt in her arms and finally understood. *You said we all got to obey, Mama.*

Lady Mae rubbed her fingertip against her thumb, pressing the nail into the skin to keep the fear that she first felt in her feet from creeping up her legs into her heart. "Mama?"

Her mother bent her head toward the window once again. Lady Mae approached her, finding solace in her mother's physical presence. Arbuckle was right: her mother would protect her from whatever she was waiting for. She looked past her mother's head out the window, toward the empty road and the fog that lay high enough to see where it started, a divide suspended just above the ground.

"Mama, what's going to happen?"

Her mother stepped away from the door and took the quilt from her daughter's hands. She folded it and draped it across the back of the sofa. Then she turned and embraced her daughter before pulling away and holding her hands to Lady Mae's hot cheeks. "Listen to what I say exactly, and please do not fear."

She took her daughter's chin in the tips of her fingers. "I am not afraid. Look at me," she said when her daughter's eyes fell to the floor, tugging her face up to her own. "There are laws, and they will come. Soon. And there's nothing you nor I can do; it is already done and was done the moment I dropped that little boy's hand and untied the tourniquet. It was done long ago, I suppose, before you was even you."

"What are you saying? You going to jail?"

"My girl, I ain't going nowhere."

She sat down. Patting the sofa seat so that her daughter might sit next to her, she wept openly and without abash. She held her arms out into which Lady Mae threw herself, pulling her mother in close enough to feel the racing of her heart.

"You going to be alright," her mother said. "We'll be just fine."

"What're they going to do you?"

Her mother gently smiled and smoothed back Lady Mae's hair, brushing it back off her shoulders and twisting curls around her fingers. "Don't much know."

"You've got to know something! Can't you remember the law?"

"Not any more than you, but I'll try if it'll calm you." She closed her eyes. "Seems I remember there being a penalty of some kind… a fine of some sort, or perhaps they'll take me to the square."

"For what? An outcry?"

"As an example. Try to shame me, us, our way. Even though it is the way the Deputies gave us long ago. Don't reckon it'll be that bad."

"But can't you just explain yourself? Can't you bring the boy back and give him his atonements? Just tell them you made a mistake, that you thought you had the wrong boy."

"It won't matter to them. Besides, don't reckon I made a mistake." She looked out the window again. They saw it at the same time: a small dot of light glowing in the distance. *That ain't the only thing that burns, Mama.* Lady Mae and her mother watched in silence as it grew brighter, bobbing up and down with each of the Deputies' steps. Had they opened the window, they might have been able to hear the boots grind in the gravel as they neared the house.

"What do you mean you didn't make a mistake?"

"I mean that sometimes one's got to do the wrong thing for the right reason."

Her mother took her daughter by the hands and pressed them to her own knees, which were thin and hard through her skirts. "Look at me now," she said to her daughter.

But Lady Mae could not look at her mother because to look at her would be to know what she had always known to be true deep down. It would be to see clearly what she knew lay behind her mother's kind eyes and tarnished hands.

"I ain't in the habit of telling you how to live your life, but I done been wrong about one thing I reckon."

"What? You ain't been wrong about nothing."

"Taught you that you ain't got no choice. Said I didn't have no choice, neither. About being the butcher."

"What're you saying?"

"True, it's our lineage—ain't no denying that. My mama, her mama, her mama before. All them women, all those years of standing by the chair. Never asking a single question."

Lady Mae wanted to ask her mother what she meant, what she was trying to say through the words that came rushing out like flooded waters. *And none of it will save you, Mama.* She felt herself barely able to breathe, to come up for air as she saw in her mother's face a calm she had not seen before.

"But that's not all that's true, my girl."

There were voices now, clear shouts and yells to *come out, we just want to talk, you know the laws.* Lady Mae's mother gripped her daughter tight. They stood, facing each other, hands in hands, and Lady Mae saw out of the corner of her eye a Deputy light a torch. They were nearly at the door.

"We all got a choice. I had one, but I chose to ignore it. To bury it down and use the laws as my cover."

"What kind of choice?"

Her mother's hands were cool and soft in her own. Lady Mae felt the fierce squeeze, the fingertips on her knuckles, as though her mother was trying to memorize her daughter's bones. The torchlight grew, and their shadows bounced off the wall of the living room, quivering, flickering.

"But I'd told you. That what I hear when they're

in the chair, well, they ain't wrong. Comes from a deep place, not one I reckon the Deputies could even know about."

There was the sound of a fist on wood. One two three it rapped, knocked, banged on the door. The planks on the shack's porch creaked under the weight of the Deputies. Their boots clacked, their tall hats illuminated by the torchlight. Lady Mae's mother grabbed her daughter and pulled her into the kitchen.

"We just want to talk," called a Deputy through the thin wood of the door. "Just got a few questions we'd like you to answer."

"Mama? They just want to talk. I don't think—"

"Lady Mae: if we all started forgiving one another, then what would be the purpose of the Deputies? If there weren't no crimes for the law to uphold?"

"We going to give you to the count of three to open this door," a Deputy called from outside. "No need to make this difficult."

Lady Mae heard three more pounds on the door. Then there was an axe through the door and the splitting of wood and the voices of the men. The first one to enter was Deputy Daniels, and he held the torch above his head. The shadows danced on his aged face. The light bore into Lady Mae's eyes as she struggled to get the words *what you done* and *don't go Mama* out of her mouth. But they were too sticky and thick to jump from her tongue. The three other Deputies of the settlement snaked in around Lady Mae's mother and encircled her, behind them a new, unfamiliar Deputy. He walked in slowly, in his hands a club, and sucked his teeth. His skin glistened, his stomach hung low over his belt. This was the one from Settlement Six—the one her mother had said was on his way months ago— but he did not seem to be in charge. No, although each Deputy held in hands a rope or a club or a chain, they waited for Deputy Daniels to speak.

"Winona, we need to ask you a few questions," said Deputy Daniels.

"I got nothing to say to none of you." Her arms hung at her sides, but Lady Mae saw her mother's gentle, small hands curl up into fists there in the glowing dark.

"Stands to seem you do. Least you need to explain yourself."

Her mother stood a meter from Lady Mae, her back to her daughter. Lady Mae wanted to reach out, grab her shoulders with both of her hands, and drag her backward into the kitchen, out the door, and beyond the settlement's edge. But all she could do was stand there, her feet in mud, and watch.

"I ain't butchering no child."

"You know your lot, Winona."

"What I know is that was just a boy. He ain't done nothing nobody else in his position wouldn't have done. He ought to be absolved."

"And you ought to know forgiveness by your own right is against the law."

"I don't much care for the law no more."

The chains scraped on the wooden floor, and the torches crackled in the stillness of the room. Three of the Deputies stared at her mother, but the fourth, the fat man Lady Mae had never seen before, stared past her mother at her, his black eyes narrowed and eager.

"Is that so?" Deputy Daniels asked.

"It is," replied her mother.

"I reckon it's your job to care."

"So you say."

"Anything less is, is—" he said, turning to the other Deputies. "That there's blasphemy, now ain't it?"

"Ain't saying nothing that everyone don't already believe."

"And what," Deputy Daniels, ignoring Lady Mae's mother, asked the other men in the room, "is the punishment for that?"

The unfamiliar Deputy spoke, his voice throaty and excited. "Judgment before the settlement."

"That's right," said Deputy Daniels, his fingers tapping upon his lips.

"I ain't standing on no scaffold."

"Seems you ain't got no choice."

"We all got a choice." Her mother crossed her arms over her chest and planted her feet squarely on the rug that covered half of the living-room floor.

"Mama—"

Her mother turned her head to the side and spoke over her shoulder, her voice clear and unafraid.

"It's alright, my girl."

The black-eyed Deputy flitted his eyes back and forth from Lady Mae to her mother as if trying to piece something together. He opened his mouth to speak, but Deputy Daniels held out his hand.

"Winona, you just come with us and do what you know needs be done."

"I ain't going nowhere with you."

"Yes, you are, Winona."

"Mama, just do what they say."

Her mother spun around and faced her daughter. The chains scraped on the floor as the Deputies inched their way toward her mother's back. She looked at Lady Mae and reached out her hand. Lady Mae took it in both of hers, tried to pull her near as if she could hide her mother in the folds of her dress. *If you let go you'll drown, Mama.*

Her mother spoke with a rushing clarity Lady Mae would never forget. "Remember forgiveness. Remember it as you would your own self."

When her mother spoke those words, Lady Mae found herself lunging and throwing her arms around her mother; she did not know what else to do. It was not the first time that day that her mother had spoken of forgiveness, but it would be her last. Her mother wriggled out of her daughter's arms and pushed Lady Mae back. The fat, eager Deputy jumped behind Lady Mae and tried to hold her, but she thrashed and clawed at him. She swiped at his face, her fingers meeting flesh. She brought her hand down across his cheek, felt skin bundle under her nails. He cried out and she kicked him and the last thing she remembered was her mother's voice rising above the thunder that bounded from the sky and the room and the marred Deputy pushing Lady Mae down and siccing himself upon her mother and snarling and grabbing and her mother's body on the floor and the club and the blood and Lady Mae *oh mama mama mama*.

PART TWO

INHERIT

6

Lady Mae took her keys out of her pocket. There were only two—one for her home and one for the depot. Before she tried the lock, she inspected the peeling and split frame for tampering just as she did each evening when she returned home. It was only one of the precautions she took as she had learned early on that despite the short distance between her shack and the depot, there were many places for a resident to hide. And while she hadn't been accosted in the nearly six years since her inheritance, she looked over her shoulder whenever she made the walk. If it was during the day, she kept her head down and listened to the chatter of residents or the cannery's whistle. But if it was night, if the low sky was black and the hills beyond invisible, her imagination took hold. She heard voices, silent footsteps running quickly and with purpose. So real did they seem that she would stop, still her breath, and turn on her heels to confront whoever had staked out after her. There was never anyone there, yet she carried her scalpel in her right hand each night, gripping it with four fingers until her knuckles turned white.

Just inside of the front door, Lady Mae struck a match upon the wall and cupped the flame around her hand. She held the burning stick between two fingers and lifted the glass of the lamp. As she held the match to the wick, the flame snaked toward her fingers. Only when she felt it on her skin did she shake her hand to extinguish the match. She set the shade gently on the table and turned up the wick. The room lightened; her shadow bounced as the flame bent and twisted in the open door's draft. She refrained from flicking the match out into the bramble that grew up against the porch. It hadn't rained for months, and one burning ember could send the dried sorghum and bluestem up in an instant. And so she pocketed the warm, burnt match and shut the door, making sure to bolt it tight.

Lady Mae sat down on the sofa and waited for her eyes to adjust to the dim light. When they did, she bent to untie her boots, which were clean as she had not seen any patients that day, and no one had brought her any animals. Finding the depot's letterbox empty was second only to Sundays and proved a much-needed respite from her duties as the butcher. She had been busier than normal lately and attributed the lack of residents' restraint to the insufferable heat, the incessant dry winds that shook the shacks from dusk until dawn. She rose stick-mouthed and thirsty, went to sleep with burning eyes. There was nothing to lessen her parched flesh and desiccated lips, no salve that could replace what was lost. It was enough to drive someone mad. Lady Mae knew that like her, the residents were on edge—all it would take would be a glance, an accidental bump to the shoulder, to set them off. Perhaps the sweat would drip one time too many into their eyes, or the sun might beat down too mightily upon their scalps. The heat, the unending and lamentable heat, had slithered under everyone's skin, and no one could get it out.

That day, however, there had been no scheduled atonements, no last-minute statements from the Deputies, no chickens or calves or swine. She spent her required eight-hour shift reading a book from Arbuckle that had arrived when the crocuses and gladioli had just started to peek through the soil. It wasn't the first book he sent her. Six weeks after he'd left, she received the first package. She tore open its paper and squeezed the book of short stories to her chest. She bent her head, breathed in the smell of the jagged pages and frayed binding knowing Arbuckle was alive, that his hands had touched what she held in her own. For over five years, he had sent her books procured from some unknown person in some unknown place. How he got them, she wasn't sure. Every few months one of the four Deputies of the settlement left a small package at Lady Mae's door under the eaves, leaning it up against the sagging screen. She never saw which Deputy it was, but Griffin and Worth, who were new in the last few years, usually patrolled. Deputy Parson, though a fixture in the settlement, tended to stay close to the square. Deputy Daniels—the magistrate for at least the last twenty years—didn't seem to leave the courthouse. It made no difference who had left the packages; it repulsed her to know they'd been on her porch and that the Deputies' hands had touched the only thing that still connected her to Arbuckle. Once the Deputies realized she would follow her orders, they left her alone. But whenever she opened her door to something once handled by one of them, she felt both a deep longing and the sick edging her tongue. The Deputy that had dealt her mother's death blow— she'd never seen him again, gone by the time Lady Mae came out of her haze. But she'd looked. She'd squinted and imagined and hoped for a glimpse, a clue, anything that would tell her where he was. And if she knew, she'd have staked out after him over the hills and peaks to the settlements she knew existed but had never seen.

I got it figured, Mama.

You best be safe, my girl.

For over five years, Arbuckle's absence had remained sharp and deep. He'd left no note, no clue as to where he'd gone. The day he'd disappeared, when he hadn't shown up for lessons like he was supposed to, she'd gone to his shack and knocked. She'd heard his father behind the door, but he didn't open it. She stood there, aimless and plagued with grief. First her mother. Then Arbuckle. She'd been right to fear their loss all along and stumbled down the steps. It wasn't until days later that she overheard the rest in Wilson's store as she crouched next to the grain bin and filled her parcel.

His father gone and went mad, Wilson said. Took an axe to his own son, heard it from one end of the road to the other. Last anyone had seen Arbuckle had been running up into the hills with only the clothes on his back. Had Lady Mae seen or heard Arbuckle's flight for herself, she would've gone running to him, begging him to take her, too. Seasons passed and he didn't return; it was just as well, as the ashes that remained would've swallowed him up.

But earlier that day, alone at the depot, she had spent her required time reading the most recent arrival: *Lessons on The Human Body and Its Health*. It was a scientific book on human physiology, and though the title promised facts, Lady Mae knew there'd be more. The book itself was a message she'd have to piece together, something Arbuckle desperately would want her to know; and so she had settled in and tried her best to decode it.

The Deputies used to examine the packages—
they told her as much, but they wouldn't have read
through the actual book at the border. They would
have skimmed the title and shook it for contraband,
waiting for a piece of paper to come loose and float
to the ground like a feather. They'd inspect it hoping
to find a reason to stake out after Arbuckle and do
away with the last of his lineage once and for all. But
Arbuckle was smart and knew Lady Mae would read
intently and with purpose, so when her eyes fell upon
a line at the bottom of the page toward the end of the
book, she made sure to read it twice: *the suffering of the
patient begins at the sentence.*

According to a study detailed in the chapter, it had
been determined that the body reacted physiologically
to any sentence given. Regardless if the criminal was
sentenced to one or ten or twenty atonements, their
bodies began to respond to the mere idea of it within
seconds. Lady Mae read slowly, twisting her hair with
her left hand, the depot silent and empty. The book
said those studied became spellbound, obsessed with
their sentence and convinced they could feel the hot
sizzle of a branding iron long before appearing for
their appointment. When she read that there was a
plummeting in her stomach and a fire on her own
skin; until that moment she hadn't thought of the days
or years leading up to the atonements. She hadn't
thought of anything. And when the patients arrived

at the depot, she steeled herself like her mother had taught her.

As she read, she was struck by an incomprehensible unease, a disquieting wave that curled under her. She searched for the origin of the discomfort, thought long about her mother and the kids that used to taunt her. Those residents that she first butchered herself. Nausea swelled up inside of her, but when she ran to the bucket that was reserved for smaller amputations, she could do nothing but spit and gag. As she crouched there at the base of the chair hanging onto the leather straps, her periphery went blurry and gray. She tried to rationalize it—the milk had gone bad, one of her patients had been contagious—but she knew it was the book, the sentence, the suffering, and such knowledge sickened her.

Once she was home and safe behind a bolted door, though, she told herself that the fear had been unfounded. And as she sat on the sofa in the dim light of the evening, she told herself that they had been thoughts and nothing more. But although she was able to keep her heart slow and her breathing soft, the gray appeared, the edges of which crackled and burned. It licked her bones, bubbled and blistered under her skin.

Ain't as thick as you, Mama.

I gave you everything you need, my girl.

Lady Mae stood up from the sofa and pushed her

thoughts of earlier aside as best she could for she had much to do; Arbuckle was arriving the next day and would be staying with her in her shack. In his last letter, he said that his inheritance was set to begin with the harvest and that if he didn't come willingly the Deputies would surely find him and drag him back anyways. It wouldn't be too bad, he'd said, saying that now that his father was gone nothing in Settlement Five could hurt him anymore. When Lady Mae read those words on the small piece of paper he'd procured from the back of a book, she felt a deep, inexplicable grief wash over her. She longed to be near him, to hear the voice she knew so well, to fold her hands over his and share in their anguish so long avoided.

He had written that he was taller, larger than he had been at nineteen and that the years since they'd seen each other had taken a toll on his body. Lady Mae doubted that such an interminable time could do much to Arbuckle, whose strong, calloused hands and broad shoulders were clear in her memory since she thought of him often and at length. Although he had said that he'd changed, Lady Mae knew she would recognize him instantly. She would see his eyes made darker by news of his father's death, his gait hurried by an invisible ache. In his face, she would recognize the child she had grown up with, the boy that found her the morning after her mother lay dead in the living room.

Lady Mae walked over to the stove in the corner and knelt down. She opened the door and pushed the silky ash around with her fingers before scooping it into the pail with a small shovel. When the pail was full and heavy she carried it out the back door to the edge where the land met the start of the rocky hills. There in the empty space beyond was the burn pile, heaving from the drought, and she tilted the pail down, dumping the ashes near the bottom. There was no breeze, and they landed noiselessly in the thick, electric air. She went back into the house, the handle squeaking as the pail swung. And as she closed the door behind her, pulling it shut and bolting it, she wondered if she'd feel safer with Arbuckle under her roof.

7

Lady Mae arrived at the depot long before her appointment the next morning. She had woken in the night and had risen with the heat. When the sun finally appeared above the eastern peaks, she set out carrying her kit of tools. Her patient, Ruby Swanson, lived on the other side of the settlement up by the canning factory. As it stood, she didn't know the details of Ruby's crime. Had she gone to the trial, she would have learned what it was the woman had done. But she hadn't been to a trial since Edith's, and while there were some that acknowledged her—Wilson, Ruby herself— she spoke to no one in the settlement otherwise. She was barred from inquiring directly, but sometimes the patients told her anyway and readily spilled their guilt. In the chair, they'd appeal to her, muttering innocence and injustice, and although Lady Mae tried not to, she heard their pleading words. She felt them worm their way into that tangled ball inside her and stay there.

This what you felt, Mama?
Don't you know it is, my girl.

She spent an hour meticulously cleaning her tools, washing them first in soapy water before drying and shining them and slipping them back into her kit. She did this ritual every morning and every night. She held and turned the instruments in her hands. The loss of her smallest fingers, taken by the Deputies as punishment for injuring the Deputy that fateful night, had not affected her ability to do her job. For a long time she wondered why they hadn't taken her toes or the bottom of her ear. But eventually she had it figured: they wanted the guilty to see the old stumps, let them know that not even the butcher was above the law.

It was in those moments that she allowed herself to think of her mother at length and with focus. Five years—five and a half to be exact—had passed, and still Lady Mae could not fully understand the last words her mother had spoken. *Remember forgiveness as you would your own self.* When she thought of it, she saw only the stretch of her mother's lips, her jaw wide, her teeth in the torchlight. The scene played out over and over behind closed eyes, and each time Lady Mae leaned in to her mother's ghost. She strained her ears, hoping to hear her mother's soft voice once again, but there was only silence. Lady Mae grabbed at the silence desperately, but she could not hold on to it.

It blew past her sounding only like the wind, like the rush of the falls or the soft beat of wings in the air.

Forgiveness. Who would she forgive? The children, now grown, that tormented her so many years ago? The other residents that had turned their own backs to her and her mother? The Deputies that had taken everything from her? She was waiting for something, some signal or sign that forgiveness was even in her at all. But nothing came, and instead the dark inside of her grew. Every time she tried to see inside of its wooly mass, it was too thick and too black to make any sense of it. And the more she chased forgiveness, the further away it got. Even when it flickered in front of her, she did not know how to pull it in close so that it stayed with her always.

Lady Mae was putting the knives and scissors and electrical box on the long table in front of the chair when Ruby knocked on the door. The electrical box was a newer tool—her mother had told her she'd never actually used it, but the Deputies had shown up one day telling Lady Mae that she was required to offer it as an atonement choice no matter the crime. Too many missing fingers, they'd said. Ain't going to have no one to do the work needed. Many of the residents had praised the advancement—they wouldn't necessarily lose any more parts of themselves. But the tool was tricky, and despite Lady Mae's best efforts, she left one resident catatonic. The Deputies had pardoned her—with advances come risks, they'd said. Still, the experience had kept sleep from her for months, and while she always made sure the patient could see the electrical box, she didn't explain what it did unless asked directly.

Ruby banged on the wooden door several more times and yelled through the small, barred window that was shuttered. Lady Mae went to the door, stood on her toes and slid the shutter open. The stout woman, her long gray hair matted and her cheeks a swollen red, was inches from Lady Mae's nose.

"Hello, Ruby."

"Miss Hilvers." She spoke loudly and moved her head to try to see behind Lady Mae.

"You're a bit early."

"Thought I'd come get it over with," she said, realizing she could see nothing from where she stood outside of the door.

"I see," said Lady Mae. "Just that it's against the law to go early."

"Don't care about no law."

"Well, I got to care about it."

"Figure you do."

Each woman looked at the other; one young, one old, facing each other through the iron bars. This was to be Ruby's first atonement, and Lady Mae expected to see some kind of fear hiding behind the woman's narrowed eyes, but her stare remained unwavering, her shoulders square.

"You come alone?" Lady Mae asked.

"Was told I had to do as much, and I ain't the kind to be dishonest. You gonna let me in?"

"You just wait there now, and I'll unlock this door at the appointed time."

"Been waiting for this my whole life. Surprised I made it this long."

Though Ruby still held her eyes to Lady Mae's, her words became hurried, her breathing fast. She was afraid, though that was not all. There was an eagerness in her voice, a burning, throaty defiance. It was not rare for patients to show up at the depot with a mind to holler, but as soon as Lady Mae opened the door, they mostly fell silent, scared and regretful. The woman had not talked back to Lady Mae, not exactly. She wasn't sure if Ruby was provoking her, if there were a bundle of brothers waiting on either side of the door to ambush her as she opened it.

The two women stared at each other, and Lady Mae waited for Ruby's eyes to drop. But they didn't. They remained unblinking and focused on Lady Mae, even as she closed the small wooden shutter of the barred window. Ruby's presence, the stiffness behind her eyes, made Lady Mae's skin crawl, and she was at a loss to understand why the woman—the only one in the settlement that ever spoke to Lady Mae directly— seemed ready to jump through the bars.

Behind the closed door, Lady Mae brought her

hand to her heart, feeling it beat against her breast. Then she pressed her ear against the door and closed her eyes. She heard Ruby's boots pacing the porch and felt the soft vibration of her steps as she walked the wooden boards. Lady Mae half expected the woman to start yelling or banging on the door again, but through the thick oak she heard a song so familiar it made her stomach plummet to the earth. Lady Mae did not move or breathe. She listened to Ruby and to her voice, which held in it not sorrow nor guilt, but a grace and ease that belied the woman's sentence. It was the same song—and of this Lady Mae was sure—that her mother had hummed the day she had crouched underneath the open window of the depot and listened to her mother take from a man what was hers to take by law. Lady Mae pulled away from the door quickly, stumbling backward until her hands hit the table behind her. Ruby's file fell to the ground, and as Lady Mae bent to pick it up she saw written in the calligraphy of the Deputies the assignment of three atonements. It wasn't a lot, but most residents ended up with only one or two at a time. What could that old woman have done to cost her three pieces of herself?

On the back wall next to the table was a black telephone. Lady Mae had never used it before, though she could easily recall being instructed in how to do so. Pick up the receiver, put a finger in the number nine—the only number on the telephone—and wait for someone to answer on the other end. She had been told it was for emergencies—blood that wouldn't slow, an uncooperative patient, an attack—and while Ruby's presence outside the door did not necessarily constitute an emergency, the small prick of fear in Lady Mae's chest thumped loudly; it was something she'd listened to since her mother's death. Perhaps had she heeded the warning drum that beat from within, the one that had been there all along, her mother would at that moment be sitting on a chair in the shack waiting for her daughter to arrive home.

Should've done something, Mama.

Ain't nothing in the world you could have done, my girl.

She brought her hand up and brushed the metal earpiece with her fingertips. It was smooth and cool against her warm skin. As she lifted it out of its cradle, the book from Arbuckle she had read the day before suddenly came to mind. The sentence; the punishment begins at the sentence. It was the message Arbuckle had wanted her to receive. She was sure of it. She let her hand drop to her side, pressing the receiver into the folds of her skirt and thought of the patient, of that woman standing outside waiting for an atonement.

With the receiver in one hand, she turned to the inquest page in Ruby's file and skimmed down to the date of her sentencing: one year ago to the day. Why had she waited so long? If what the book said was true—that the dread and panic was there from the outset—wouldn't residents want to come and get it over with? For over three hundred days and nights Ruby must have thought about it—what it would be like to walk up to the depot whole and leave with something gone. Had she cried? Had she begged the victim or their family to spare her just this once? Or was she resolute, finding inside of her a strength she never knew she had? She straightened up, and when she hooked her finger in the number nine, she saw the crescent moons her fingernails had carved into her palm.

"Settlement Five, Iverson here."

So the fifth Deputy had finally arrived. Deputy Daniels had announced only three days before that a new Deputy was on his way. Got some changes in store, he'd said. The residents, afraid and uncertain, had spent the time since making preparations. They'd went to their lots early in the morning and stayed late into the night, and if they were like Lady Mae, had made sure that nothing under their roofs could be seen as blasphemous. They dusted the framed bylaws, hung straight their own certificate of inheritance, made sure their porches were tidy. They shined their boots and ironed their best clothes so that when they met whomever had been sent to Settlement Five, they'd appear no different from anyone else.

Lady Mae had stopped hoping any new Deputies would be the same as the one that took her mother.

Deputies changed now and again—perhaps a handful had come and went in the last five years, but it was never him. Even still, she was wary of them all—had been since she could remember. Her revulsion had grown over the years, though—after her mother, after the burning of Arbuckle's shack and his father along with it, after what they'd done to Edith so long ago. That last one stayed with Lady Mae more than she'd thought it would; the girl had just been a child, terrified and unable to control the hatred that her parents had poured into her. And when the settlement had descended on the square to watch the torching, Lady Mae had looked at the ground, at the residents' tired feet in their worn boots. She hadn't looked up, not even when she heard the girl scream her name as the flames consumed her toes; not even then. Had she been there, Lady Mae's mother would have pressed her close, would have held her hand over her daughter's exposed ear. But she wasn't there, and so Lady Mae had heard everything, had seen it all even though she hadn't raised her head once.

"This here's the butcher," she said into the receiver. She was facing the room, her eyes on Ruby's file.

"What is this regarding?"

"There's a patient here. She's early. Says she wants to get it over and done with. Says her name is Ruby Swanson."

The clock ticked, and Lady Mae heard the woman

on the porch, the planks creaking as she paced outside of the door.

"Yes, and?"

"And she just seems suspicious is all."

"How you mean?"

Lady Mae licked her dry lips and tasted salty sweat on her tongue, felt the slow drip down the back of her neck. It was hot—hot like it hadn't been in years.

"Wanted to see if there's anything I ought to know," Lady Mae said into the receiver. "Anything I should've been warned about. There ain't nothing in her file."

She heard the rifling of papers and the sucking of teeth, and as Lady Mae waited for a response, she leaned up against the bare wooden wall and wrapped the telephone cord around her fingers.

"Where are you?"

The words left her mouth before she had time to think, and in an effort to distance herself from them, she stepped quickly away from the wall.

"Lady Mae, I believe you more than anybody ought to know about asking questions."

The hairs stood on the back of her neck at the mention of her name, spoken slowly and deliberately, the Deputy's voice stringing out each syllable in a growl. She tried to push down the salty panic, but her breath caught, the alarm thick on her tongue.

"What do you mean?"

Perhaps she had spoken defensively, the initial reaction to preserve her mother's reputation both immediate and innate. She wanted to say *was you in my house*. Her lips moved and her eyes widened. Over the years, she'd examined the faces of each Deputy that came and went, hoping to see four jagged lines upon his left cheek. Then she'd know if he had been in her home under her roof or if he had watched them bash her mother's head in or if he had done it himself. To her it mattered not; they were all guilty, no one any more than any other, each beholden to the crime. There was a lurching in her chest as though her insides were metal drawn out by nickel, and though her mouth remained closed, her teeth found the inside of her lower lip. She chewed softly at first, feeling the slick bumps and frenum with her tongue.

The Deputy—Deputy Iverson—sucked his teeth again, let out a long exhale that rushed into her ears. The crackling papers in the background fell silent. "Lady Mae," he said. "You know the law."

When she heard her name again, she bit down. As she pierced the flesh she held between her teeth, she tasted the blood, felt the iron pool in the pocket of her cheek. The Deputy sounded far away suddenly, like he was down a deep tunnel that lay beneath the earth. He had said her name too many times. And she'd had enough.

What if I could, Mama?

What good are you dead, my girl?

"You there, Lady Mae?"

She closed her eyes and tried to sear the sound of his dripping voice in her mind so that one day when she was heading into town or in the square, she might recognize it. She'd take something from her kit—something small that she could fit in her hand—and approach him from behind, working quickly and without thought as she had been trained to do. She'd put a needle through his heart—undetectable and instantaneous—and she'd watch him fall like a rag doll to the dusty road.

The clock struck the hour, and Ruby banged on the door again. She hollered outside, and it made Lady Mae think of Arbuckle and the way his father would yell in the night. But when she opened her mouth to ask, all that came out was, "What do you advise?"

"Advisory falls outside of our jurisdiction."

"Do you think she is—" she began, and then the breathing and crackling and sucking of teeth ceased. Lady Mae stood there with the silent receiver up to her ear for a moment before untwisting the cord from her fingers and placing it back on its cradle. She stood there, the wooden door shaking under Ruby's furious fist, the clock ticking seven eight nine ten. When it fell silent, she went to the door and unbolted the lock.

Ruby looked over Lady Mae's head and shoulders in an attempt to see inside before even entering the depot. She must've heard the stories and likely knew well a resident or two that found themselves at the mercy of the butcher. Was it what she had imagined?

"Where do you want me?" Ruby asked.

Lady Mae pointed to the black leather chair that sat in the middle of the room. She was sure not to take her eyes off Ruby who examined the tools laid out on the table against the wall.

"You going to use all those?" she asked. Her arms were crossed over her breasts, and she hinged at the waist peering at the items, no doubt so that she could make her selection carefully.

"Depends on what you want. Says here you've got three." Lady Mae held up her file and waved it back and forth.

"So it does."

Ruby did not look at Lady Mae. Instead, she stepped slowly, carefully, from one end of the table to the other, her eyes falling upon each tool. But she did not blink.

"You doing just one? Or you want to do all of them?" Lady Mae asked.

"Doing all of them," Ruby muttered. "Ain't no chance I'm ever coming back here."

Lady Mae motioned for Ruby to sit in the chair, which she did, the leather creaking and squeaking underneath worrisome weight. She looked at the straps that hung from the arms and lifted one up with a wrinkled hand. Her fingers stroked the cracked leather, and then she let it fall to the side. It swung back and forth, its buckle clanking against the chair.

"You sure about that now? Once I start, I've got to finish." Lady Mae pulled her stool over next to the chair and sat down quietly.

"I'm sure."

"Alright, then. What'll it be?"

"These," she said and held out her left hand and wiggled three fingers. "I figure I can get by without them." Her eyes then looked over at the electrical box still on the table. She tilted her head toward it. "What's that?"

"It sends an electrical current through you. Kind of like lightning, but not as strong."

"Does it hurt?"

"Some say yes, some say no." Lady Mae spoke softly; she held behind her breath the dread that swelled in her stomach.

Ruby took her hand back, placed it in her lap, and thought of her options. She'd known for a year. She had dreamed about it, asked about it, thought about it; that day was finally upon her and all she could do was seek out that which she thought the least painful.

"And that counts as one?" Ruby asked.

"Each time, yes."

"And it won't kill me?"

"Shouldn't. Anyway, it's against the law to kill you."

Ruby looked down at her fingers. They were old and fat and rough. She thrust her hand back at Lady Mae.

"Just this finger," she said, pointing to the one with her wedding ring. "Been trying to get this off for years."

Lady Mae took up her chart and began writing the treatment. Her hand shook, and she thought it was because she was afraid. But Ruby must not have been that dangerous. If she were, she'd be accompanied by a Deputy or two and they would stand on either side of her dressed in their black coats and tall hats. They would make no motion, no movements when the screaming began. They would simply stare ahead at some imaginary spot on the wall and deafen their ears to the howling and begging. They would stand mercilessly and without regard.

"Alright, that's one. What else?"

"I'll do the current thing for the other two," she said, and tilted her head toward the electrical box.

"You sure now?" Lady Mae shouldn't have been asking and as such she spoke low, her hands gripping the sides of the chart.

"Yes," Ruby said.

Lady Mae returned to the chart, wrote down the other treatments and signed the bottom. When she handed the chart to Ruby their hands touched, and Lady Mae thought of what Ruby must've done to end up in front of her.

She held on to the chart, pulled at it even, wanting

somehow to release Ruby from her sentence. Had the woman kept track of her days, marking them off with chalk on the wall as each one passed?

"I'll do the currents first," Lady Mae told her. "Might help numb you for the finger."

Lady Mae got up and took the electrical box from the table. Wires came out of two of the sides, at the end of which were small metal squares. She licked each square and put them on either side of Ruby's forehead. "Just have to get them into place. Now don't move or they'll slip, and we'll have to start over," but as she said this she felt a deadening in her feet and a spasm in her belly.

The woman sat rigidly, her chest still and her eyes closed. "Your mama…" she said.

Lady Mae's heart tumbled, and she froze. Her hands were on Ruby's head, her fingertips tapping the small metal squares to flesh. They stayed there, unmoving, trembling, a deep, anxious taste on her tongue.

"Say again?"

"She was a good woman."

"Aye, she was." Lady Mae moved her hands again and adjusted the metal, tucked the wires behind Ruby's ears.

"Always tried to do right, no doubt." Ruby spoke loudly as if Lady Mae were not just inches from her.

"That she did."

"Them Deputies called blasphemy on her."

Lady Mae did not answer but took her hands away from Ruby's head and turned to the electrical box.

"Were it true?" Ruby asked.

With her back turned to the woman, Lady Mae felt as if she were on fire. If she said yes, then what kind of daughter was she? What kind of woman? She'd be just as guilty as the scar-faced Deputy, just as to blame as the others with their chains and torches and tall hats that fell from their heads after the first whip. If she said no: what then? Was it a trick devised by the Deputies—or worse, the residents? Were they waiting right outside the door for her to say it was all lies and she saw them and they took her life because?

"Just want to say, we was all grateful she spared that boy even if were only for a spell."

If Lady Mae moved, if she spoke, what would come out of her? Would she pour herself onto the floor beneath the chair, float like ash up into the sky? She picked up the electrical box and held the black metal, which was heavy in her hands. The sides were smooth and cool, and she rubbed the tip of her thumb across the switch, the gauge, and back to the switch again.

"Aye. She was a good butcher," said Lady Mae as she turned back toward Ruby. She tried to level her voice.

"I ain't talking about that. Talking about what she had in her." Ruby brought her hand to her chest, made a fist, and held it there. She lowered her chin and closed her eyes. Then she spoke again. "I reckon you got the same thing."

Her mother had talked of what patients said while they were in the chair—had said she'd heard it all and that the residents would likely do anything to stave off the first atonement. Was that what Ruby was doing? Trying to draw out time so that she kept her finger for just a little more?

"Reckon it's time to begin," Lady Mae said.

"Aye. But listen here—we all know you got it, too. You just ain't got no idea."

"I'm gonna count to three."

"Ain't got no idea."

"One, two—" and Lady Mae flipped the switch. Ruby shook and her mouth slacked and her eyelids parted revealing the whites of her eyes. Her fingers curled and twitched. Her feet floundered, stomping the floor and kicking wildly at the air. After five seconds, Lady Mae turned the box off. Ruby's head hung down as they usually do after a surge, and Lady Mae took her wrist to check her vitals. Then she lifted her eyelids and checked her pupils, waiting for her focus to return. When she thought Ruby coherent enough she asked, "Shall we continue?"

Ruby nodded, but Lady Mae knew it was an involuntary gesture from the lingering electricity. She wanted Ruby to say no, but she couldn't speak. She wanted Ruby to change her mind, but she couldn't think, her brain muddled and dim.

8

Lady Mae was late meeting Arbuckle that day; the surges she had hoped would help with Ruby's amputation were not enough to keep the woman still. Though the leather straps were pulled as taut as possible without cutting into her skin, the woman's hand shook and twitched when the blade touched the fourth finger of her left hand. Her mouth opened instinctively as she tried to scream with the first incision, but the electricity had made her weak and her moans, guttural and low, betrayed her earlier demeanor. When it was all said and done, Ruby had looked at Lady Mae. Her eyes, suffering and unclear, had held to Lady Mae's face as she cauterized the cut and then wrapped it in cloth. Ruby stared at her as if trying to see something lying deep down in Lady Mae's bones. What she'd said about her mother, about her—her mother had told her as much. Someday you'll know, she'd said.

This what you meant, Mama.

Clear as day to me, my girl.

As Lady Mae walked the crescent road toward the square, she saw Arbuckle up ahead sitting by himself on a bench. He was waiting for her even though she had told him to meet her in the square. She paused, smoothed her hair, and tucked the stray ends behind her ears. He had only one suitcase between his legs and looked in the direction of the courthouse. What would she say to him after all this time? That each time she'd dreamed of him it was nearly the same; the two of them standing in a field of nasturtium, the red petals brushing against their limbs? Would she say that she had held him still so as to not crush the tender leaves and stems, and that in doing so their lips came close enough to feel the heat of the other?

Her throat seized as if it were trying to wrap itself around her loneliness, for she had not allowed herself to think of the emptiness his absence left in its wake. Because then what? He was gone then, and though she knew that he would return immediately at her words *come back* and *why'd you go*, she did not wish to be the thing for which he relented. She'd been angry for a long time; he'd left her, or so that was what she'd understood to be true after he'd gone. But since the fire, her anger had diminished. She was not surprised by this, but what she found, what was unaccounted for, was that the other feeling—the one she purposely hadn't named— unraveled the tangled mass inside her just enough.

Maybe I won't need them no more, Mama.
Careful what you let go of, my girl.
"Arbuckle!" she called.

His head turned in her direction, and when his eyes met hers, a relief washed over her so mightily that her legs went weak. Her heart leaped, and her stomach pitched. It was not just Arbuckle in front of her; it was her childhood, her own remains she thought long gone sitting and waiting for her. It was her own existence, and it burned her eyes bright. It was that she'd been there, and he hadn't. It was what she saw that he knew but wouldn't say directly. It was all of it, a deafening cyclone of madness that engulfed her there in the square in the late afternoon sun.

They walked toward each other with trepidation, as if the other might disappear should they move too quickly. When they neared, their eyes took in the other's. It was Arbuckle after all, the same boy that had watched her mother burn beside her. He was only slightly different—taller, more muscular. But the crease in his brow had remained, and though the scars from his father so long ago had faded, she could see them, knew which was from a fist, which from a glass bottle, a wooden beam. To Lady Mae he was as handsome as could be, more than she remembered. She put her hand to her stomach, took in a deep sip of breath. What would he think of her in the early evening light? Five and a half years ago, she'd been a child. Would he rustle her hair as he used to, tease her when she ran after the chickens? Perhaps he too had thought of her long into the dark night, remembering how their shoulders touched as they sat on the sofa, how close their hands remained during lessons.

But then, as if they'd been doing it their whole lives, their arms found each other. They held each other tightly as if they were drowning, sinking down into the murky waters of memory. Lady Mae's head fit just right into the curve of Arbuckle's neck. They stood as one, pressed together by an unseen force, and when they pulled away from each other, they found themselves alone in the square, the hot wind blowing from the west and carrying with it the promise of rain.

When their bodies broke from each other, Arbuckle cupped her chin in his hand, which was rough and warm. It had been years since she was touched in such a familial and loving way. Her eyes went hot, her teeth ground as she tried to stave off the welling sorrow working its way out of her. But it was of no use. The tears came, fell from her lids to the dust, and when she looked down, she saw the wet earth at the tips of her toes.

"Lady Mae, what's all this?" he asked as he brought his thumb to her cheek. "Thought you'd be mad at me."

"I was. I am." She brought her forearm up to her face and wiped her cheeks with the rough fabric of her dress.

"I know it."

Three birds circled overhead in a westward current. Their wings beat against blue sky, and Arbuckle looked up. He kept his palm on Lady Mae's cheek, and while he stared after the birds, she studied his face. His lankiness was gone; he was a man, no longer a child under his father's thumb. There was a tumble deep down, a knocking at her ribs; Arbuckle was back, and the fullness of it all nearly took her breath away.

"Look at us," Lady Mae said.

"I'll say."

"You look well."

"As do you. How high are them boots?"

"Ain't much. I grew is all."

"So you did, so you did."

"You as well."

He pushed up his sleeves to his elbows and dropped his eyes. "Well, I am newly twenty-five."

"That'd be right."

Their eyes held, squinting but not daring to blink. She was afraid to look elsewhere, as if even a momentary disappearance of his face would set her back nearly six years. How had she managed all this time? Bit by bit, cut by cut. In each she felt both a relief and an unrest—this was what she had to do to live. And that's what her mother wanted. She assumed Arbuckle, too. So she had done it over and over again until it was like running her hands under cool water at the end of a day, both mechanical and necessary.

"Well, what now?" Arbuckle asked.

"Thought we'd go back to my shack. Unless—"

"You ain't got to go to the depot?"

"I was already there. That's why—"

She cast her eyes toward the dusty earth and stared at the tips of her tattered boots, at the dirt lining the edges of her skirts, hoping that he did not notice the splatters of dried blood that could never come clean. A shame rose, knotted and lead-like.

He ain't going to understand, Mama.

Not if you don't give him a chance, my girl.

"That's why what?"

"There was a woman, and she—"

"Someone come at you?" Arbuckle asked. He brought his hand to her arm and squeezed it gently.

"No. Ain't no one lay a hand on me since the inheritance," Lady Mae said.

"They don't need to lay hands on to hurt you." In his eyes she saw the concern and for that she chastised herself. She did not want his pity.

"I ain't hurt."

Arbuckle said nothing in return, but she watched his chest rise with each breath, watched him work his jaw like he always had. She wanted to grab his arms, press into him the words *you got your own lot* and *just as bad*. He'd talked in his letters how things would be different once he was in charge at the cannery, but Lady Mae understood that not all things intended took hold, and not all that took hold was intended. Arbuckle would do what he'd need to do just as all the other residents had, including Lady Mae herself. But he was not made of the same mortar as the others; he had risen out of his own mother's ashes with hope in his heart. And Lady Mae feared it would kill him dead.

"Just wanted to tell you why I was late is all," Lady Mae said.

He didn't believe her. She never could lie to him, but she didn't want to have to explain—not there. There was Ruby's talk of her mother, the Deputy on the telephone, and they both sprung in her a fear so mighty that though she tried, she could not push both back down into the bubbling mass.

"This place changed much?" he asked.

She knew what he wasn't asking. She'd told him herself, the letter written and sent even before the timber stopped smoking. His father's shack had caught fire and there had been no water to put it out. The flames were too hot to see if his father was still in there, but when it had burned to the ground, Wilson took a long pole and walking around the scorched perimeter, poked at the ash until he found bones. And so while Arbuckle did not mention his father, Lady Mae understood how the absence of an only parent, even if they'd been a monster, left a chasm that nothing could fill. He'd ask after his father when he was ready; perhaps when night came and they were safe in her shack together, she'd tell him about that night—what she'd heard about it at least—and say we both got ash now.

"Want to go by it?" Lady Mae asked.

"Don't know," he said and tucked his lower lip under his teeth.

"I'll come with if you want."

"It ain't that." He shook his head and looked down at the ground.

"Then what?"

Arbuckle then raised his head toward the hills, at the switch grass and salvias that still bloomed despite the heat. Although his face was turned away from her, she knew his eyes worried. His shoulders hunched, and he took his suitcase from one hand to the other.

"Well, I've made up the cot for you. Let us just go on there," she said. "Never you mind anything else."

"Sure did miss you," he said.

"I know it."

"What, you ain't miss me?"

"Stop messing. I did. Nice to be talking to someone else."

Lady Mae had not said what she meant; the truth, hidden behind words she had practiced and rehearsed and made sure gave nothing away, was there right at the edges. It simmered in her periphery, a longing so instinctual and prolonged, she felt as if it would swallow her up.

There were few other residents out, but those that were walked hurriedly toward the square. Out of the corner of her eye, Lady Mae saw them turn their heads toward herself and Arbuckle as they passed. Perhaps they were afraid that when he took over at the cannery in just a few weeks' time, it'd be just as bad as when his father ran it. Maybe worse. They would no doubt go back to their own shacks with the news of Arbuckle's return and around their tables, the families would talk. Would he work them until they could stand no longer, until their knees buckled underneath them, their lips bloody and raw from the heat? Would their hands be blistered and peeling from the steam? When Arbuckle's father had been in charge, the Deputies let him do anything he wanted as long as profit was involved. And despite the wretched human that he was, he did turn a profit. Not that the residents saw any of it. The Deputies kept from the residents what was rightly theirs, and instead sported new hats and shiny canes. Their chains glistened brightly in the sun. Their torches burned longer. The scaffold was sanded and scrubbed.

Lady Mae and Arbuckle walked for several moments in silence; the earth, salty and dry, held them gently as they did. There was the sound of the horses' hooves in gravelly dust, her skirts flapping in the wind, the squeak of the suitcase's handle as Arbuckle shifted it from one hand to the other. There was so much she meant to tell him, but all she could do was count how many footsteps were in stride with each, telling herself that if she got to twenty he'd stay for good.

"Been this hot long?" Arbuckle asked.

"Since the solstice. Storm's coming, though."

She licked her index finger and held it up to the sky. The wind blew against the pad of her finger, and she squinted to better see up toward the mountain ridge.

"There," she said and pointed above the white specked peak. "It's just on the other side. See them clouds?"

"When'd you learn about them clouds?" he asked. He took her hand in his; it was not the first time in her life that he'd made such gesture, but as she absorbed his warmth and strength she became aware of her body, of her heart leaping quick and untethered. It'd been so long since anyone had touched her, and in that moment there on the crescent road not fifty paces from the square she felt the weight of the absence as if for the first time. Her eyes stung and she grit her teeth together; she did not want to give into it there, did not want Arbuckle or any other resident to witness her weakness, gray and muddy and thick as hide.

Lady Mae had long dreamed of their reunion— she'd planned what she'd say, how he might answer, where the words they spoke to each other might take them. The thing, the weighty question that burned at the edges—how could she ask that? What would he say to the *why* and *how* and *could you* that she so desperately needed to know? She'd resolved that morning that she'd ask, that she couldn't move beyond anything without an answer. And so in a clear voice she asked, "Why'd you leave?"

Arbuckle sucked in a breath, but did not immediately speak. Instead, his mouth twisted as though to not let the words out. She pulled at his hand. "It's okay," she said. "You can tell me."

"Don't reckon I can say, exactly."

"What'd he do to you? Before you left?" She asked this gently and brought her other hand to his arm.

"Ain't nothing he hadn't done before."

"They said it sounded like murder."

"Who's they?"

"Ruby Swanson, Wilson. Overheard them a few days after you'd gone."

"What'd they say?" Arbuckle asked. Behind his voice was both a curiosity and a disdain that surely pulled at him; he did not wish to know what was said of him for he had spent his life trying to unhear the torment into which he had been born.

"That the hollering bounded all through the settlement."

"I suppose it must've."

"When you got to the edge—them Deputies didn't try to stop you?" asked Lady Mae.

"No, they did not."

"So they just let you go?"

"Aye. Said I still had my lot and to not go getting any fancy ideas."

"You could've waited—could've told me you was going to leave."

She didn't mean to say it so sudden and accusatory-like, but she had, and now it was done. She had not said the words *why did you* and *all alone*, but she might as well have. His absence all this time—had it mattered to him as well? Did he feel the suffocating void of her as she did him? He would not think her foolish, though.

"Been lonely around here," she admitted. Doing so surprised her, and it was as if she wasn't even herself. But still she could not help but let the truth fall from her lips.

"Up there, too."

"We're here now, though."

"So we are."

Arbuckle lifted her hand and brought it to his chest. She heard birds call from above, their song floating down around them, and felt his heart through his thin shirt. The wind shifted and kicked up the dust around them. Arbuckle took his handkerchief out of his pocket and held it to his mouth and nose.

"You know I been meaning to say," he said through the fabric. She looked up at his face, at the lines that had appeared near his eyes. She opened her mouth to say *you came back* and *didn't never think* and *all them prayers*. But the wind carried with it a clamor of voices that came from the direction of the scaffold. They dropped their hands and peered toward the end of the road.

"Let's go," Lady Mae said and turned on her heels. "We can take the hill path."

"Why? What's going on?"

As she tried to pull him away, she heard clearly the chanting, the low calls, beastly and berating. "Come on, Arbuckle. Ain't nothing for us over there."

"Seems like something," he said.

It was Saturday—market day. It had slipped her mind what with the preparations of Arbuckle's arrival and then Ruby's alarming demeanor. She never went to town on market day if she could avoid it. She'd told Arbuckle why in her letters, but she'd mentioned it only briefly and without opinion as she worried the Deputies would read her letters and disallow the correspondence. Outcries—that's what they called what happened on the scaffold most market days. Residents that were beyond the butcher's hand, their crime blasphemy.

"Go on now," she said, and elbowed him to the side. "We don't want to be there." But his legs were longer, his gait wider, and so he strode out in front of Lady Mae to get a better look. "Arbuckle," she said over and over again. "Don't you remember? I told you in the letters how—"

Lady Mae's explanation, her pleading, was drowned out by a large roar that erupted from the square. A throng of residents had converged across from the courthouse—it looked like nearly everyone in the settlement was there. Arbuckle grabbed her hand and pulled Lady Mae toward the back of the group. They could not get closer, but Lady Mae saw the shape of a Deputy up on the scaffold, a steel megaphone in his right hand. The residents, who stood dozens deep, pushed up against the wooden steps and platform, their arms spreading across the beams, touching and writhing as though they were snakes in a pit. Many had children on their shoulders. Some of the women sobbed, others raised their fists and punched the air.

The residents stared at the two of them as they walked along the edge of the crowd. Arbuckle was back, and that girl was next to him. The two of them joined at the hip as anyone could be. But Lady Mae noticed the difference between a blink and a shift of the eyes, the rigidity of the residents' bodies as they drew near; they were not welcome there despite the expectation that all residents attend the outcries.

"Come on," said Lady Mae.

Arbuckle, though, was looking toward the scaffold. They were closer now, and Lady Mae could see that near the edge was Deputy Daniels, Deputy Parson, too. The other two Deputies—Griffin and Worth—held a man by each arm. But over to the left, near the edge of the scaffold where the stairs met the ground, there was the fifth. From where she was, he looked no different than the others. He stood with the megaphone poised at his mouth. The brim of his tall hat covered his face. The crowd hushed, and he spoke.

"We, being dead to sins, should live unto righteousness!"

His voice boomed through the speaker that he held tightly up to his mouth, rushing over the heads of the residents to the ears of Arbuckle and Lady Mae who stood perhaps a meter behind all of the other residents. His voice—she couldn't be sure. It was obscured by the echo off the square, made tinny by the megaphone. But still. She felt Arbuckle's arm press up against hers as he put his suitcase down in the dusty road. The Deputy adjusted his tall hat and said something, but the crowd had cried out with his last statement. They were cheering still, and the Deputy again raised the megaphone in the air. The crowd quieted quickly, and the children, who were normally raucous and feral, fell silent, their eyes wide and lips closed.

"By the butcher's stripes ye were healed!" the Deputy called. "For the life of the flesh is in the blood: and we have made an atonement for your souls: for it is the blood that maketh an atonement for the soul. And it is the propitiation for your sins: and not for yours only, but also for the sins of the whole world!"

He stood rigidly on the wooden stage as he spoke, his body fighting itself, trembling as though something was about to explode inside of him. It was not unlike how the Deputies were in court, and Lady Mae knew such behavior was meant to rile the crowd. It was a frenzy that was contagious, one that jumped from the body of a Deputy to a soul of a resident as easily as a common sickness. It was happening then. She saw it. The way their feet dug into the dirt, their clenched fists, the way they raised their fingerless hands and stubbed arms into the sky. Dust floated up between bodies dressed in gray and black, feet pounded the hard, cracked ground. Lady Mae kept her eyes on the Deputy as best she could, but she could not make out his face under the brim of his tall hat. The sun, which was directly behind the scaffold, turned his body into an indecipherable shadow.

"Neither by the blood of goats and calves, but by your own blood you obtaineth eternal redemption," the Deputy continued. "And so we sing a new song, saying, for thou hast redeemed us by thy blood out of every kindred, and tongue, and people, and settlement; and almost all things are by the law purged with blood; and without shedding of blood is no remission!"

There was movement from the side of the scaffold. Two of the Deputies—Griffin and Worth—still held the man by his arms. The man thrashed and tried to throw his body forward over and over again. The

Deputies held on, but then the man broke from their grip and lunged forward, tearing at the air with his hands. It was sudden but not surprising. The Deputy holding the megaphone, unaffected by the resident's actions, did not flinch nor stumble, but stood stoically, assuredly, even as the man began to shout and rush at him, pointing his fingers at the other Deputies. The noise from the crowd quieted and then ceased altogether. Children atop shoulders were gently lifted to the ground. Lady Mae heard the crunching of gravel and the brushing of stiff fabric. She saw the residents back up, distancing themselves from the Deputy and the man facing each other on the scaffold. A few of them—those on the edge by Lady Mae—turned and walked away from the square, back toward their shacks or their shops.

Lady Mae watched the Deputy lower his megaphone. "It ain't safe, Arbuckle," she said. But her eyes stayed on the Deputy, who had stepped aside and out of the sun. She squinted, scrunched her eyes up as tight as she could without closing them. "Come on," she said again, barely hearing the words spill from her own mouth.

There's something, Mama.

You'll know it when it's right, my girl.

The man on the scaffold stood defiantly, hands on his hips. "I ain't done nothing that you all ain't do! Thomas! You's a coward!" He pointed down at the crowd, though from where Lady Mae was she could not see to whom he was referring. A loud roar came up from the crowd. It was not uncommon to blame others, to try to figure who gave them up to the Deputies. But as he scanned the residents for the likely culprit, he must not have heard the other Deputies quietly creep up behind him carrying with them their chains and sticks and torches. Lady Mae watched as the Deputies quickly surrounded the man, who, upon discovering that he was trapped began to lash out, animalistic and full of rage. The Deputies danced around him, around their prey, waiting for the man to make a move. And when the man finally realized that he was outnumbered, he let out a wail that could wake the dead and ran headfirst toward the Deputy with the megaphone still in his hand.

Lady Mae pulled hard on Arbuckle's arm. "We got to go now," she said.

"Okay, but is this—"

She grabbed him by his coat just as the men and women and children in the crowd turned around to run; they'd been to enough outcries to know that the Deputies spared no one when provoked. The eyes of the residents were wild, their faces flushed, and as they tore past Lady Mae they spat at her and shouldered their way around her, slamming into her arms and stepping on her toes. Arbuckle put his arms around her and attempted to pull her out of the way, but old Edmonds broke through their embrace and pushed

Arbuckle who staggered, surprised and unready, and fell to the ground.

"Arbuckle!" Lady Mae cried.

The small man kicked Arbuckle in the side as hard as he could, but he was thin, and even with all of his weight, he could not keep Arbuckle down. The man scrambled behind Arbuckle, hooked his arm around his neck, and pulled with all his might. There in the dust they tumbled, a pile of limbs and grunts and boots digging deep in earth.

"Go," Arbuckle yelled, his voice thin and whisper-like. "Get help."

She looked up and saw that they were the only ones left in the square. The five Deputies atop the scaffold stood tall, their shoulders back, chains hanging across arms and dangling from their hands. Lady Mae dove at Arbuckle and the old man, tried to rip them apart with her small, strong hands. The man flailed and struck Lady Mae in the side of the head. But she did not feel it. She tore at Edmonds' face, put her arm around his own neck and pulled with all her might. It was enough to loosen Arbuckle, who jumped to his feet coughing. The man fought. His face reddened and swelled, his throat garbled, but still he thrashed at both of them.

"Help!" Arbuckle cried toward the Deputies on the scaffold. "Help!" he called again, louder, but they either did not hear or would not hear for the Deputies stayed where they were, spinning their chains and lighting their torches. Lady Mae saw the veins in Edmonds' forehead, his bulging eyes. She couldn't kill him even if he'd come at them, even if she wanted to, and so she let go. Arbuckle grasped Lady Mae's shoulders, tried to pull her from the man who lay in the dust choking on his own sick. He lifted Lady Mae off the ground, held her up with his strong arms and made sure that she was steady on her feet.

"We need help!" Arbuckle yelled toward the Deputies on the scaffold.

By this time, the square was silent but for the cries of the man the Deputies surrounded. He lurched and fell and climbed to his knees, which were bloody and raw. Lady Mae and Arbuckle watched him, and though Lady Mae knew what would happen, Arbuckle did not; his self-imposed exile had sheltered him as much as it had exposed him to the harsh realities beyond the settlement's boundaries. They watched as the Deputies wrapped their chains around the man's feet and wrists, looked as they laid him out on the wooden planks.

"No, shhh—be quiet," Lady Mae said. She began to brush off the dust that covered her skirts, but Arbuckle dragged her toward the scaffold. She pulled back, tried to twist out of his grasp, but he held tight. As they neared, she heard the man, stretched out on the wooden stage with a Deputy at each limb, cry out. She looked up and saw the Deputy nearest his head—the one with the megaphone—kick him in the skull and the man's shrieks abruptly ceased. Lady Mae heard the clanking of chains, watched the Deputies slinging them over their shoulders and turning to face away from the man. They hoisted the chains, pulling them taut before standing still.

"He shall be redeemeth!" the Deputy called not arm's length from Lady Mae. She looked away from the man on the scaffold and toward the Deputy. She couldn't breathe, and the heat and wind danced around her. She strained to get a better look at his face, but the sun obscured her sight again. Was that him? The one that— Maybe it wasn't him, but did that matter? She was so close to him, to his head in which coursed blood the same as her mother's. Would it pour out of his skull the same way, bubbling and pulsing its way out of him? His words scattered and dripped around her, and she remembered that day in the road long ago when the children had accosted her. A strength, however brief, had revealed itself, and she felt it again there in front of the scaffold. The Deputy looked at her then, just as a cloud passed across the sun. Their eyes met, and she felt the fire on her skin and a searing in her heart, for there on his face were four long scars.

The Deputies holding the chains gripped them tight and began walking in opposite directions. They must not have heard Arbuckle above the man on the scaffold being stretched to his death, his guttural screams straining toward the sky. Lady Mae looked up. The birds dove down and landed in the settling dust. There was another scream, curdling and grotesque, and when she looked back up at the scaffold she saw that in the hand of one of the Deputies was a long piece of fabric to which another held a torch. The fabric caught and drew the flames upward. The Deputies, satisfied with their work, looked at Lady Mae and Arbuckle, the only two left in the square, and threw the fabric out toward them. It landed near their feet. Only then did Lady Mae realize that it wasn't fabric at all, but the skin of the man they had pulled apart, the remains of which glistened underneath the hot afternoon sun.

9

Arbuckle paced in the front room of Lady Mae's shack. The floor creaked and its pine boards bent under his feet. She stared after him as he moved back and forth from one end of the small room to the other. From where Lady Mae sat on the sofa, she could see with each thundering step how he worked his jaw, trying to unpick what she had tried to say in her letters. But he did not speak. He could not, had not since they had returned to the shack. What he had seen—what words would be enough? As it was, Lady Mae tried not to think of the savageness of it all. But when she looked at his gritted teeth, lips in two thin lines, all she could say was, "I told you to get, Arbuckle. Said we got to go and you didn't listen."

She sat down on the sofa and pressed her unsteady hands down on her knees that were bony and thin until she felt muscle.

"I was hoping things might've changed," he said

and gestured to Lady Mae. She knew he wanted her to say that things had changed, that what they saw in the square had been an exception, and the man on the scaffold was a man who deserved whatever he got.

"Nothing's changed. Gotten worse more like it. That was the ninth," she admitted. "The outcries. Five men and four women."

"But that—that—what they did to that man? That ain't right—killing him right in the square like that. They don't even try to hide it no more?"

"Guess not."

"You guess not? This what you been trying to say in your letters?"

When he sat down next to her on the sofa, the cushions gave under his weight and his knee knocked hers once. "You ain't tell me this," he said.

"You know right as I do I couldn't."

She hadn't because to write *killing* and *murder* and *stay there*—there would be repercussions for that. The Deputies would question her and put their thick hands on the letters she kept behind a drawer, carefully stacked and tied with a string. They would not see what was, only that which they wanted. Arbuckle and Lady Mae had always been careful with their words, but it'd make no difference; to punish her they would set out after him and find him with his pen and paper, and the earth would eat his bones.

LAURA KAT YOUNG

"Ain't nothing you could do anyhow," she said to Arbuckle.

"Ain't nothing I could do? I would've tried to get you," he said.

"To get me? And then what?" She looked up at him from where she sat, watched as his own eyes worked the room for the answer he did not have.

"I don't know. We could've left—we could've—"

"You know I can't leave. Not now, anyway."

As she said it—the thing she had known but had never said aloud, that her mother and grandmother had known but had never spoke of—she bit her lip and crossed her arms over her chest.

"I know," Arbuckle said. "I know. But this here, what we saw out there? That's different. What's to say that ain't someday you or me up there on the scaffold?"

"That ain't going to be you or me."

"How you figure?" he asked.

"'Cause you ain't going to say nothing. No more questions, Arbuckle. No more what-ifs like you used to talk about. It just ain't safe no more."

"Weren't never safe," he replied softly.

In her mouth was the taste of *it was him* and *what can we*, but she worried that Arbuckle would stagger, bewildered and unforgiving, out the door. He might lay his hands on the first Deputy he saw, and then what? He'd be torn apart just like the man on the scaffold, and she'd be forced to watch the last thing on earth she had rise white and hot up into the sky.

What if he goes too, Mama?

We all go sometime, my girl.

Arbuckle let out a long sigh, and she turned to see him put his hand on her great-grandmother's quilt, which hung on the back of the sofa. It was a small gesture, but Lady Mae knew he was thinking of when he had found her standing in the middle of the living room screaming nearly six years before. She didn't remember—didn't still to that day—but Arbuckle had told her the rest. From his own shack, he'd seen her mother running down the crescent road, the Deputies following not far behind. He had snuck out of a window and crept along the asters on the settlement's edge until he got to Lady Mae's lot. He inched his way toward the back door and peered through the cracks in the wood. There was shouting. Chains on wood. The high peal of laughter. A thump. Lady Mae's tiny voice growing into a stone gull's song. Arbuckle had waited in the dark until the Deputies were gone and went around to the front of Lady Mae's shack. The door was open, and from where he stood, he could see her mother's feet splayed apart, boots on. He knew before he crossed the threshold that she was dead. And when he entered the shack and saw Lady Mae still but for her mouth that opened and closed with each deep breath, he thought only to cover her, to wrap her up and lift her to her feet. This is what he told her.

Arbuckle wrung his hands together and then touched his fingertips to his temples. "I mean, my heavens, they were skinning him alive!"

"We don't know what he'd gone and done." She was trying to soothe Arbuckle, who had worked himself up good. What would come of her telling him it didn't matter what the residents on the scaffold had done? Or that maybe, just maybe, they hadn't done anything at all?

"If he had done something, wouldn't you know it?"

"No."

"But you're the butcher."

It was the first time he'd ever called her that. He said it softly, as if he didn't want to remind her of what she was. He said it gently, as if the weight of his words might knock her down quickly and without strain. He'd named it, finally, eighteen years after they'd met in the dust, each ostracized for their lineage. She'd never mentioned how the residents feared he'd grow into a violent man like his father, and he never said anything about the fingers and toes she'd take. They had an unspoken bond, an implicit agreement between two children that did not have the right words.

"Don't mean they tell me nothing," she said.

"Well, they should. You got more sense than the lot of them."

"I know it."

Arbuckle turned his body toward Lady Mae and rubbed his eyes with his knuckles. He breathed in heavily through his nostrils, whistled the air out between his parted lips. If she told him about the Deputy, it'd be the last thing he heard anyone say. The blood would boil in his ears, the rage, all of it he would take with him as he ran into the square yelling. They'd hear him, and they'd come out, their fingers curling around the wood and metal they held in their hands.

"You okay?" Lady Mae reached up to Arbuckle's face. It was scraped and bloody, but nothing seemed broken.

"Aye. Didn't much like you diving in and trying to stop it. You could've been real hurt."

"But I wasn't," she said.

"This time. I don't want you doing nothing like that ever again. No matter what happens to me."

"You ought to report it."

Arbuckle didn't say anything, but behind that silence was his belief in redemption and a justice that wasn't just about punishment. He'd want to talk to Edmonds, understand why he'd lashed out. Was it just that Arbuckle was there? Or had the old man seen him and taken to him as he should have done his father?

"Maybe if I just talked to one of the Deputies—I'm sure they saw it. I could just say what he'd done and that there ain't no need for further involvement."

She felt the ends of the ball inside her tighten, little tendril-like fingers poking at her guts. There was her mother and there was the Deputy and there was her kit and there was the fall of night. When Arbuckle fell asleep that evening, she could slide out through the window, land quietly on her feet. She'd go back to the square, behind the scaffold, and up the courthouse steps. That Deputy was in there somewhere—that's where they slept, somewhere in the belly of the jail, a room full of heaving bodies shrouded in darkness. She'd get to him, kneel by his bed with the needle to his heart.

"Let me fix you up," she said to Arbuckle.

Lady Mae rose and went to the kitchen. In the cupboard was antiseptic and cloth bandages. She grabbed her kit, too; he might need a stitch or two as well. When she walked back into the room, Arbuckle was holding his head in his hands.

"Now hold still." She opened the antiseptic and placed the cap on the table in front of the sofa. "This is going to hurt. I ain't gonna lie."

"Go on now," he said.

She tipped the brown glass bottle and poured out a small but steady stream of the liquid onto the cloth. Arbuckle winced when she touched his face, his cheekbones, above his brow. But as she cleaned his wounds, he stared at her.

"How long them outcries been going on?" Arbuckle asked.

"Don't know; a year, maybe. Two."

She stood and went around to the back of his head, blotted his neck where the antiseptic had dripped, wiping and pressing a small towel to his skin. Even though there was a layer of fabric in between, she could feel his strong muscles. She stared at his skin, the small, tanned sliver that showed between his collar and hairline. There was the sudden urge to lean down and press her lips upon it, to wrap her arms around his shoulders and breathe in.

"They always kill them?" Arbuckle asked.

"Aye." She cleaned around the wounds as best she could. She put the rag down, opened her kit, and took out the string and scissors. "Just a stitch or two. Need anything first?"

"No," he said. "What they done, anyway? Them residents on the scaffold?"

"Blasphemy—at least that's what they say. I tried to tell you, but… I just. I didn't. Don't know why."

"I knew you weren't telling me the whole truth."

"Oh? How is that?"

"I could see it. Read it by your hand. You can't lie to me no more than you could've lied to your mama."

"Why didn't you say nothing then?" She squinted and thread the string through the needle, cutting it off at its end with her teeth. Then she put her hands on either side of Arbuckle's head to still him.

"What good would've come of that?" he asked before falling silent.

They had both tried to protect the other knowing that, no sooner had they put onto paper their suspicions, the Deputies would have come. They would have intercepted the letters and walked to her shack in a small group, their tall hats bobbing along the horizon, the same way they had nearly six years before. They would have knocked quickly at Lady Mae's door waiting only but a few moments before bashing it in with their clubs and shoulders and feet. They would have come for her first in an effort to lure Arbuckle back to the settlement so that they would not have to search the hills and mountain. They would have made him come to them where they would be waiting with their chains and torches. No, she would not tell Arbuckle any of it.

Lady Mae put the needle through the top layer of skin on Arbuckle's scalp. He took a sharp breath in and held it as long as he could as she went back and forth with the needle and string, stitching him back together again. When she finished she dabbed it once again with antiseptic. "Keep them wounds clean."

"I will," he said.

"It's getting late. We should turn in."

She put her scissors and thread back in her kit and closed it up. She tucked it and the antiseptic under her arm, balled up the rag, and placed it in the burn bin next to the stove.

"Don't reckon I'll be able to sleep at all," Arbuckle said.

"Me neither."

"Then at least I'll have company," he said and stood. He put his arm gingerly around her small shoulders as if she would break should he pull her in too close.

That Deputy, Mama.

Now you see, my girl.

10

When she woke, she was glad it was Sunday—the only day the depot was closed—and that she might ignore for a moment the image of the Deputy on the scaffold the day before. She'd seen him—in her shack that night so long ago, in the deep black of her dreams—and she was sure of it. The man on the other end of the telephone, the voice thick as mud through the megaphone; it was him. He'd been there that night. She felt it deep inside, this knowing, as if it had been there all along just waiting for the chance to swallow her. A slow, hot rage gathered in her belly and seeped out of her there in the space between sleep and waking.

But what should I do, Mama?

Tread wisely now, my girl.

She brought her hand to her breast, pushed against the bone underneath her thin skin, and leaned into the discomfort. The sensation was familiar and was as it had always been, long before her mother burned and her childhood lay buried in ash.

She walked over to her dresser and dipped her fingers in the wash basin. The water was warm from the hot night but felt good still as she washed her face. She blotted her cheeks with an embroidered towel and, as she hung the towel on the hook, she caught a glimpse of her hands. They were young enough, and to a stranger's eye looked nothing out of the ordinary. But Lady Mae knew that the dark corners of her nails were not from cleaning the coop or digging for potatoes. That Deputy on the scaffold—her own hands had seen as much blood as his, maybe more. They weren't too different, she and him, and it burned like a lightning bolt gone straight through a deadened tree, like half of her was already scorched.

When she made her way into the living room, she saw Arbuckle's cot was empty, its sheets pulled up neatly and her great-grandmother's quilt folded and stacked on top of his pillow. The thick smell of griddlecakes came in from the kitchen where she heard him putting logs into the stove. She went to the doorway and watched as he stacked the wood with just enough tilt so that the fire could breathe. When he stepped back to examine his work, he stood rigidly with his arms grasped around opposite elbows, his strong shoulders flexed. The wood burned hot and fast, every drop of moisture sucked out of its flesh in the unending heat.

It popped and crackled, and Arbuckle took up an iron with which to stoke the wood. The flames caught and leaped up the bark, and he closed the stove door.

"Arbuckle, what're you up to in here?"

He turned his head toward her and smiled at her appearance in the doorway of the small kitchen. "Learned how to cook while I was away," he said.

"Did you now?" Lady Mae pulled a chair from the table and sat down, rested her elbows on the wood, and leaned her chin into her hands.

"Had to. Ain't no way I was going to eat mush for six years. Learned how to hunt, too. Didn't like that part much, though."

"Ain't had no choice I reckon," said Lady Mae.

He didn't reply. Instead, he checked the fire again even though the logs were blazing, and the heat rose in the room. Lady Mae's hairline was soaked already and the neck of her blouse, too. It was sweltering in her shack, but she did not mind; it meant she was not alone. "How's your head?" she asked.

"Fine. Just sore a little."

"Best you change those bandages, though."

"Aye."

"Here. Let me help."

She stood from her chair and motioned for Arbuckle to sit down. He did, and Lady Mae took a towel and dipped it in the water that he had already boiled for the day. First she examined the stitches. Then, with careful hands, she pulled the bandages off his face, revealing weeping, raw skin. She lifted the towel to his face and gently dabbed at the wounds. The fire snapped, and Arbuckle closed his eyes.

Lady Mae took a good look at him. How was it that he was really there in her kitchen, her hands upon his face? He was the same Arbuckle that he'd always been, so why did her stomach flutter when her fingers touched his skin? She looked at his lips, his beard, and wondered what it'd be like to press her flesh against his.

"Can I ask you something?" Lady Mae asked.

"Anything at all," he said, his eyes still closed.

"The night my mama died. You saw them Deputies coming, right?"

"I did."

"Did you see any you hadn't seen before?"

A silence followed, interrupted only by the snaps of the fire. Lady Mae put new bandages onto his wounds, and Arbuckle opened his eyes.

"Don't reckon so, no."

"But you did see them?"

"Not directly. I remember it was dark," he said. "What're you getting at, Lady Mae?"

She wished with her heart that beat faster and faster that she could tell him *it was* and *did you see his face*. But then what? They might sit knees to knees as they used to, trying desperately to come up with a way to help themselves.

Can't do nothing, Mama.

You can do more than you know, my girl.

"There's a new Deputy. Spoke to him yesterday at the depot before I got you."

"Thought you seemed rattled. Now why didn't you tell me before?"

"Don't know. Just trying to think on it, I guess."

"What'd you talk about?"

"The patient—the one I was worried about. But then he mentioned—"

But she paused. To tell Arbuckle of the strings that stretched out from her insides—that this one was her mother, and the next the Deputy, and so on, each one tied so tight she nearly suffocated from their grip. She dragged them with her at all times, pulling the weight of the loss and wonder behind her. So long had she carried it, but she did not wish to worry Arbuckle any more than he was. She was afraid of his worry, what he'd do with it, and where it would go should he not be able to contain it.

"Come on, I know you ain't telling me everything," he said.

"Brought up my mama," she admitted.

"That it?"

"Said I ought to know better than to ask questions."

She looked at him then, at his beautiful eyes and strong forearms. What she saw was no surprise, though had she really expected it? Who he'd been before he left, who he was now—he was one and the same and she was glad for it, she supposed; she could count on him like daybreak, feel him close even when he was far away. But a flash of panic was there in his stare.

"Don't necessarily mean nothing, right?" she asked.

"Nothing means nothing, Lady Mae."

He was right. Whatever the Deputy had said or didn't say sat heavy and hard. But how could she tell Arbuckle that he was on the scaffold? Of his scars made bright by the sun? To tell Arbuckle would make it true. All those years wondering, all those nights spent wishing for just a glimpse; if her suspicions were right, he was but arm's length from her, close enough to get at with her eager hands.

The fire spat and the griddlecakes smoked on the stove. Arbuckle stood and took up a fork. He made his way to the stove slowly, his body sore from the beating. "Someone say something like that to you—that's a threat. Don't matter if it was a Deputy."

He turned back to the stove where the griddlecakes smoked. He flipped them one by one onto a plate and put the plate on the table. But as he did so he shook his head slowly, deeply, as if what Lady Mae had just told him weighed more than he could withstand. "Just ain't right," he said with his back to her. "You got to do something. Or I'll—"

"You ain't doing nothing. This is just the way it is."

Arbuckle spun around. His eyes were wild, and in his hand he held the spatula tightly enough that Lady

Mae could see the veins and bones in his hand from where she sat. "And that's enough for you?"

"Got to be," she said.

"But—what they did to your mama—how—"

"I know it. You think I don't? Every day I see it; it's in here till the end of time," she said, and touched her head at her temple.

"Okay, Lady Mae, okay," he said and sat finally. The light was just coming up through the eastern window, a smoke-filled shaft floated above the small table. They sat close, silently, and their forks scraped the metal plates as they cut into their griddlecakes. Arbuckle's cheeks were flushed from tending the fire, and his hair fell across his forehead. Lady Mae kept her eyes on her plate so that she would not stare at him and wonder what it would be like to have him there always.

"I never meant," Arbuckle began, clearing his throat, "I didn't mean to upset you. Thought about it endlessly last night before I finally drifted off; I know you ain't got no choice, no more than I."

"We all got our lots. Least you got out for a spell," she said. He must've heard in her voice the deep betrayal that sat unmoving and invisible. He placed his hand over hers gently. His fingers found their way between hers, and she could not swallow the piece of griddlecake that she had in her mouth. He moved his index finger and thumb softly upon her own hand,

and she could not move. Though she had tried to ignore it each time it came to mind, she had thought of Arbuckle. Thought of his eyes, the way he smiled when she joked, his laugh. She thought of the sound of his voice, dreamed of the whispers he might say to her in the cover of night.

"You mad at me for leaving, ain't you?"

"Don't know," she lied. "Don't really matter now, does it?"

He opened his mouth to say something else, but then smiled instead and took his hand back away from hers, crossing his arms over his chest. "Just want you to know I did what I had to do. Might not have been the right thing, but it's what I did."

"I know it," she said. "We all do what we got to do."

But the words *how could you* and *why not me* skittered up her throat. She wanted to grab his hand and tell him how it broke her when he left. Didn't he know how she had drifted all that time, her head barely above water?

"I was glad to get your letters," he said.

"Me too."

"Got pretty lonely, I admit."

"Where were you, anyways?"

"In the hills. Straight eastward. Up there's a clearing."

"And the Deputies let you be?" she asked.

"Mostly. Came around a few times a year."

"What'd they want?"

"Make sure I was still there, that I hadn't run off up and over the mountain," he said.

"Could you have?"

"Sure. Few times I was out pretty far for weeks at a time laying traps. Didn't see nobody that high up."

"Did you think about it?"

"Nearly every day."

"Why didn't you do it?"

"'Cause you were here. Thought lots about coming to get you."

He said it without hesitation, as though the words had always lain upon his tongue. It was immediate and she heard in his voice the truth. He could've gone and left for good, could've escaped. He could've gotten away. A guilt, fulsome and unyielding, seeped in. It was because of her that he'd come back when he might've found the forgiveness he searched for somewhere beyond the hills and mountains. Perhaps there was a place beyond the settlements that stretched far and wide. And even if there wasn't, perhaps he could've made a place for his own. If he had, would she have had it in her to find him?

"Arbuckle—I, I mean—you'd have been a fool to try to come back and fetch me. What then?"

"Don't know. Guess I would've tried to get you out of here. Away from this. From what you got to do."

"And how'd you plan that?"

"Not sure, I reckon. But I bet we'd make it. Just need to be smart is all."

The sun finally burst over the horizon, and for a moment Lady Mae could see it: she and Arbuckle up on the mountain, far enough up where no one would go. There they'd live, survive, make love. They would wake together with the sun. A hope sprung in Lady Mae's chest. What if she said right then and there *could we*... But Lady Mae was not that naïve. Though the two of them might rise side by side, they would live on constant alert, worried if the freshly fallen snow had simply covered the tracks of Deputies lying in wait.

"You better be careful those words don't fall out of your mouth in front of anyone else," Lady Mae said.

"I know, I know. I ain't going to saying nothing to nobody."

She had an urge to reach for Arbuckle's hand when the deep shame rose up inside her. It was always there even when Arbuckle wasn't, a shadow she just couldn't get in front of no matter how she tried. And it pulled at her like quicksand, made her feet heavy and her heart sour. Maybe Arbuckle felt it as well. It was what joined them together in a world that had cast them aside. They were the children of miscreants, heirs of misfortune and sadness, and so she found his fingers again and curled her own around them, feeling a rise in her heart when he squeezed her hand three times in a row, their secret code from so many years before.

"Arbuckle."

"What's that?"

"So why'd you leave, then?"

Lady Mae asked it softly, gracefully, as if she could with her words shelter Arbuckle from the storm that brewed inside him. She saw it in his shoulders, saw it resting just underneath his eyelids. She had asked the thing she'd wanted to ask for over five years, not because she could no longer hold out but because she saw that he needed to tell her. And so she welcomed it, willing to hear whatever she might so that he could finally rest, his mind no longer spinning a tale that he kept from her.

"Maybe I shouldn't have left. Maybe if I'd stayed— that man in the square, it wouldn't have happened. Maybe I could've kept you—"

"You couldn't have done nothing for me, Arbuckle," she said, and though that was not entirely true, it was mostly true. "Besides, been getting on fine without you five years and counting."

"That night when I left," he began. "I had to. My pa was out to get me."

Arbuckle had never written about why he had set out in the darkness nor had Lady Mae asked. She had wanted to many times, but many times felt the prickling of dread just underneath the surface. What if what he said proved irreparable and cruel? What if he'd said he couldn't stand to see her take her inheritance, to know that she walked to and from the depot each day with her kit under her arm? But now he'd said his father; it hadn't been her after all and for that she was grateful.

"What do you mean 'out to get you'?"

"He didn't want to bequeath to me, said I wouldn't be any good there at the helm. Yelled it across the whole settlement."

"Well, he didn't have no say in that I reckon."

"I told him as much. But he weren't wrong. What I got to do at the cannery, not sure how I'll fare. He... I—"

"It's okay, Arbuckle. You don't need to tell me."

"I do, though. Got to just come right out and say it because I've been holding it in here." He brought his hand to his chest. "Ain't no good in there, and if anything happened to you I just don't know what I'd do."

"What's anything got to do with me?" she asked.

"He came home late in the night. Been drinking. I'd been asleep and all of a sudden he's got his hand around my throat." He brought his own hand to his neck.

"Arbuckle! Why ain't you never tell me this?"

"And say what? My own pa tried to kill me?"

"You could've told the Deputies—they would've—"

"They'd had made me inherit then and there. And I ain't gonna lie. Don't want nothing of this inheritance at all. But that's not the worst of it," he said.

"What d'you mean?" Lady Mae pushed her plate away and leaned forward.

"Told me that if I didn't disappear, he'd make sure you ended up like your mama."

"End up like her?"

"Yes."

"What'd that mean?"

"Not sure. Figure dead is what."

"Why'd he want me dead?"

Here Arbuckle paused, though he kept his hand in Lady Mae's. He wasn't telling all, and although she could sense that the words were there in his breath, he kept them in. "That weren't all he said, Lady Mae."

"Go on now. Ain't no use keeping it from me."

"He said if I didn't get, he'd sic after you. Said he'd only be doing what the Deputies wanted all along."

"What? Kill me dead?"

"Aye."

"Why'd they want me dead?"

But she knew why they'd want her dead. What Ruby had said was true: in her pulsed the same blood as her mother's, and there in the kitchen she felt it. She was her mother, her grandmother, her great-grandmother, and their goodness was in her, too. And try as she might to avoid it, she felt the soft touch of their ghosts. She'd long believed the residents despised her for being the Deputies' minion, but now that Ruby had said her piece, even if it was out of fear and compliance, maybe it weren't all true after all.

"Don't know," Arbuckle said. "But he knew something."

"Well, I'm glad you're back," she said finally. She swallowed that which she didn't know how to say, leaned in to his presence, and kept her fingers on his.

"Me too," he said, and Lady Mae watched the small joint on his jaw move outward and inward, over and over again, as if the answer to her question was there in his mouth, in the gentle spaces between his teeth.

11

The next day Lady Mae set her kit down inside the door of the depot, and the light shone through the window, which was dusty and brown from the drought. She grabbed a pail and brought it out to the pump. Up and down she moved her arm and watched the water slosh into the pail. She reached in her pocket and took a fistful of cleaning granules that she had taken from inside and tossed them in with the water. The water foamed and bubbled. She turned off the pump and carried the pail with two hands back up the three steps of the depot and went to the only window. She moved slowly, dipping a rag in the water and then washing two full rotations clockwise before putting it back in the pail. Her sleeves darkened, and the water found its way up her arm. She was thankful for the respite.

She and Arbuckle had spoken late into the night, and when she woke that morning she knew one thing for certain: the swelling in her heart, the fullness that came from being so close to him after all that time—his return meant more than just that he was back. One day was all it took, and the hovering mass in her periphery was nowhere to be seen. Gone were the tangled strings that had floated just beyond her reach, the gnarled and frayed ends that had almost bound her interminably. Instead, what remained, what had been unearthed, was a sudden hope that came on so quickly it stung.

That hope had lifted her out of bed, and though she could not calm the thoughts that swirled around her tongue, she had gone to her dresser to ready herself. But whatever she had felt or thought or wished to be disappeared when she saw herself in the mirror. Her hair, uncombed, fell to nearly her waist. She wore a long nightgown that hid her full breasts and hips. She did not look like herself but did not know who herself was. Two days before she'd been just the butcher, still a child in her own mind. And now, now. It was a feeling she could not name, one that had hung heavy behind her eyes.

Will I always be, Mama?

No such thing as always, my girl.

Lady Mae wiped the final streaks dry from the window that she was cleaning. When she bent to pick up the pail, she caught a movement behind her. She stilled for just a moment and held her breath. There was the slip of gravel and the clearing of a throat, and in the window, she saw a reflection in addition to her own. Her pocket watch had read nine thirty last she checked, and her patient was not set to arrive until ten o'clock.

"You the butcher?" a man's voice asked.

She kept her back to the resident as she picked the dirty rags up off the porch and put them in the near empty pail. "Aye," she said. "You're early."

"Not here for an appointment," he said, and cleared his throat.

Lady Mae looked more closely at the reflection in the window. She saw the tall hat that he held under his arm and watched him blot his bald head with a white handkerchief in his other hand. She stiffened. She'd been waiting for a Deputy to show himself for two days, his boots kicking up the dust and leaving a cloud in his wake. And she'd been hoping it'd be the one, just so she could see once more to make sure. But she had been thinking of Arbuckle, haphazardly cleaning the window, and hadn't heard him come up behind her.

"I'm Deputy Iverson—we spoke the other day on the telephone. Seems I came from Six just when I been needed most. You the lady that was attacked in the square on Saturday?" he asked.

"I weren't the one attacked," she said, and spun on her heel. The bucket swung and banged against her leg.

"Even still, I'm here to take a statement." He put on his hat, placing his handkerchief back in his pocket. "Get your version of events."

Lady Mae heard the redemption in his words, the long drawl of salvation. And when the wind carried his voice to her ears, she felt a prick, like someone had blown hot ash onto her skin. She squinted, held her hand up over her eyes, and looked closely at the Deputy's face. As she stared after him, she watched him tilt his head back, and though he was saying something to her, she could not hear him. Her ears, which had heard the howling of the wind and the beating of her heart, filled with a silence muddy and thick. She watched the Deputy's mouth move around in that mud. It was cold and dark and slow, and when his mouth moved again she saw the four long lines clear as day. She watched them stretch as her mother's mouth had, watched them move up and down as he spoke. Lady Mae hovered, her heart beating up against her breast. She balanced there, delicately, her toes crunching up on themselves in her boots. She felt her knuckles tighten and her stomach fall.

"Lady Mae?"

"I got nothing to say." She spoke through nearly closed lips, her jaw tight and her teeth clenching against each other.

She did not know what she meant other than *you should be* and *dead like my mama*. Because there in the morning light she understood what stood before her. Pail in hand, her toes just barely visible from beneath her skirts, she waited for the anxiousness that had been with her always, counting the seconds until it bubbled up inside of her. But as her words fell into the dust the sour panic didn't come; she felt only that which she remembered from that day long ago when she lay on the ground, her ribs broke, her head split open, when she had crawled back up to her feet and called after the vicious children.

This what you're saying, Mama.

Let it rise inside of you, my girl.

"Everybody's got something to say," said Deputy Iverson. The notebook he was writing in dropped to the ground. When he bent to pick it up, Lady Mae watched him straddle the earth, his engorged stomach down to his knees. The wind lifted the pages of the notebook, and they flapped against one another. As he hunched further down he lost his balance and pitched forward too far. He stuck both arms out to break his fall, but it was too late, and he toppled over into the dust.

Lady Mae watched him scramble on the ground, lunging after the notebook and pencil, and she switched the water pail to her other hand. She gripped the handle, pressing the metal into her flesh until she felt a pinch. "Well, I ain't the one you should be talking to."

But as she spoke the words, which sounded far away from her own ears, she saw closely then his hideous figure, his body bent and twisted, as she did that night so long ago when she had still been a child. Her breath caught, and the wind lifted the hair from her neck. The pages of the notebook waved once again before Deputy Iverson grasped it with his other hand and stood upright. He looked at her directly with a pencil in his hand. His knife hung at his side. She knew she could get to it first, get it before he even knew what was happening. Her fingers gripped the pail harder, trying to cut open her skin with the rusty, bent metal.

"But you is the one I'm talking to," he said.

Lady Mae saw for a moment the nothingness high up on the mountain of which Arbuckle had spoken. She was far enough away from the square that she could get to at least the edge of the settlement before anyone came for her. They'd unleash the dogs, but the river would break her trail. They'd still go up into the hills looking for her, but she'd have had a good start. The pail felt heavy in her hand—if she swung it just right she could split his head open. She gripped the handle tighter, the metal pressing into the creases behind her knuckles, and moved her wrist just enough for the pail to move. Lady Mae's toes reached out over the edge of the top step, and there she teetered but a stone's throw from Deputy Iverson. He was writing in his notebook and did not look up at her. Lady Mae slowly and carefully descended one step.

"Lady Mae?"

Her name. The name her mother had given her. The name that had leaped from her mother's lips two times before there was nothing but the loud breathing of the Deputies who circled around her lifeless body. The cicadas had just emerged, and Lady Mae noticed them only after the first blow. She saw her mother try to lift her head and her lips moving, but she heard only the insects, which after so many years deep in the dirt finally woke. And as she remembered her mother as she lay silent on the wooden floor, she heard again the low drone that rose and fell from the trees. Their song had lifted up into the night sky, and even nearly six years later she could not picture her mother without hearing the insects, too. She heard them then as she stood on the second step as if they surrounded her still. The handle of the metal pail creaked as the wind blew, and her skirts snapped.

Deputy Iverson looked up, and their eyes met. She did not blink nor avert hers, not even when she felt his stare burn into her own. On her lips were *my mama* and *kill you dead* and *six years I been waiting*. She took another step.

He let out a *huh* and a thick laugh as his lips curled up into a smile. He held the pencil between two of his fat fingers and pointed it toward Lady Mae. "Spoke with Arbuckle just now on my way to you," he said. "Had to get a statement, of course."

"Then you ain't need nothing more from me," she said.

"He was poking around what's left of his place."

"He's got every right."

"Well now," he went on, ignoring her. "Let's just hope he does what he's told and doesn't go causing more trouble than he's worth. Be a shame if he went the same way as his pa."

A sudden terror found its way into the space between her bones. She felt it deep inside, primal and innate. Her feet, heavy and hot, ground into the rotting wood of the last porch step. The stench of the dirty rags wafted up toward her, and a single drop of sweat found its way down her temple and into her eye. She tried to blink it away, but it remained, salty and burning underneath her lid.

"What's that supposed to mean?" she asked.

The Deputy looked to his left and then his right as if wary, as if to make sure that no one was around to witness the words he spoke. Lady Mae did, too. But there was no one there. Then he refocused on Lady Mae, squinted in the bright light, and said, "Just noticed is all."

Her hand cramped and stung from holding on to the pail so tightly. It'd just take one swing—she had good aim—and even if it didn't do the trick it'd at least knock him out. Then she could bring the pail to his head three times the same way he'd brought his club to her mother's; he'd shown no mercy, and mercy he would not get.

But then she thought of Arbuckle. They'd find him and string him up if she tried anything. If she ran, they'd use him as bait to get her to return. They'd kill him either way and tell the other residents that he was just like his father, no better than a scoundrel. Though vengeance coursed through her, wave-like, and brimmed in the bottom of her eyes, there was nothing she could do. She was looking at the man who murdered her mother on that late summer's night. They held each other's gaze, each knowing what the other knew, and neither looked away.

"So how many, Lady Mae?"

"Like I said, he ain't attack me."

"Did he lay hands on you?" he asked.

"Aye, but only 'cause I was in the way," she replied.

"You know the law. All involved got a right to punish."

"Alright then, one atonement."

The Deputy sucked his breath in through his small nostrils and squinted up at her. "Twenty's the limit," he said.

"I know it."

"So how many you want?"

"One," she said again.

He looked up at the sky and then spat into the dust before licking his pencil once again. "Four atonements," he replied, and wrote it down in the notebook. He ripped out the paper and put it in his mouth, holding it there while his hands put away the notebook and pencil. Then he thrust the paper toward Lady Mae, who went down the last step and took it out of his hand. The wind kicked up again, and he put his arm up to his hat to keep it from blowing off.

"If I see Arbuckle again, I'll tell him you said hello." He had her then, and she knew it. "Court's at eight a.m. tomorrow," he said. "Don't be late."

Lady Mae was washing the floor of the depot when Arbuckle knocked hours later. She'd hoped to have the place in order, but her appointment had run long and the patient, old Herschel from the cannery whom she'd thought would be easy to subdue, had jerked and seized in the chair even though it was his sixth and final atonement. She knew him a little by now, knew his family and his children and what he had done to protect them years ago when Arbuckle's father was still around. She might've done it, too, and thought about it as she sliced into his skin first with a scalpel and then again as she shimmied the bone cutter beneath his flesh. It had been difficult to get the entire hand quickly. She'd been distracted, worried that Deputy Iverson had passed Arbuckle again on the way back into town and had gotten to him. Herschel had bled significantly but not dangerously, but Lady Mae thought only of the four lines across Deputy Iverson's face and the drip in his voice and the pail in her hand. So when Lady Mae heard Arbuckle's knock—a knock she knew like the back of her hand—she let out the breath she'd been holding inside. He was there, and he was alive.

"I'll be just a minute," she called through the door. She could see his silhouette, shaded by the eaves and leaning against the frame.

"Alright," he said. She was glad he wasn't allowed in, that he wouldn't see up close the stained tools or the red drops that went from the chair to the door. Herschel had refused the bandage and said he'd rather die of an infection than let her touch him again, and so she sent him off having only cauterized the severed stump with gunpowder and flame.

When she finished cleaning the floor as best she could, she threw the tools into her kit—she'd clean them up later at home—and went to the door. A hot gust of wind came, and Arbuckle reached up to keep his hat in place.

"Hello," she said, keeping her eyes low and studying the keys she held in her hand. She locked up the door quickly and then moved to the side out of the glare of the setting sun.

She had thought all afternoon whether she would tell Arbuckle that Deputy Iverson came to see her. That he was the one. And if she did, would she tell him all of it? Of how Arbuckle's name had fallen off the Deputy's lips? Of how with just one mention of her only friend she saw again that summer's night, her mother's body, heard the cicadas reverberating in the cottonwoods? She'd wanted to kill him, but then what? She'd have to have run, leaving Arbuckle to wonder after her or worse. No, the mention of his name had kept her thinking clearly, even if the pail handle in her hand pierced her palm.

"Arbuckle," she said and looked up at him. As her eyes adjusted to the light, she noticed that his brow was creased, his eyes red and swollen.

"What is it?" she asked and instinctively reached up to place her hand on his cheek. She felt the soft hairs of his beard and the crisp line of his jaw. Arbuckle brought his own hand to hers, and there they stood looking at each other, the wind pounding against them, its howl interrupting their silence.

"Went by my pa's place today," he said.

"And?" she asked quietly.

"And it weren't there. Knew it wouldn't be, but still."

"I told you I'd go with you," she said. "Didn't think you should be going alone—"

"It was like I could smell the smoke," he said as if he hadn't heard her. "Like it was in me. I could taste it. Made me think of you."

"Me?" Lady Mae brought her hand down to her chest. Her fingers fiddled with the button of her collar.

"Well, I didn't mean—it's just with your mama and all. Can't imagine what it was like for you."

"Yes, you can. You was there. For a spell, anyways."

"I was," he said, and reached up with his other hand, grasped hers, and lowered it to his chest. He held it there, and she felt his heart beneath his shirt, saw the droplets of sweat on his chest. Though the day was ending it was hot still, and beyond them in the distance, she could see the rippling waves of heat rise up toward the sky. "I was always there," he said, "even when I weren't."

She wished to take his face in her hands and say *don't matter now* and *could we be*. She wished to bring his eyes to her lips and gently place them upon his eyelids, hold them there until the pain passed. But what tumbled in his heart had to run its course; even if he hated his father all this time, he still had sought love. And Lady Mae reckoned that it wasn't hate Arbuckle felt for his father, after all. It was a deep pity and a stretching of his heart, an anger down in his belly. It was the nameless rage understood so long ago, now flapping and floating at his seams. Lady Mae knew because it was in her, too.

They turned toward her shack, their hands still touching, and began to walk down the dusty road. On the horizon, the sun was low in the cloudless sky. It was going to be another hot evening; they would eat whatever was in the cellar for dinner so that the shack would stay cool throughout the night.

"You put in for old Edmonds?" she asked him. "That sure was something."

"I did. Didn't want to—pretty sure my own pa was the reason why his son ain't around no more. Understand why he came at me." He walked next to her and their fingers brushed up against one another. The sun peeked out from the dusty mountain ridge beyond the valley. "But I don't like it one bit. What was going on in the square? That were enough to make anyone act crazy. Them Deputies riled everyone up. Ain't Edmonds' fault he got swallowed up by anger."

"We all got anger. Just need to try to keep it inside. Not let anyone see."

"What about you?" he asked.

"What about me?"

"You put in? Edmonds struck you, too."

She did not answer at first. She wanted to tell Arbuckle that it was the Deputy that had killed her mother. She could warn him, tell him how the Deputy said like his pa. But there she was inches from Arbuckle and all she could think was *can't lose you too*.

"A Deputy came by the depot today. He ain't give me much choice."

"How you mean?" Arbuckle asked.

"I said one, he wrote four."

"But he can't do that!"

"He can do whatever he wants. They all can."

"What if you went to Deputy Daniels and told them that—"

"There's more," she interrupted. She spoke quickly, let the words rush out of her mouth as though she might suddenly lose her nerve. "I'm gonna tell you something, but you can't go and do nothing. Can't say nothing neither. Promise me."

"Well I can't exactly promise—I mean it depends on what—"

"Promise."

"Alright, alright. I promise," he said and held up his hand. "But I don't like where this is headed. It's bad, ain't it?"

"Not sure I can say for sure," she said and brought her hands together in front of her.

"Go on, then," Arbuckle said.

"It was him."

"Who was him?"

"The Deputy that came to see me today. It was him. One from that night."

She brought her shaking hand to her eyes hoping to flick away the tears before Arbuckle could see, but he reached out and put his hand on her forearm, stopping her there in the road.

"How sure are you?"

"There's four lines across his face from where I scratched him. Back then, in my living room. I know it's him. Got to be."

Arbuckle straightened up and looked past Lady Mae as if he were studying the empty shacks behind her and the hills and mountain peaks beyond. He kept hold of her arm with one hand and then, turning his eyes back to her, he wiped the tears from her cheek with the other. He let out a long sigh and scratched at his beard.

"I wanted to kill him, Arbuckle. Thought all afternoon how, and I think I got it worked out—"

"And you ain't see the problem in that? Then they'd come after you."

"He don't deserve to live."

"No, he don't," said Arbuckle. "But then what? Killing one, killing five. Don't matter. There'd be other ones, and they'd do to you exactly what they did to your mama. You say anything?"

"No. But I think he knows I recognize him."

"How would he know?" he asked.

"Not sure. Just felt it is all."

"Did he say anything else to you? He threaten you?"

"No," she said because if she said *your father* and *burn up the same way* and *you'd be just ash* Arbuckle might leave again or worse. He was there and there is where Lady Mae wanted him always. And so she kept to herself the laughter she'd heard on the Deputy's lips and pushed down the dread that crept up the back of her neck. She remained silent knowing that when night fell she would lay wide awake thinking of Deputy Iverson and the what and when.

Arbuckle gently moved a piece of hair that had swept into Lady Mae's eyes. "Listen," he said softly. "I know I came back to take the helm, but that ain't the only reason I'm here right now."

"What, then?"

"I don't want this for you, and I don't rightly think you want this for you, neither. I wrote you something, Lady Mae," he said and patted his breast pocket.

"What's that now?"

"I wrote you a letter because the only way I knew I could say what had to be said was putting ink down. When I'm near you, it's like I can't remember everything, like the things I know I got to say to you—well, just seems like they float away," he said.

He reached into his pocket to pull out the letter, but Lady Mae put her hand on his. "You know you can tell me anything. Tell me everything if you got to," she said.

"You and I—we could be out there," he said, and tilted his head back in the direction of the hills and mountains. "I told you, just you and me, and as long as we stay high up through the winter they won't be able to find us. Won't ride that far come the cold. I know you got it in you, to leave. Know you got other things, too."

"Go on now, hush," she said. But she had wondered what was out there, especially when he'd written of the snow and the bears and the quiet—it was always so quiet—and she thought of the white of winter and in front of a fire the two of them curled into one. She wanted to go there—wherever there was—and in the hot sun of late summer she stared at the boy from her childhood who was now a man. His lips moved as he told her *it ain't right* and *trust me* and *I wrote it all down here*, but she did not hear him. Instead, her hands found his, and she pulled him into her. She buried her head into his chest, pressed her lips into his rough shirt, breathed in the smell of home. Her hands glided up his arms and over his strong shoulders, and she clasped them behind his neck. The wind stopped, the last of the sun fell behind the ridgeline, and she pulled his head down to hers. Her lips found his, shyly and gently at first, and as they kissed in the falling light of the summer's evening it was clear: everything that was in her heart was in his, too.

12

When Lady Mae opened her eyes, it was still dark. Arbuckle breathed softly next to her in the small bed. Their feet touched, and Lady Mae drank in the smell of him as he lay beside her. She gently placed her hand upon his chest, careful not to wake him, and felt the rise and fall of his breast, the rhythmic beating of his heart.

She had been nervous but certain the night before when she took Arbuckle by the hand and led him to her bedroom. She was no stranger to what would happen—her mother had taught her the many ways of which love looked. And when her lips fell on his she wanted all of him—not just in that moment, but forever. They stood facing each other; they did not speak, not exactly, but there in the dark of night their hands found each other's buttons and hooks, bumping into each other and laughing shyly. They made love slowly, tenderly, as if the moment itself might vanish right in front of them. It was nothing like Lady Mae had expected, but had been everything she had dreamed of.

"Arbuckle," she whispered. "Arbuckle."

He took a deep breath in and opened his eyes. Lady Mae raised herself and leaned on her elbow. With her other hand she traced her finger along his arm.

"Morning," he said.

"Morning to you."

He rolled over and brought his hand to the back of her neck, gently bringing her head to his. He kissed her forehead, her eyes, her lips. And there, just as dawn was about to break, he kissed her again and again. "Lady Mae," he said when he finally pulled away. "All them nights up there... I don't know..."

He drifted off and kind of smiled, one side of his mouth higher than the other. "I ain't ever thought this would happen—you and me. Thought on it, sure. Be lying if I said I hadn't."

"And I'd be lying if I said I hadn't thought of you. But guess I didn't know for certain till I saw you in the square."

"Are you telling truths now?"

"When you left," she said and sat up on her elbows. "It was like half of me was gone," she admitted. "I thought of you up there, all alone. Pictured myself sometimes there, too. What it might be like the two of us with no one else around." She leaned her head down and kissed his shoulder.

"The way I thought on it," she heard him say. "All those years apart, they just too long. You're my family, Lady Mae. Only thing I know that's true in here," he said, and touched his heart.

"Ain't much space for nothing else in mine but you neither," she said.

"And now here we are."

"So what do we do now?"

Arbuckle brought his face to hers, touched her cheek with the back of his fingers. He brushed her hair behind her ear and found her lips in the dark of the early morning.

"This," he said.

The day broke hot and unrelenting and already the earth was scorched when Lady Mae and Arbuckle set off for the courthouse. They walked from her shack in the same broken, comfortable silence that had accompanied them at breakfast. She had taken his hand as she descended from her porch and did not let go on their walk to town. She spoke with him about the weather, about the empty shacks they passed, about the birds crying overhead. She spoke around and around her love for him, too afraid of its fragility and consequence to say anything directly.

As they rounded the curve of the crescent road, Lady Mae saw in the distance a crowd gathered at the bottom of the courthouse steps. From where she was, it seemed small, maybe ten residents at most, but large enough that Lady Mae gripped Arbuckle's hand tighter and slowed her gait. He followed the direction of her gaze and said quickly, "Don't worry about nothing." He squeezed her hand three times. "They won't do nothing to you."

The residents' eyes were on the two of them, all grown up yet childlike still. Lady Mae straightened her back to steel herself against the words that she knew would erupt as they crept closer to the crowd. Her mother would've told her to keep her head up, that the residents don't know nothing about anything. And on the nights when her mother had held her young daughter's cold feet in her warm hands, she would say *your grandmother and hers* and *me and you* and *the law's got to count for something*. So although Lady Mae was afraid of the residents in front of the courthouse and could taste the sick in the back of her throat, she grasped Arbuckle's arm and walked ahead.

There were men and women both, and from behind the legs of one a young boy appeared—maybe he was ten or twelve, but a child nonetheless. They made no sound; the birds above called out, and the boy looked up. The residents stood chain-like and unmoving, their arms entwined. But once Lady Mae was near enough to the crowd their stillness ceased. They began moving slowly, twisting and bending their bodies up and down, their shoes scuffling in the dust. Taken by their slow and purposeful dance, she did not hear Arbuckle calling to her, did not feel him tugging at her sleeve. She was mesmerized by the motions, which at first she did not understand, not until her eyes focused in on one man's hand raised high in the air. He had spread his fingers wide enough that Lady Mae could clearly see three were missing. Her eyes darted to the woman to his left who had lifted her skirt to her knee to expose empty space where a leg should have been. Behind her was another woman whose only foot stuck out from underneath her dress.

One by one, they revealed to Lady Mae the pieces of themselves that they'd lost, the parts that she or her mother or grandmother or great-grandmother had taken from them by law and without hesitation. She knew all of them—some better than others—but it didn't matter if she'd been gentle with a knife or the bone cutter. They hated her and their hatred burned under her skin. Arbuckle tried to pull her away but she resisted, planting her feet in the road and wriggling her hand out of his. She watched the group that stood frozen once again in silence, their clothes undone and their shoes off and their hats cast aside. On their bodies, they had written the words *vile* and *pig* and *thief* in coal dust, the black of which had already smeared in the sticky heat.

"Go on now, get!" Arbuckle called toward them. He put his arm around Lady Mae's slight shoulders and pulled her away from the residents. She went reluctantly, slowly, watching the residents' eyes follow them as they went up the courthouse steps. She wanted to say something—call *it ain't my fault* and *it's them Deputies*—and so at the top of the steps she turned toward the noiseless crowd. But then, nothing. For what if she was vile like they said? After all, what of her hands? All those residents' missing parts—she did that and would do it again. And although her mother had spoken softly *didn't question* and *all got a choice* and *forgive as you would your own self*, she had hated them, too. She tried to push it away, but there it stayed, blistering and hot.

I know I ain't supposed to, Mama.

Can't help what makes you, my girl.

"You okay?" Arbuckle pulled Lady Mae close to him as they approached the wooden doors of the courthouse that were worn by the handles, faded and smoothed from years of use. She leaned in to the smell of his safety. "Just wasn't expecting that," she said.

There was a tremor in her voice. She was used to the name-calling—heard it all the time up and down the crescent road. She was used to the stares and curled lips, the flickering eyes. But never had residents come together like that, knitted together by a singular hatred. To them she was loss. She was imprisonment. She was chains and torches and rope. Lady Mae looked up at Arbuckle and in her mind said *what if* and *what have* and *these hands*. Though he already knew what her hands had done, the pity for which Lady Mae saw balanced upon his eyelids.

"How is that allowed?" he asked as he pulled open the wooden door. "I'd think the Deputies would—"

"Ain't no law against what they're doing."

"Ain't no law? Lady Mae, the other day in the square—what we saw—the man on the scaffold. What was that, then? What law was he breaking?"

"Blasphemy. But the Deputies were involved directly. That, outside just now, that was about me. Just me."

As the heavy door swung shut behind them Arbuckle said, "That ain't about you. You ain't none of those things. No matter what you've got to do."

And though he spoke those words with a soft earnestness, she felt the truth deep in her stomach. "You say that," she said, "but look at what you think. Think I don't know."

"What do I think?"

"That I'm not far off from what all them are saying."

"No, I—" he began but then fell quiet. A look of deep shame came across his face. "I didn't mean—look, I don't think—"

"I know it. Didn't mean for it to come out like that, but that don't mean I didn't mean it."

"Alright, then," he said.

They stared at each other without speaking, their gaze broken only by the noise at the far end of the corridor. Where Lady Mae and Arbuckle had themselves entered, the group of mangled men and women were slowly making their way inside. They would sit in the courtroom—along with whomever else showed up—and listen to the proceedings, watch as Arbuckle and Lady Mae took the stand. As the residents moved nearer and nearer in the corridor, Arbuckle grabbed her hand and pulled her behind him as if he alone could protect her. He could not, though, and so she pulled her hand away from his grasp.

"It's okay." She looked over her shoulder at the crowd as it drew nearer still. "What choice do I really got? Run off into the hills with you?"

She had the words *he said your name* and *your pa* and *everything burns* ready on her tongue. Maybe then he'd understand why she was acting the way she was. After all, he'd do anything to find out answers to his father's death; it pulled at him more than he let on. But she would not put Arbuckle in harm's way to justify her actions. If she said something to him, anything at all, he might go after Deputy Iverson. And though she wanted Arbuckle to, wanted him to say *you took them from both of us*, he was no match for the Deputies. If he went up against them—she could not think of that. And so she hid her fear behind the law, her love behind her weakness. What else could she do?

The church bells on the other side of the square rang one, two, three. The crowd was but steps from Lady Mae and Arbuckle, who watched them as one would watch the thunderous sky, hopeful and afraid. Four, five. And then Lady Mae found herself holding the heavy, creaking courtroom door open. She stood there, her foot up against the bottom of the door, and studied each resident as they filtered inside. Some were solemn and others' eyes gleaned with excitement, but none looked directly at her. They passed her as if she were invisible, and while she was long used to the treatment, shame swirled inside of her when she saw Arbuckle's pitied brows and crease in his forehead.

"Let's just get this over with," she said, and motioned for Arbuckle to go in first. The bells rang six, seven, eight, and the door, heavy and creaking at the hinges, swung shut behind them.

Deputy Daniels came in from his chambers. The bottom of his long, dark robe flapped and snapped against itself as he walked up to the bench. He'd been the Deputy Magistrate since she was a child; that he was there was no surprise to her. She quickly examined the other Deputies. Griffin and Worth sat on either end of the courtroom. The other two—Parson and Iverson—must've been patrolling the square, though nearly all the residents were in that courtroom. Part of her wished

Iverson was there. That there in a court of law she could question him about her mother, ask him the why and what then.

Deputy Daniels stood behind the bench and towered over the room. He nodded at Deputies Griffin and Worth, looked briefly at Lady Mae and Arbuckle who sat behind a large wooden table, but did not address anyone else. He took his seat, cleared his throat, unrolled a piece of paper, and began to read from it.

"Whereas from and after the publication of this law it shall not be lawful for any resident to carry or arm himself with any club, staff, gun, sword, or any other weapon of defense or offense, and it is further enacted by the authority aforesaid that if any resident shall presume to lift up his hand in opposition against any Deputy or resident, shall for every such offense, upon due proof made thereof by the oath of the party before a magistrate, have and receive a maximum of twenty atonements." Still standing, he turned toward the man on the stand. "Mr. Timothy Edmonds, are you of sound mind and body?"

Edmonds was shackled and in the loose, gray clothing of a criminal. Though his head had been shaved upon processing, his eyes were wild. Whatever his punishment, it will have been worth it. "I am," he said.

"And," Deputy Daniels continued, "do you declare that your admissions in this court of law are yours and yours alone?"

"I do."

"Let us begin," said Deputy Daniels.

Edmonds stared at Lady Mae who sat at a table with her hands folded in her lap. He did not look at Arbuckle, only Lady Mae. Afraid that if she let her eyes fall on the man she would crumble, she kept her own eyes on Deputy Daniels and watched him arrange his gavel and papers. Arbuckle sat straight and rigid next to her, but she did not turn to look at him. She was ashamed—ashamed at what she was, what had happened to Arbuckle no doubt because of her. She wished to say to him *I know it* and *you is right* and *do you think we can.*

But what if he never understands, Mama?

Won't know until you say, my girl.

"We are here to sentence you for the crime you committed: assaulting Arbuckle Anfield and Lady Mae Hilvers. Are you aware of said crime?" asked Deputy Daniels.

"Yes." Edmonds' body shook slightly from the nervous bouncing of his foot on the courtroom floor.

"Well, then, please put it into your own words for the court." Deputy Daniels motioned to the residents sitting stiffly in the rows of wooden benches.

"I guess—" he began. He cleared his throat, but Lady Mae did not turn her head; she had steeled herself, and though she could sense his eyes in her periphery, she still did not look toward him.

"It were an accident. I was running, fell on the two of them, I guess. I tried to get up and keep running, but Anfield over there threw me down, started in with his fists. Just like his father. Ain't had no choice but to swing back, I reckon."

"There is a discrepancy in your version of events," said Deputy Daniels. "Both parties claim you laid hands upon them without cause."

"I was only trying to defend myself."

"Did you or did you not knowingly lay your hands upon the two residents sitting there?" He pointed directly at Lady Mae and Arbuckle.

There was a pause, and Edmonds looked down, perhaps at his hands or feet, and stayed like that for a few moments. Deputy Daniels waited calmly for him to respond. It was a long pause, as if he were mustering up the courage to apologize. Not that it would deter his sentence, but maybe he felt remorse or at least a slight sense of sorrow. Maybe the other residents weren't that hateful after all.

"Aye," he said softly. His head hung, and Lady Mae thought she imagined his admission. His shoulders shook, and underneath the creaks and snaps of the residents in the pews, she heard a laugh.

"Aye," Edmonds said again, louder and with authority. Lady Mae allowed herself to look at him, at his flushed cheeks, his hair matted wet against his forehead. It was sweltering but that was not all.

His voice skittered across the courtroom, and the residents, though taught to disregard anything an assailant had to say, could not help but turn to those next to them and whisper, nudge their spouses in the ribs with elbows. The bustling grew, and Deputy Daniels picked up his gavel. Edmonds narrowed his brows and turned his head toward Lady Mae. He was seething, trapped in the stand like an animal waiting to pounce. "And I'd do it again," he said in a low, slow voice. "I'd rip their hearts out if I could. They ain't nothing but a torturer and a fiend."

He brought his fist up as if he were going to strike at them right then, but the shackles attached to his wrists caught, and his body yanked back against the chair. Deputies Griffin and Worth stood behind him and restrained each shoulder so that Edmonds could not hurt himself. Lady Mae did not look away but instead held her eyes to his, suddenly overcome by the man's admission.

"What you would or would not do is not the question. Did you knowingly lay your hands upon those two?" asked Deputy Daniels.

"Yes," Edmonds hissed.

"Are you sure about that, Mr. Edmonds? You sure you didn't accidentally fall like you said in your statement?"

Edmonds said nothing, but instead tilted his head back. Out of his mouth came a slow laughter. It rose up in the courtroom, bouncing off the chamber's plaster walls.

"I see. Your behavior will be taken as a guilty plea. As you know, Mr. Edmonds, such an act is punishable by law," said Deputy Daniels.

"I know it," he replied, his unwavering eyes still on Lady Mae. "Don't much matter. Ain't got nothing to lose anyhow."

"Well, then. Mr. Edmonds," Deputy Daniels turned a page in his book, "I must read the following: any resident victimized can and will sentence the perpetrator to a maximum of twenty atonements. Is that something you can understand?"

"Aye," he said. He nodded slowly once, twice, then over and over again. With each dip of his head, he brought his fist to his forehead as if trying to put his admission back into his brain. But his body betrayed him; every few seconds a high cackle came bubbling out of his throat, and he shook his head like a dog.

"And atonements, by law, may be taken in their entirety or parsed out on a yearly basis," said Deputy Daniels. "Which do you ask for?"

"Yearly," Edmonds said. He said it loudly, his head bowed but his mouth turned in Lady Mae's direction. "Yearly," he said again.

Lady Mae was struck with a flash of panic—she'd have to see him five times. Four years for her, one for Arbuckle. She'd have to touch him, push into his thin skin. Maybe there would be a Deputy accompanying him, or maybe it would be just the two of them in the depot at the end of the empty road, her hands on his body. Would she want to rip his hair out? Claw at his heart like he had hers? Or would she simply cut too deeply an artery and watch?

"Yearly it is," said Deputy Daniels. Then, to Lady Mae and Arbuckle, "Please rise. What is your sentence?"

She looked at Arbuckle and saw his squared jaw and folded arms. He'd want her to tell the truth—that she'd wanted just one—but that kind of truth was treacherous. All she had to do was think of how Arbuckle's name had rolled heavy off Deputy Iverson's tongue and echoed in the dusty air.

"Four," she said.

"Mr. Anfield?"

"One," Arbuckle said.

"A fair judgment indeed." Deputy Daniels brought the gavel down to the table and struck it three times, each one ringing long in Lady Mae's ears. Mr. Timothy Edmonds said nothing, but he did not need to; the upturned corner of his lip was enough.

By the time she and Arbuckle left the courthouse, the crowd had gathered again on the courthouse steps. It had grown and was now two, perhaps three residents deep. Others who had not been in court had joined the group, and when Lady Mae saw this, she reached again for Arbuckle's hand. The two of them walked down the steps and away from the crowd, even though it was in the opposite direction of both her shack and the depot. Lady Mae didn't care—she wanted only to get away, to be invisible and small. But everyone knew her face, her walk, her hair, her hands. And there was no escaping them.

When they neared the southernmost corner of the square, they turned right and headed down the small alleyway behind the shops in order to get back to the road that led to the depot. She took one last look at the crowd before disappearing behind the building and felt a strange relief at seeing the residents heading north. She wasn't running, but she was glad to be away from them. She'd never run from anyone; she had only avoided as her mother had taught her. She'd heeded those words, the *careful* and *eyes down* and *their loss* for so many years— for what? The residents watched her, spat at her as she walked by. They denounced her and forsook her name. They shunned her and ridiculed her, and she had done nothing except be her mother's only daughter.

"Lady Mae," Arbuckle said, the concern rising in his voice. "This is crazy! This how your life is?"

"No," she said and glanced back over her shoulder, seeing nothing but the trash heaps and soiled mops that sat outside of the shops' rear doors. "Not really.

It's not—I don't go into town much." She fumbled for the words that she couldn't grasp and couldn't say, the same ones she couldn't see, couldn't read in Arbuckle's letters. They were there all around her, but to put them together—what then? Her throat tightened and her eyes stung hot. Arbuckle's hand held hers tightly.

"This ain't right, Lady Mae. I know it. You know it. They treat you like, like—this ain't no way to live, running like this," he said.

"I ain't running."

"What do you call what we're doing back here?"

"They don't—" she began, turning once more to make sure they weren't being followed. "It's just that—"

But up ahead the crowd appeared at the end of the alleyway. One by one they came out from behind the rotting wood. They walked slowly, limping and dragging their uneven legs, holding on to the side of the building with their only hands. They walked silently, cracking the dry gravel beneath their feet.

"Come on." Arbuckle tugged at her hand, pulling her back in the opposite direction.

"No." She took her hand out of Arbuckle's. "I ain't scared." Her dark curls lifted softly in the wind, and she tucked her hair behind her ears as her heart rushed quietly in her chest. Her mother's warnings held strong in her mind, as if her mother herself were where Arbuckle stood. She heard them all those years later still, but she was tired of taking the long way into town and the fear that pressed down on her as she returned home each night.

Is this it, Mama?

Might be if you let it, my girl.

"We don't want no trouble," Arbuckle said.

"Maybe I do." She put both hands on her hips. "Maybe it's time I do."

"What are you saying, Lady Mae?"

"Tell me about them hills."

From the middle of the crowd ahead, which was then five or six residents deep, a handful of children appeared. She could see them clearly, their little bodies and small heads and tiny feet. Aside from those still upon their mother's breast, they were the youngest in the settlement. But they were no longer children, not really, having been warned about the butcher from creation, having grown up on bedtime stories of Lady Mae and her mother, having wakened in the night to see their mothers changing their fathers' bandages, throwing the soaked and soiled rags into the fire.

"The hills?"

"Up there," she whispered and tilted her head toward the eastern mountains. "Think we could?"

"Lady Mae, what are you asking?"

The crowd grew nearer, and Lady Mae began to make out the singular features of the residents. She tried to remember their faces from time spent in her chair.

But she couldn't, for they were strangers to her despite the settlement having only three hundred residents. They had become unrecognizable, a result of a life spent in solitude. They recognized her, however, and she saw upon their faces the pious hatred she'd never escape.

Lady Mae remained still despite the crowd flowing toward her. Her mother had said forgiveness, but she'd also said *didn't question* and *do better* and now Arbuckle was back, and his own thoughts had unearthed something she hadn't known was buried. It rose up like a blade, and though she heard his voice calling to her from behind, she couldn't reply, her mind too muddled to fathom the danger that was headed her way.

"Lady Mae, come on. Let's go back the other way." Arbuckle tugged at her hand.

But Lady Mae didn't move. She stood there, her feet dug into the ground, her hips squared to the crowd. This was her chance to show the residents she couldn't be beaten. She leaned forward on her front leg to brace herself against the first blows that were coming her way. She balled her fists and steeled her shoulders. She was no match for all the residents, but she'd put up a fight. Her mother had fought, and Lady Mae still saw it as clear as day. She had kicked and punched and thrashed and when they'd bludgeoned her, she had called to her daughter the words *promise me always*; those words, so puzzling and permanent, carried Lady Mae to sleep nearly every night.

"Arbuckle," she said. "What if we did?"

"Are you saying…?"

"Think so."

The sound of the residents' feet grew as they shuffled through the red dust of the alleyway toward her. Some had canes, others crutches propping them up. They lugged their good feet along the road, swung their dismembered legs forward, pulled their bodies closer and closer to Lady Mae. Arbuckle leaned his head to hers, and they stood as one as the residents inched forward. She could feel Arbuckle's heart racing against her back.

The children passed them first. They did not look up, did not speak as they circled ghostlike around Lady Mae and Arbuckle. They made no physical contact; Lady Mae felt only the breeze off their bodies as they moved. The others were almost upon them; she could see their sunken, thirsty eyes. The adults were only a few feet away and Lady Mae felt the heat coming off their filthy, sweaty skin. They were old and worn, worked hard by the Deputies for little in return.

"Do you mean…" he said as he huddled in close.

"Arbuckle," Lady Mae said, and then the crowd dispersed all around them, weaving in and out of each other like snakes, silent and knowing and satisfied.

13

They returned to Lady Mae's shack both soaked in sweat. They had walked quickly, arriving with an unearthed determination. Once safely inside, Lady Mae bolted the door and put her finger up to her lips. Then she moved to close the windows and pull the curtains shut, and when she was satisfied, she sat upon the sofa. Only then, in the hot dim of the room, did she speak.

"I mean it, Arbuckle. I want to go. Up there," she said and nodded to the east. "Where you were."

Arbuckle wiped his brow with the back of his forearm, and when he brought his arm back down his eyes were wide. "You mean it now?" he asked softly.

"Never meant nothing more than I do right now," she told him. "Don't think I can do it no more. I can't just up and go to the depot tomorrow as if it were nothing but an ordinary day. Not after old Edmonds— you see him in there? What's to stop him from doing something?"

"He ain't going to do nothing to you. I won't—"

"You won't what? Ain't nothing you can do."

Arbuckle held out his hand to Lady Mae, but she did not take it. To take it would be to say *they want your hide too* and *everything I touch just goes up in flames.*

"Look at me," Arbuckle said. "You ain't do nothing that you didn't have to."

"Says you who ain't gone and done nothing to nobody."

"Yet," he said. "And you didn't—"

"I could've tried," she said. "Could've made them see what my mama said."

"And what was that?"

Arbuckle sat down on the sofa next to Lady Mae, but he did not move to touch her. Instead, he leaned forward onto his thighs and dropped his head.

"Forgiveness. She said it was the answer. That without it there weren't much point to anything."

"It's true," he said.

"It ain't that easy."

"I know it."

"And they ain't ever going to forgive me."

"You might be surprised," he said softly. "What people can do when they put their mind to it."

She looked around the living room of her shack. Her eyes danced from the iron stove to Arbuckle's cot to the darkened spot on the floor that was still visible no matter how many times Lady Mae tried to get rid of it. She leaned back against her great-grandmother's quilt. Arbuckle sat up straight and slipped his fingers between hers and together they fell silent. The windowpanes rattled quietly. Lady Mae half expected the Deputies to come to her door, as if they somehow knew of their plans. She pulled back the curtain and peeked out. There was nothing there.

"I want to go." Lady Mae spoke quietly but with certainty. Deep down it glimmered, the thing from the dust, from the square.

"You sure now?" he asked.

"Sure as I've been about something near I remember."

"It ain't going to be easy," he said.

"No such thing as easy, anyways."

"All them years I sent you books," he said. "I wasn't trying to convince you—didn't mean to press you or nothing like that."

"You ain't the only one thinking this whole time," she replied.

"Then you tell me. What are you thinking?"

"The way I figure is them Deputies? They ain't ever going to leave us be. My mama, your pa—might as well be you and me. Might well be, too."

Arbuckle put his arm around Lady Mae's small shoulders. "I ain't ever going to let anything happen to you," Arbuckle said.

"So we go up there." Lady Mae said it with a rushing

clarity as if, should she speak too slowly, the hills might crumble before they could reach them.

"We go up there," he said. "And we'll stay on the move. Over the ridge, down into the other valley. Like I said, I got it figured—know them mountains like the back of my hand."

She thought then of the Deputy—Deputy Iverson, of his shining eyes and high-pealed screams and the stick he used to crush her mother's skull. He was there, in the settlement. He breathed the same air and walked the same dust. She had waited over five years to see him again, and now that she had, she wanted to run out of her shack and down the crescent road and bang on the residents' doors. She wanted to yell what she'd discovered, how the Deputies were wrong about nearly everything. But the residents already knew, didn't they?

"He was baiting me," Lady Mae said suddenly.

"Who was?"

"The Deputy. The one that came to see me."

"How'd he bait you?"

"Just think he was trying to get me to do something, say something. Heard it in his voice, the way he just showed up at the depot and talked about your pa."

She slipped. "Arbuckle, I didn't mean—he didn't—"

But there, in her living room, it was done. Arbuckle sat stock still, his chin taut, and stared at Lady Mae as if he had never seen her before. She thought he was furious, but it was not anger that he worked in his jaw. No, it was a heavy sadness.

"Arbuckle, I—"

"What do you mean talked about my pa?" He moved his arm off of Lady Mae and turned on the sofa to look at her.

"He was just trying to get to me—knew talking about you would—said he saw you by your—where your shack was."

"And?" he asked.

"Said something about you going the same way as your pa."

"That all?"

She wished she could lie to him, but he was Arbuckle and knew her no doubt as well as he knew his own heart. And so she admitted, "Weren't just that. Something about the way he said it—don't know, sounded like something, though." She was just talking, unsure of what she was even saying. How could she describe the thick warning that he spat at her, how it had tumbled toward her like a weed? "My mama," Lady Mae said. "She hadn't thought—didn't think to ask the why or the how. And I guess for a second she was there doing the asking. I couldn't stop myself."

"Go on now. What did he say?"

"Didn't say nothing, not really. Said something about hoping you weren't more trouble than you're worth. Don't know. Maybe I imagined it."

A look that she would remember up until her last moments came across his shadowed face. It was not one of curiosity nor alarm as she expected it to be. Instead, a kind of revelatory satisfaction danced about his chiseled features, as if the thing she said he had known all along and had been merely biding his time until she realized it herself.

"You didn't imagine it. I knew that fire weren't no accident."

"How do you know? He could've meant anything by it—"

Arbuckle brought his hand up to her cheek, brushed his fingers on her skin. "Same as I know what I got to do right now."

"You ain't doing nothing. And that's why I didn't want to tell you."

"Well, it weren't yours to keep from me."

Lady Mae wished to put her arms around him and say *of course it was him* and *he took them both from us* and *even though he was a bastard, he was your father still.* She wanted to pull his head down to hers and kiss his cheeks and his eyelids. But then he said, "Go on and get some things together. We'll leave as soon as it's dark."

"What are you going to do?"

"I'll be back by sundown." He stood and walked toward the door.

"Don't you say nothing to them Deputies," she

warned and followed him. "I told you, they're worse than they used to be."

"I reckon I've a right to know what happened to my pa once and for all. I'll find Daniels, ask to see the file. That's it."

"I still don't think—"

"Lady Mae," he said and turned to face her. "I've got to do this. Don't you see?"

And she did. The same was in her own heart. The urge she'd had—to kill, to maim, the hot hatred in the back of her throat. Arbuckle felt it, too; just because his father was vile didn't make him not his father. It only took two fingers to strike a match that night, and Arbuckle must've heard it catch all the way up in the hills.

"Promise you'll just ask."

"Promise. I'll be okay," he assured her. "You just be ready to go come sundown."

"We really doing this?"

"Seems we are," he said. He tipped the front of his hat back and reached his arms around Lady Mae as his face came within an inch of hers. "I'd be lying if I said I didn't think about it—you and me away from this place—for all them years I was gone."

Lady Mae encircled his waist with her small arms and pulled him close. His lips touched her forehead, and she felt the soft hair of his beard on her unopened eyes. In his arms, it was safe, and she felt maybe for the first time in her life a sense of ease deep and pure. Then Arbuckle stepped back.

"Arbuckle—be careful. You don't know what they can do."

"Don't worry. I'll be back soon," he said and closed the door behind him.

As the day drew on, she could not help but feel a festering grief build inside of her. She tried to tell herself that it was because she was leaving her shack, the only home she had ever known. She'd need to carry her mother's memory with her now. After all, her mother was not the threads of the quilt or the splinters of the floor. She was not the skirts and corsets Lady Mae wore, nor the tools she sharpened each night. Her mother was in her, buried underneath her own skin.

Am I doing right, Mama?

Only time will tell, my girl.

She spent the morning tidying up the shack; she dusted the beams and swept out the stove, folded the blankets and made the bed. As she did, she took in the memories—the small collection of painted plates, the letters from Arbuckle. She'd leave it all; that power—the same one from all those years ago in the dust, from the other day on the steps of the depot—rose in her and she breathed it in as if it were the last drop of air in the world. Everything she was, she had always been. Her mother had been right.

As she packed a large satchel—for she did not own a suitcase—she did so slowly. She placed her petticoats and the warmest dress she had in the bottom of the sack, and caught a glimpse of herself in the mirror. The light through the bedroom window outlined her figure in a late summer's halo. She looked like her mother; she had lost the look of childhood without noticing, but she did not feel like the person she saw in the reflection. That person was beautiful and full of grace, and though a satisfying resolve had been with her since she returned home from the courthouse, she was no less haunted by her own self. She would carry her satchel up into the mountains, but she would also carry what she'd done, the blood of which she'd never scrub clean from her hands. She had resigned herself to walking away from it all—the tangled mass, the blood in the pine, the bones in the ground. She'd receive no closure, and though her days and nights might be filled with a rage she could not diffuse, what else was she to do?

The sun was low in the sky when there was a knock on her door—Lady Mae went to it but did not look out the window. Even if she had, it would've made no difference, for when she opened her door she saw in front of her Deputy Iverson. His shoulders twitched and jittered, and he put his small hands in his pockets and hoisted up his pants underneath his large belly. She stepped back as if she had been struck, and he lurched his body across the threshold. There he stood in her living room, the hot wind blowing behind him.

He took off his hat, and as he did, she saw the four lines, felt his flesh underneath her fingernails still. He mopped his nearly bald head with a handkerchief and placed it back in his pocket. He sucked his teeth and kept his eyes on hers, and a joyous urge rippled on his face. Hot dread pooled in the back of her skull and inched its way down her body until she felt the prickling fear in her fingertips; the Deputy was there and she was there and the two of them were as alone as could be. To her right, just inside the door where the Deputy could not see, was an umbrella, the tip of which was sharp enough—she could make it up into the hills. But Arbuckle had not yet returned and so in the steadiest voice she could muster, she asked, "Can I help you?"

He licked his plump, glistening lips and spoke. "Your boy," he said. "He's been making trouble."

"My boy?"

He reached his finger to his teeth. As he stuck his rotten nail in the cracks he said, "Come now, Lady Mae: Arbuckle. Came charging up to the courthouse claiming this and that, mighty heavy claims at that. Reckon you know anything about it?"

"I do not."

His chin quivered with the excitement boiling inside of him. He licked his lips and rubbed his hands together, darted his eyes around her shack before falling once again on Lady Mae. "You sure now?"

"I am," she said.

His laugh, the one she remembered on the darkest of nights, started low and soft, and she could not be certain that she wasn't imagining it. But as the wind kicked up behind him, it carried to her the marrow-deep sound of her mother's death.

"I'm here to tell you your boy's standing trial tomorrow morning."

"Trial? What's he done?"

"Them questions, Lady Mae. Again with them questions."

"I got a right to know."

"Want to hear something?" he asked after a moment. "You're right. In fact, you ought to know what that scoundrel has up his sleeve."

"He ain't done nothing."

"I wouldn't say 'nothing,' now, Lady Mae," he said, and from within the inner pocket of his coat procured a small piece of yellowed paper. "We found this on him."

He held it out in front of his face with his right hand, and in the distance, the clock tower rang. The sun had gone behind the peaks, and the glow of dusk blanketed the settlement.

"What's that?" she asked.

"I reckon you know."

"I don't know nothing."

He unfolded the creased and worn piece of paper and his shoulders shook. He leaned from one foot to the other as though he were about to pounce right then and there. Sweat dripped down the curve of Lady Mae's back, her corset tight, her breath short and labored.

"Dear Lady Mae," Deputy Iverson began as he read from the paper. "As I sit here the wind howls outside of my window, and I think of you. I try not to, for thinking of you has brought me as much misery as happiness in the years since I've been gone. Many nights I've sat above the settlement thinking about sneaking back in and getting you, waking you in the middle of the night and running up into them hills. Thought long on it, but each time I did, I couldn't help but think of your mama on the floor. What if you ended up the same way? Wouldn't be able to survive that. So I didn't come, and though I might've sent you letters and books, I ain't never said the thing I wanted to say. Which is that you got it, too, what your mama had. The knowing of the difference between right and just, that them Deputies got everyone fooled. She gave it to you, birthed it as she did your own self. People ain't gonna fight each other if they ain't provoked, and who does the most provoking? Them Deputies, that's who. And you know it. Been seeing that understanding in you all these years—I know that's what it is. So here I was setting down, but now I see. It's already in you, ain't it?"

Lady Mae stood still. She did not take her eyes from the Deputy, but she did not see him either. Instead she saw the hills, the wintry mountain on the darkest of days, Arbuckle's smile, her mother's gaping mouth. She stood, unable to speak or respond, unable to do anything but softly teeter on her own two feet.

"Any truth to this, Lady Mae? You been doubting in your heart?"

Truth. What was true at all anymore? All this time she had been ignorant, up to her elbows in blood, her heart sour and alone. Arbuckle had left without telling her, wrote without admitting, returned without suggesting. And now she knew why he'd never been quick to give her answers in her studies nor offered his opinion before she asked it. He simply waited for her to get there on her own because—and in that moment she understood—he believed in her goodness. She was a butcher, yes, but he saw in her all that she was and could be and loved her as she wished to be loved— down into her soul she felt it. The Deputy had read the words, but she'd heard only Arbuckle's voice pure and strong.

And if she said it was the truth? Her eyes dropped and she bowed her head to look at the floor. The rug, which had covered it for five years, was threadbare right above the invisible stain. Lady Mae had lain on the floor at night for years tracing the motifs with her nails, the pile worn down and faded. If she said yes there was truth, then what? What then if she said no?

What am I supposed to do, Mama?

Why you got to choose, my girl.

"What say you, Lady Mae?"

"I—I don't know—I didn't know—"

"I, I, I, I—spit it out, girl."

The umbrella was close. But they had Arbuckle and they'd kill him. They'd kill her, too. The only way was to lie. She'd say no—Arbuckle would be charged with falsification, he'd get atonements. And when he came to the depot she'd have their bags ready. They'd stay there into the night; it wouldn't be the first time the butcher was with a patient in the dark. When it was safe, they'd sneak out the back and quietly run toward the hills holding their small bags tightly to their chests. They'd run until they could run no more, until the sun rose and their feet stopped underneath them. There they'd collapse, spent but alive.

"No," she said.

"You speaking truthfully, now?"

"Aye."

"Court's at eight, then."

He turned and walked out of her shack, down the gravel path, along the dusty road, and there in the emptiness of a darkened room, Lady Mae whispered Arbuckle's name, touched her heart, and closed the door.

14

When the sun rose the next morning, Lady Mae was sitting on the sofa in her living room. She stared at Arbuckle's empty cot, felt her great-grandmother's quilt around her shoulder blades. The night had brought with it dreams fearsome and wild, and every time Lady Mae closed her eyes there was only Deputy Iverson, her mother's ghost, the discolored knots in the pine floor. She saw it all again, watched it over and over as she had nearly six years before. A fear—the same one that had lived in her since—crept out of the dark chasm deep beneath her heart. She tried to disregard it; after all, Arbuckle's crime was different. He hadn't gone against his inheritance, just said the thing Lady Mae supposed she'd always known to be true: that she knew what was just and what wasn't. She felt it there as the sun inched its way above the peaks to the east. The trial would be quick; they'd cry falsification and atonements and after he arrived at the depot she'd wrap her arms around him, bring his lips to her own, and whisper *it was in me* and *you always known* and *how could I ever live without.*

Certain of it now, Mama.

Always were; just didn't know, my girl.

When the clock struck seven thirty, she rose from her seat and went to the door, next to which was her satchel. Before retiring for the night, she had packed several items in it. There was a photograph of her and her mother, the edges of which were curled and yellow. She had boots. A thick blanket. Three tins of canned food. It was all she could fit. They needed more, but they needed to get away, to run up into the hills while the earth was still warm and hospitable. They'd figure it out—she'd hunt since he disliked it, and in the glow of a night fire deep beyond the tree line, they'd feast on their spoils in a comfortable silence. Lady Mae placed her hand on the bolt of the door and turned it until it clicked.

As she walked down the crescent road, others came out of their small and dirty shacks. Word got around quickly; the residents had watched Arbuckle and Lady Mae for over twenty years and were no doubt eager to see the two of them together in the courtroom again. It was no surprise; the residents insulted Arbuckle as well, insinuated many things, all of which were equally terrible, but he and Lady Mae never spoke about it. That they did not repeat the words in each other's presence helped quell the embarrassment and shame Lady Mae felt. Arbuckle had been called a bastard and a misfit when he was young, a scoundrel and vagabond as he aged and went off into the hills. He was none of those things, but still, she saw how it smote him, how he carried it upon his shoulders. He hurt like her, and on the dusty road, she realized it for perhaps the first time. She'd be glad when they were free, even if it meant a life without a guarantee of survival.

Despite being awake since before dawn, she was the last to enter the courtroom on that sweltering day. The crowd, who sat facing the bench, turned as she opened the large wooden door. The residents' eyes fell upon her face, her skirts, down to her feet, which sweat in her tightly laced boots. Her throat went dry, and there was a surge in her chest that would follow her to her seat and stay with her long after the stares had subsided. She walked down the aisle and took the seat third from the back as the front was brimming with bodies already too warm for the room. She could see the accused's stand, and it was empty. Deputies Griffin and Worth stood before it. Arbuckle was somewhere in that building beneath her. He had spent a night under the watchful eyes of the Deputies. Maybe they'd already gotten to him and Deputy Daniels would come out from his chambers and tell the residents to go home. No one would object—Arbuckle and the ghost of his bastardly father would finally be gone. But then the large wooden doors behind her opened, and she turned her body to see Deputy Iverson, the four lines, his fat, sweating face underneath his tall hat. Behind him walked Arbuckle, flanked on the right by Deputy Parson. All five of the settlement's Deputies were in the courtroom; what if Lady Mae struck a match and sent them all into the sky?

Arbuckle walked across the threshold. He was bound at the wrists as she expected, but around his mouth they'd placed a scold's bridle, which was not uncommon but alarming still. Lady Mae clenched her teeth together and made sure to hold his eyes as he went past. As he proceeded down the aisle, she followed him with her gaze and tried unsuccessfully to disregard the other residents whose own eyes were upon her. When he got to the stand, Deputy Iverson on his left unlocked his shackles and Deputy Parson, the bridle; Griffin and Worth swung open the small wooden door so that Arbuckle could take his seat. The metal of the shackles and bridle clanged and jingled in the nearly silent courtroom, and as Arbuckle stepped up onto the stand, he turned and looked over the heads of the other residents to Lady Mae. The furrow in his brow softened, his shoulders loosened. She smiled at him and bent her head in his direction as if to say *it's all ready* and *only a few hours still* and *ain't nobody going to find us*. He looked away again and sat, his body and the wood meeting with a creak.

Deputy Daniels appeared at the door of his chambers. While he was not the worst of the Deputies, he had a reputation of baiting the accused. He had a tell—the way his voice would lilt in question—and typically the accused played right into his open hand. Arbuckle would not know that, and Lady Mae worried that he'd be drawn in like he was in the square the day he arrived. She'd warned him as best she could that day, though there was much more she would've told him had she known he'd end up in court only four days after having returned. The Deputy Magistrate sat, picked up his gavel, and as he did the residents packed into the viewing area grew still.

"In session, in session," he called and pounded his gavel on the bench three times. "Whereas from and after the publication of this law it shall not be lawful for any resident to willfully blaspheme the name of the Deputies or the law, by cursing or contumeliously reproaching one or more, and it is further enacted by the authority aforesaid that if any resident shall presume to reprove, they shall, for every such offense, upon due proof made thereof by the oath of the party before a magistrate, receive atonements in accordance with the law."

Deep down in her breast, farther than she had ever felt or thought of, a flame caught. It grew slowly, flickering and bending and licking the underside of her skin. She could not breathe, could not move her eyes from Deputy Daniels who sat with the gavel in his hand. He had said the word—blaspheme—the weight of which tried to pull her under the earth. Blaspheme. She thought of the Deputy reading Arbuckle's letter to her the day before—she'd heard it correctly and had wagered it all on what she knew: those who lied were charged with falsification. Atonements were given. But blasphemy, while still under atonement law, was what got residents up on the scaffold. And in the nine outcries Lady Mae had witnessed, no one—not a single resident that once stood on the scaffold—was still alive.

Deputy Daniels turned to Arbuckle. "State your name," he said.

"Arbuckle."

"In its entirety for the court."

Lady Mae watched his lips carefully as he spoke the name that carried with it all that he wished to forget. "Arbuckle Anfield."

"And how do you plead?"

"Not guilty," Arbuckle said.

"We are here to sentence you for the crime you committed yesterday. Are you aware of said crime?" asked Deputy Daniels.

"Yes." Arbuckle turned his head to look at Deputy Daniels as he spoke, and as he did he met Lady Mae's widened stare. He did not know—could not know—that once blasphemy had been spoken there in the stifling courtroom, there was no way out. It didn't matter that Lady Mae's satchel sat in her shack next to the door—that she hadn't brought it with her to stow at the depot. Arbuckle would never make it to the depot.

"You may put said circumstances in your own words for the court," said Deputy Daniels.

"I wrote a letter, and in it I questioned the how just the law is."

"That is all?"

"I reckon."

"Deputy Iverson?" Deputy Daniels called across the still courtroom. "Approach the bench with evidence."

He walked over to Deputy Daniels but held his eyes to Lady Mae. He reached into his breast pocket and took out the worn letter. He licked his lips as though he was thirsty for the accused. His throaty breathing rose and fell as he made his way to the bench. He handed over the letter to Deputy Daniels who then passed it to Arbuckle. Lady Mae wanted to shout *don't say nothing* and *you didn't mean* and *it is what I think*. For he had not simply questioned the law. Perhaps he thought he did, saying there had to be more for her and didn't she wish it, too. She did—but she had taken an oath to inherit her mother's lot, the butcher's oath that her mother and grandmother had taken as well. If she should waiver, she would pay for it with her life. She had blasphemy in her blood, dissent in her bones.

LAURA KAT YOUNG

And the Deputies weren't going to take any chances. But Arbuckle didn't know about that, and so when he wrote the words *I saw it in you* and *in you still* he unwittingly accused her of blasphemy, and in doing so committed blasphemy himself. And for that they would both hang.

"Could you read the letter? Aloud, please," said Deputy Daniels.

Arbuckle unfolded the piece of paper in his hand, and as he did, he looked up at Lady Mae. She held his stare, tried to shake her head no. But she could not obstruct the law any more than he could get around it. He cleared his throat and spoke.

"Dear Lady Mae. As I sit here the wind howls outside of my window, and I think of you. I try not to, for thinking of you has brought me as much misery as happiness in the years since I've been gone."

He looked up at her again, past the residents who sat with their backs to her. They tried to restrain themselves from turning around, though some feigned a coughing fit so that they could twist their body just enough to catch a glimpse of her. What did they wish to see? What was it that they so badly wanted from her? Tears balanced on the trembling, burning lids of her eyes. She did not dare raise her hand to wick them away but instead let them drop weightlessly, falling down her cheeks. Arbuckle saw, and his voice softened. He did not take his eyes from her.

"Many nights I've sat above the settlement thinking about sneaking back in and getting you, waking you in the middle of the night and running up into them hills. Thought long on it, but each time I did I couldn't help but think of your mama on the floor. What if you ended up the same way? Wouldn't be able to survive that."

He spoke the words without looking down at the letter. They spoke of an improbable future, one of which she had dreamed as well. She had no idea when he had written the letter, but—he had tried to tell her, hadn't he? The morning before, as they lay spent from a night of finding in each other what they'd been missing all along; maybe if he'd read it then and there this wouldn't be happening. She would've warned him, cautioned him against his words that were true after all.

"So I didn't come, and though I might've sent you letters and books, I ain't never said the thing I wanted to say. Which is that you got it, too, what your mama had. The knowing of the difference between right and just, that them Deputies got everyone fooled. She gave it to you, birthed it as she did your own self."

The words, which he knew by heart, came at her, and though she had heard them before, that moment in the courtroom she heard them as if for the first time. He had wanted her—her—in the hills and up the mountain. He'd left, and she'd understood why. He'd wanted to save her and the only way he could was to protect her from her own self. But those thoughts in her he spoke of—they were there all along. She had only been too afraid to see it.

"Been seeing that understanding in you all these years—I know that's what it is. So here I was setting down, but now I see. It's already in you, ain't it?"

His voice rose, clear and deep, and Lady Mae held on to it as best she could. But with each syllable, with each breath, he drifted farther from her, cast out alone by her own hand.

I thought and figured and weighed, Mama.

They weren't never going to leave him be, my girl.

As Arbuckle lowered the piece of paper to his lap, Deputy Daniels spoke. "Are these," he asked, "your own words and yours alone?"

"Aye," replied Arbuckle.

"And do you believe them to be full of truth?"

"Aye."

"May I ask how you came to such conclusions?"

It was his chance to clear his own name. All he had to do was say that he had spoken to Lady Mae over the course of days, months, years. She'd be called to the stand, and there she'd be charged with blasphemy. But he'd never do it, never. It had been in his voice; a stoic confession that held much more than the words he had written. "Just knew is all."

"And did you ever hear Lady Mae Hilvers state directly any of the things you claim?"

"No, I did not."

"Has Lady Mae Hilvers ever given you reason to doubt her allegiance to the Deputies?"

"No, she has not."

"I hereby declare that the accused has admitted to speaking on behalf of a member of our lawful entity and in accordance shall and will be charged with blasphemy. The court shall seek the maximum allotment of twenty atonements. In an effort to keep you from writing any further blasphemy, the butcher will take both of your hands. That will count for ten atonements. The other ten are at your will. Do you understand, Mr. Anfield?"

Arbuckle had looked at Lady Mae the entire time Deputy Daniels spoke. He did not blink nor flinch at any of the words but instead had held fast to her own eyes. The sentence wove in and out of her and pulled her down down down through the filthy floor and into the dank earth.

"You must report to the depot tomorrow at ten o'clock in the morning," said Deputy Daniels. "Two Deputies will escort you to your place of lodging to tend to anything necessary before your scheduled atonement. They will remain there throughout the night to ensure that both you and Miss Hilvers obey the law to the greatest extent. Is this understood?"

Lady Mae saw the Deputy Magistrate's lips move as he continued reciting the full sentence, but she did not hear him. Slowly she moved her eyes to Arbuckle and saw not the fear she herself felt brimming, but a calm that enveloped him in that dusty courtroom. It remained even as the Deputies retrieved him from the stand and led him down the aisle and out of the courtroom on that late summer's morning. Lady Mae, who heard nothing but the whooshing of panic underneath her skin, instinctively reached out as he walked by. Arbuckle grabbed her hand and before the Deputy could pull it away, he'd squeezed it three times, each one pressing up against her beating, breaking heart.

15

Lady Mae waited outside of the courthouse for Arbuckle. She sat on the steps, uncaring of the crowd that had gathered below. Though they pointed and whispered, she ignored them and instead stared at her hands. Two things were true. The first was that she could never harm Arbuckle. The second was that the Deputies would never let her recuse herself. She saw it clearly then, how the Deputies had finally found a way to make them all pay—her mother, his father, the two of them. They were pitted against the other, each having to follow a law they no longer believed in. In the end, the Deputies had them, and she felt the bending of her fingernails on the wood step. How much would they give until they snapped? She tested it, pushing down into the sawn oak so slowly that she felt certain they would bend entirely. Her nails lifted away from the tender skin underneath, but it did not hurt. Blasphemy. An eye for an eye, just as the law says.

She'd set her mind to it. When Arbuckle walked out of the courthouse, she was going to take him by the hand, and they'd walk down the steps and through the crowd side by side. Whatever was waiting for them they'd tend to it together, and when the sun rose the next day she was certain they'd know what to do. Twenty atonements—sixteen was the most she'd ever performed, eighteen the most she'd heard of herself. But his hands. What of that? If she could do it, he'd survive—would she? Or would she drown in her own life as soon as blade cut skin, her blood pouring into his own until he too choked? She couldn't lose him again.

I ain't alone no more, Mama.

You never was, my girl.

She heard leather soles on dust and the creak of the hinge, and she stood, brushing off the back of her skirts with her fingers. She wanted to turn to him and say *I can't* and *never harm*. But what would he say? Perhaps he would protest her worries and pull her in close, whispering that he'd thought of it the whole night through and had a plan. But what if her lie had turned him to ash? Would he believe that the conflict was still there just beneath her flesh?

"Morning, Lady Mae."

It was not Arbuckle's voice; instead what she heard was a familiar drip, liquid-like and hot. Instead, it was the one she knew like the pine floor grooves that lay

under the living-room rug. It was him. Deputy Iverson.
The one who—

Lady Mae turned slowly and saw Arbuckle standing
in between two men, one of whom murdered her mother.
The steps gave and the sun flashed and her heart lunged
toward the earth. It stilled for long enough that she
brought her hand to her chest, but she did not look at the
Deputy. She didn't need to; his eyes pressed into where
she touched her breast, and there they remained until
she felt a beat under her skin. Her mouth opened but no
words came out. If she moved or started at all, he'd have
her. And what then? She and Arbuckle were so close;
they had but one night left in the settlement. If they
could make it until dusk of the next day, then maybe.

Maybe, Mama.

You got more than maybes, my girl.

The hot sun glared down onto the four of them as
they stood on the courthouse steps. "Been assigned
watch," Deputy Iverson said. "I got it in me to make sure
the law is followed. Do anything that's necessary, too."

"What's that supposed to mean?" asked Arbuckle.

"Means I stand watch. Means I escort you to the
depot. Means you best shut up now, boy, lest you end
up like your pa," Deputy Iverson said, then tilted his
head toward Lady Mae. "Or her mama."

He'd said it. It was both a confession and boastful,
and as Deputy Iverson's words circled above, the black
scourge smoke-like and thick, she saw how it would

unfurl. They'd follow her back to her house and cross the threshold and stand in the exact spot where her mother's life was taken. Would he remember it as she did each day if she let herself? Or had her mother been just another resident who disobeyed the law? Perhaps there was a deep wake of bodies that carved its way through the valleys from settlement to settlement. Maybe there were other mothers out there, their brains beaten and bones left for meal. And what had their daughters done when they, too, watched their own flesh burn into the night sky?

Vengeance pushed at her. She heard her mother's whispers to forgive, but how could she? She could not forgive the Deputy any more than she could harm Arbuckle; but to act on it—to kill him with all her might—would only endanger her and Arbuckle. And so in that moment under the scorching sun, she decided to hate quietly and without abash; she would save her violent fantasies for the pitch black of night, and there it would play out. Her hand around his throat. A needle through his heart. His face in the dust. What she had loved had been taken from her, and no matter her mother's words, the dark odium remained just beneath her, lapping at the tips of her toes.

Deputy Iverson spat on the ground by Lady Mae's feet. "Go on now," he said. "Sure there's someplace you ought to be."

Arbuckle stepped forward and took Lady Mae's

elbow, but she did not feel it. Instead, there was only the hot breath of Deputy Iverson upon her neck. He followed behind the two of them, close but not too close, and as they walked in the direction of her shack, Deputy Iverson whistled low and long. Deputy Worth said nothing, but swung his watch at his side. He was bespeckled and thin, the quietest of the bunch, but he'd splay a man on the scaffold quicker than the rest and for that he was notorious.

Arbuckle wiggled his finger into the crook of Lady Mae's arm and pressed down through her sleeves. He was trying to tell her that it was all right—but there was little comfort in it. Unless Arbuckle had a plan, getting away would be nearly impossible, what with the Deputies standing watch. And it was her fault. She had lied, and though it had been a calculated one, it didn't matter. Twenty atonements. Both of his hands. Even if they stayed, even if she cut into him twenty times and left him limbless, would the Deputies be satisfied? Surely they'd find some way to get Arbuckle up onto the scaffold. Blasphemy. No one was left alive.

When they arrived at her shack, all four were wet with sweat. It slipped down their foreheads and their cheeks, sat trembling on the edge of their upper lips. Lady Mae did not dare raise an arm to wipe it away. She held on to Arbuckle, each step desperate and full of dread. It was a dread that had lain dormant since her mother died, the same one she had felt during that day so long ago when she mistook her mother's hesitation for—for what? She had been too young to know what questions to ask and would have been ill-equipped to handle any true answers her mother could have given. The only thing she had known was the suffocating alarm that tried to swallow her as she watched her mother run and stumble in the dusty road.

The Deputies stopped just short of the porch and watched them with silent eyes as Lady Mae and Arbuckle walked across the old drooping wood.

"We'll just be out here—wouldn't want to impose," Deputy Worth said.

"No, we don't want that," said Deputy Iverson.

Lady Mae opened the door, and Arbuckle stepped through first. She went to follow but heard Deputy Iverson clear his throat behind her. Without turning around, she hesitated, her hand on the frame, and listened.

"We'll be here, Lady Mae," Deputy Iverson said. "Don't you go getting any ideas."

"I ain't," she said.

"Good to hear. Specially since I know there's truth to that boy's letter. Don't think you're hiding it, Lady Mae. You ain't nothing if not like your mama. Might've fooled Daniels, but you ain't fooled me."

She did not reply but instead entered the house. As her eyes adjusted to the change in light, she closed the door behind her with a shaking hand.

"Arbuckle," she said. "You alright?"

He reached his arms around her and pulled her close. "Aye," he said.

"What'd they do to you?"

"Just asked me questions is all."

Lady Mae brought her hand up to his face and placed her palm gently upon his cheek. She felt his beard, thick and soft, and the muscles work beneath it. He was not telling her the truth.

"But you had a bridle on."

"Guess they didn't like how I was answering."

"Arbuckle," she said, pulling away from him. "It's my fault—that you got so many atonements, that your hands—I, I thought—the letter. What'd you think coming here with something like that? You know them words get you in trouble."

"I was going to give it to you, least tell you what it said. I started but—"

"I ain't let you finish, did I?"

"No."

"And then?"

"And then. Never thought about the fact I had it on me in my coat. Was thinking of other things." He bent and kissed her long and slow, and she gave into it, leaned in to the fullness of it all, her flesh alive with his touch. His hands found her body—his hands. She grasped them then and pulled him close.

"Arbuckle, if I'd heard what you said in that letter,

I would've burned it right then and there. When Deputy Iverson came and read it—I thought if I said it were true they'd hang me. Reckon I thought you'd get falsification. I didn't know—blasphemy—I didn't know, Arbuckle. I'm sorry, I'm so sorry."

"Hey now. You ain't done nothing wrong," he said and held her head to his chest.

"But you got twenty. And your hands!" She cried into him, let it come as it might. All those years stored up inside of her flipped quickly past, mournful and choking.

"Don't matter, right?" he asked and gently lifted her head. "I got your hands now, too, don't I? And I think I got a plan."

"But the Deputies are right outside—front and back. They're going to follow us—"

"I know it. I figured it. We'll play calm, wait it out through the night. Long as we stay inside, they should leave us alone. Tomorrow we'll go to the depot and you'll do one, and then they'll go. They'll see you going through with it, that I'm abiding. You've said it yourself; only time the Deputies stay is if a patient is violent, and I ain't that. They'll see you start, and they'll leave, and then we just wait till nightfall."

"I ain't going to be able to do it," Lady Mae said and stepped back, breaking their embrace.

"You'll have to," he said.

"Ain't no way I can hurt you."

"I ain't looking at it like that. And I reckon I'd gladly give up a hand to be with you."

"I can't."

"You're going to have to."

Lady Mae wrapped her fingers around one of his. It was warm and slender and rough to the touch. She bent his fingers down into his palm and held his hand in hers. If it meant they could get away—but as she was about to say *don't know* and *might be* and *hard to say*, another thought crossed her mind. It was quick and picture-like: she and Arbuckle standing over the lifeless bodies of the Deputies that stood outside of her shack. In the corner were the fire irons—it'd only take one blow to the head to knock them out, one pierce through the flesh to stop their hearts.

"I want to kill them," she whispered. It came out suddenly and with force, and Arbuckle lowered their still-joined hands and pulled her in close again.

"We ain't killing nobody. Don't got need to. Tomorrow you'll take my hand, and then when night falls we'll go."

"But my mama—"

"I know," he said. "And my pa—wasn't going to tell you but when I left here yesterday I found him—the one out there standing watch in front. Deputy Iverson. I asked him how it happened. How my pa died. I mean, I know it was a fire and all, but how'd it start? I asked him if they'd ever investigated."

"What'd he say?"

"Said my pa had started the fire himself on the stove, and when the walls caught he must've been too drunk to wake. But the thing is, Lady Mae, that he ain't never use that stove. The pipe was clogged and it ain't never get enough air to stay lit. Ain't no way a fire would live in it."

"Maybe he cleaned it out," Lady Mae suggested.

"Not likely. Hadn't been used in years."

"Did you tell anyone that?" she asked.

"No."

"But if that's true, then that means—"

"Means what we've always known."

"Your pa."

"Your mama."

"But why would they want him dead?"

Arbuckle shrugged. "Same as anybody would've wanted him dead," he said. "He was a terrible man— all them residents maimed under his eye. All the times them Deputies had to set out after him."

"What are you going to do?"

"Ain't nothing to do."

"But he's there," she said. "Right outside that door. We could do it—we could get up into the hills and—"

"And what?" he asked.

"But what he's done to us. To you and me both."

"It is our lot," he said. "But we'll get away, and both them Deputies will have to live with that fact—

might even be persecuted for it, them standing watch and all."

The room darkened suddenly, and they both turned to look out of the window. The sky, which had been clear and bright for so long, held gray toward the west. In the distance, they saw a cyclone of dust rise and fall from the ground. The wind had changed and with it would come the rains. If they could get away before the first drop fell, then it could be. Might be.

But what if we make mud, Mama?

Then mud is what you'll be, my girl.

"Lady Mae." He pulled at her hand. "We got this. We wake in the morning and go to the depot. Then this." He held up his hand. "It'll be quick and I'll be no worse for the wear. The Deputy will go away and then—"

But he could not finish the words for Lady Mae's lips reached for his and pressed gently against his flesh. She kissed him as she had always dreamed of— as if he would turn into dust should she pull back. If he turned, then she would, too. If she kept her lips on his, though, on the warm skin, faces touching, then they'd stay forever, their mouths and hearts dancing slowly until the end of time.

16

Lady Mae woke the next morning to sound of rain. She rolled over and let her arm fall to the other side of the bed, but it was empty. She sat up, saw the indent of where Arbuckle had laid his head after they had made love. She leaned into it, breathed in his scent, which was now mixed with hers.

Thunder cracked in the sky, and the rain came down in sheets so forceful that she rose and looked out the window to make sure it wasn't hail. The sky was gray and low; the drought had broken and the earth drank up the water greedily. The dusty road was thick and dark, and from her bedroom window, she could see the edges of Deputy Iverson who stood underneath the porch eaves. The rain whipped loudly against the shack; she could slip out her window and walk around. He wouldn't hear her. It would take only a moment, just one motion to slice his neck from ear to ear. The blood would be warm and would drip down into the mud. He'd be part of the earth. But her mother was already earth.

Won't let him near you again, Mama.

Ain't your cross to bear, my girl.

She moved away from the window slowly and began to dress. Although it was still warm she made sure to wear both pairs of stockings—it could get cold in the hills quick, especially when the winds changed. Arbuckle had often written of the snow and ice, of how the weight of it snapped branches and bent limbs as if they were simply the arms of a child. It was hard to imagine; although the temperature did fall with the seasons, the settlement never received more than a thin blanket of snow. She had already packed what she could, and that satchel sat at the back door. She could not bring another without raising alarm, and so she took the extra pair of gloves she held in her hands and tucked them down into the waist of her skirts.

As Lady Mae made her way toward the kitchen, she saw her great-grandmother's quilt neatly folded on the cot in the living room. She went over to it and stood quietly for a moment before picking it up. It was worn and soft and felt heavy in her hands. It would be difficult to leave it behind. She brought the frayed edge to her face and inhaled deeply. It smelled of Arbuckle and her childhood and the sooty ash of fires past. She buried her head into it, and though she could not recall exactly, she thought of Arbuckle wrapping it around her all those years ago and the hollow loneliness that followed. But she'd be lonely no more; she'd have Arbuckle and together they'd climb their way through the thicket and brush until they came to trees so tall and dense that there would be no way for the Deputies to find them. She folded the blanket, laid it on the cot, and went into the kitchen.

She saw the tips of his boots first. The worn, brown leather toes and mottled soles stuck out just beyond the table legs. They tilted outward, each toe pointing in a different direction as if he were asleep.

"Arbuckle?" Lady Mae asked as she stepped across the wood floor to the other side of the table. "What're you—"

She fell silent. It was a loud silence, hollering and rushing and wild, and it came at her fast and without warning. It filled her, stuffed her ears with its roar, and as her hands grasped and clawed at the fabric at his wrist, she saw where the cleaver had met skin again and again, the frayed muscle of his wrist, the half-severed hand on the floor nearly floating in a thick slick of his own doing. Lady Mae pressed her palm on his wrist, but it was too late; the blood had poured out of him already, and her gesture did nothing but darken her own skin. When she brought her fingers to his neck to check his pulse, the blood, sticky and wet and no longer warm, smeared on his skin jagged and rust-like. It was old blood, sour and deep.

"Arbuckle! Arbuckle! Wake up!" she cried and tore at the belt he had fastened above his elbow. She pulled it, felt it give, and as she did this his upper body moved, tilting toward her as she tugged. His eyes were open, but they did not fix upon her own. Instead, they stared at some far-off place. The cannery, maybe. His father's shack. Lady Mae's own kitchen table years before. She held his shoulders gently and pushed him back against the wall. There was a sweat on his brow, a sallow yellow underneath his lids. She picked up his injured hand, wanted to whisper *how could you* and *what've you done*, but instead she brought his hand to her cheek and pressed it upon her skin. It was cold and heavy, the fingertips already darkening.

This is how you started, Mama.

I know it, my girl.

"Arbuckle, come on," she whispered, but her words, which held in them a familiar fear, betrayed her. She had said his name, but what she meant to say was *you are my person*. She had called to him, but she could not pull the language from the sky to say *don't go*. To say *always it was you*. She wiped his upper lip, the sweat cool, and drew her lips to his. She held his limp, hand in hers, his bone shredded, she did not move, not even when the blood seeped through her skirts. If she didn't move. Then. He would be alive. Then.

"Arbuckle," she whispered. "Please."

It had taken half the night for her mother to die.

Lady Mae had waited, cradling her mother's head in her small hands long after they'd gone numb. The once warm skin of her mother's scalp had chilled her fingers even on that summer's night. She knew the weight of the flesh, understood when the breath became the soul. "Oh, Arbuckle," she said, her lips still lightly touching his. "What have you done?"

For just a moment, she thought his eyes held hers. She opened her mouth to scream into his soft ears that *I know now* and *I'll go with you* and *we can find* but the words wouldn't come. "Arbuckle," she whispered instead. She brought her hand to his cheek and leaned in, kissing his lips over and over again as if it would revive him, as if she could give a piece of her own life to him. She pulled away and placed her hand upon his chest, felt the muscle and give of flesh underneath, wishing for the beat of his heart one, two, and then nothing but the trembling of her own hand. Everything went still—her breath, the rain, the drips that fell from the ceiling into pans. She heard nothing but a muted hush, a soundless quiet so deafening she threw her hands up to her own ears and pressed them hard. She still heard it, though, and she wretched, heaving the hot spit out of her mouth over and over until there was nothing but the taste of sick in her throat.

Thought I'd have time, Mama.

We always think that of what ain't ours to hold, my girl.

He was gone—and she would've stayed forever by his side but for the Deputies outside her shack—and she unraveled the fabric that he had wound around the incision. She undid the coppery layers; his blood was sweeter than any she'd ever smelled. It was comforting, earthy and rich. Arbuckle's blood, her mother's blood— perhaps the way a person bled revealed their truest self; both Arbuckle's and her mother's had flowed quickly, and they were of the same mind. Forgiveness. Understanding. If it were true, that the blood was nothing but a reflection of what lay inside, then maybe Lady Mae's would boil instead of flow, thicken instead of run. Maybe it was slow and stuck, trapped underneath open wounds.

So this is what the Deputies made them do—cut each other and themselves till there was nothing but a pile of flesh on the floor. She lifted her hand from Arbuckle's chest and brought it to her mouth as she gagged again, a silent cry breaking through.

He'd been right all along; he'd seen who she was when she couldn't see it herself. She'd thought she was just the dust, the children, the scaffold, the spurning, the loneliness, the leaded weight of her inheritance. He'd known what was invisible to herself, and a rueful grief barreled through her, and she remembered that day in the road when the stones flew at her. They'd taken everything from her but her own life, and she'd had enough.

She leaned over Arbuckle's body and placed her lips against his one last time, pressing hard onto his cold skin. She held there, and murmured *I love you* and *it was always you* and *what'll come of me now*. And when she pulled away, a panic took hold. There she was in the abyss, and try as she might she had no one to hold on to. She stumbled to her feet, pulled the blood-soaked fabric of her skirts off her knees and shins, and stepped backward, her hands twisting into themselves, until she was up against the door. There, leaning up against her mother's cabinet, was her satchel. Beside it, her kit, opened. The cleaver still lay by Arbuckle's hand; Lady Mae instead pulled from the kit the heading knife. It was long and heavy in her hand. It gleamed, for though it was a butcher's tool, she did not use it often.

Then she peered through the kitchen window curtain and saw the brim of Deputy Worth's hat just outside the back door. It was the other one. She'd take him first, and her thoughts were wind through her ears, a tunneling of cries so loud she was sure Deputy Iverson could hear in front of the shack. She put her hand behind her and felt the iron of the knob, the cool touch of metal on her sweating palm. She turned it, and the door swung open.

Before Deputy Worth could even turn around, Lady Mae bore the heading knife straight over his head. A guttural cry came from him, a garbled plea to stop, but she didn't. Again she brought the knife to his head, slicing and cutting into his skin, his scalp. Over and over she hacked at him, the blood spurting and spraying onto her hands, onto the back steps. She kept going even when his voice ceased and his body went limp. One was for her mother, two for Arbuckle, three for his father, four for herself.

She stumbled back, the knife fell to the ground, and the rain whipped through the settlement. She climbed up the steps again and grabbed her satchel and kit. She looked through the doorway into the front room and saw Deputy Iverson just as he turned to look into the window. She threw herself to the floor beneath the cabinets so that he could not see her. From there she could see straight into the living room. She had only a moment before he would realize that the back door was open, and so she took it all in: the cot where he once lay, her great-grandmother's quilt, the ash pail, the sofa where their knees touched, the table she and Arbuckle had sat so many hours together. She scrambled to her knees, pressed her kit to her chest, felt the soft nudge of her mother, and then she ran one two three down the wooden stairs and onto the earth and one foot and then the other and faster still until her breath broke, her legs fire beneath her.

PART THREE

RELINQUISH

17

Lady Mae made it to the brush before the bells carried their song through the rain to the edges of the valley. There she crouched in the mud among barbs and thorns trying to catch her breath, and when she heard the bells ring out she stilled. It wasn't the ring of an hour or the announcement of a union; it was a frantic ringing, over and over, iron against iron again and again. It was an alarm, a call of caution that the residents had all been taught to heed, even Lady Mae. She knew how it would go: the women and children and men would hear the bells from inside their shacks and shops, or, if they were still sleeping, awake to the clamoring. The ringing would continue, and they might slip on their shoes and put on their coats, or, if they had already ventured away from their shacks, they would stop whatever they were doing and walk in the direction of the scaffold. Mothers would drag their children behind them, hurrying along in hopes of standing near the front. As they rounded the crescent road, they would see the tall hat of a Deputy who would be pacing the wooden planks. As they neared the scaffold, they would hear him spout *Arbuckle* and *Lady Mae* and *just like her mother*. There would be whispering among the crowd, low and hushed, their lips moving out of one corner, their hands still. But before long the words of the residents would rise, their chants loud enough for the Deputy to hear. He would raise his hand and point toward the hills, and at that moment the residents would erupt, their voices a roaring battle cry of obedience.

Get her, they'd cry. Take what she's took from us. And then they would charge, pushing into each other, scuttling around the children who were small and easily knocked to the ground. They'd chase each other down the crescent road, past Lady Mae's shack, to the edge of the settlement where one by one they would crawl through the same brush and scale the same rocks hoping to be the one who got to Lady Mae first. There was nothing to gain from being first but the satisfaction that they had finally gotten their hands on her after so many years. They'd take that anger, that simmering rage that flowed through them even in the womb, and they'd do with it what they would.

Maybe she should let them. After all, she'd done things; it was true. She'd done them because what else was she to do? It was her life or their limbs. She had felt the weight and strength of it as she held on to Arbuckle's wrist, rubbing the tip of her thumb across the lines in his palm. She hadn't the chance to make it right like her mother had, to hang forgiveness above one's own life; she had only the misfortune of watching her most beloved take their last breaths as she knelt helplessly before them.

Maybe she should go back, turn toward those that rushed at her and meet them, chain to chain and torch to torch. They would burn just as easily, their vengeful flesh meeting the sky. An eye for an eye. Would it be enough to levy the grief in her heart? Or would it do nothing but turn her own skin to ash?

She took a breath and wiped her brow. Though the blinding, flood-like rains blurred the mountains beyond, she knew they would shelter her as they had Arbuckle. And so she grabbed onto the branches that scraped up against her, pulled them taut and slid on her stomach until her head was through. She pushed her hands into the earth and sank, her face inches from the steaming ground. The rain fell harder still, and her feet slid in the clay-choked mud. Heaving herself forward, the branches and sticks cut along her arms and whipped the backs of her legs. But then she was through. She scrambled to her feet. Her skirts were soaked and weighed her down, and in front of her were the rocky hills. She stumbled forward and did so heavily, sick and slow in her guts.

What you gone and done, Arbuckle?
Weren't going to let them make you, my love.

She started climbing the rocks, reaching up as far as her clothes would let her, and pulled herself up little by little. The stone was sharp and scraped her palms and the insides of her wrists. There was the hot burning of open flesh to air, and she rested for a moment to hold her hands faceup toward the rain. The drops fell fast but barely washed away the blood stuck in the cracks of her skin. She lurched forward, stood high on the tips of her toes, and continued to climb. She counted her breaths, her hand over hand, the sound of her boots knocking and grinding into the rocks. One two three four five and she was over. The black gums and yellow birch stood before her, and into them she ran and ran until she could see nothing but the shedding limbs and furrowed bark that surrounded her. When she could run no more, she fell to her knees in the wet leaves and spat. Her chest pinched, and she brought her hand to her ribs, taking in long sips of air until her breath steadied.

Lady Mae held her ear in the direction from which she came. There was only the cry of birds seeking shelter and the slowed patter of rain on the canopy above. She climbed to her feet and went up the mountainside. It wasn't too steep yet, though she knew it'd get rocky quick. Arbuckle had said he'd been high up—the clearing, he'd said—but with the settlement still in view. She'd find it. If he were there she'd ask him *how far* and *was it always*, but he was not. She'd have to find it herself, remember the clues in letters written by his own hand. Crawl on her knees, claw at the clay-choked soil until she found his shack, the only thing left of him, if it was left at all. After that, she did not know. Arbuckle had said there was a farther still, past the valley and over the easternmost ridge—maybe she could go where Arbuckle had not, up and up to where the mountain met the sky.

She slung her satchel over her shoulder and walked. The ground gave softly under her boots, but the fallen leaves of the hemlocks, which carpeted the forest floor, kept the mud at bay. She walked quickly up the hilly earth, stopping every so often to turn around and cover her tracks. She might not fool the Deputies, but no resident would be able to pick up her trail. Even if they did, what would they do once night fell? Would they keep going in the thick darkness holding their hands out in front of them? No, they would fall back, retreat to their shacks and shops and be satisfied believing that they'd finally gotten rid of Lady Mae once and for all. She'd rest when evening came; until then she would keep going. It didn't matter that her thighs burned, that her breath was short and labored. She would not let the residents nor the Deputies get her. And so she walked quickly and with purpose, weaving in between the trees until the rain stopped and the sky darkened.

When it became difficult to see without a lantern or even a match, she stopped next to a large patch of sumac. On her hands and knees, she climbed under the shrub, breaking off the larger branches until she had made a space big enough in which to lay down. By the time she was finished, she could see nothing at all. She leaned back onto the blessed earth and let it cradle her to sleep.

Lady Mae woke with the birds. The sun had not yet fully risen, but the grosbeaks and orioles were already calling to others through the trees. In the space between sleep and wakefulness, she felt a peace; gone was the weight of her heart, the malaise that sat unmoving just underneath. But then she rolled over, and it all came back: Arbuckle, his shredded bone, the heading knife through skin, the weight of the Deputy, her feet in mud. It choked her, and the heavy sadness made her sick. She spat into the mud, coughing, heaving until the seizing and gagging subsided. Then she slid out from under the red blooms and pulled her satchel out from underneath the shrub.

She had clothes, but they were wet still. She pulled them out of the bag one by one until she lifted the last piece and placed it on the ground next to her. She took out the canned foods, no more than two, maybe three days' worth of rations. She'd have to be resourceful, careful, and eat only if needed.

Ain't got no right trying to save me, Arbuckle.

Only thing I knew to do, my love.

The clearing was southeast from where she was. But as it stood, she couldn't see the sun. She'd have to keep going until the canopy broke, though she hadn't had any food for over a day, and she was weak. At the bottom of her satchel was her kit. The knives would help her cut open an animal should she trap one; without them, she would not survive. But that was not all that it was. It was the only thing of her mother's she had. She had meant to take something more, but there was the rain and then his boots and marrow and silent heartbeat and—

She opened her kit and remembered: the cleaver next to Arbuckle's body, the knife in the Deputy's head. The only tools remaining in her kit was a small scalpel and the cutting scissors. She stabbed the tip of the scissors into a can of tomatoes over and over until she had made a hole big enough for the fruit to get through. She pried the metal back with her thumb. Then she tilted the can up to her mouth and drank the contents down, barely even stopping to chew when her teeth and tongue met the fleshy pulp. When she had emptied the can, she wiped her hand across her mouth and then her stomach, but in the morning light she could not tell where the juice ended and the Deputy's old blood began.

Her feet throbbed, and she was stiff from tip to tail. As she sat in the damp leaves, she levied it: she could turn back, meet those who had hated her one last time. She could wait until dark and then find her way back down the hills to the edge of the settlement in hopes of getting her hands on supplies—a trap, maybe, the cleaver and heading knife. Her great-grandmother's quilt. Or she could keep going up in hopes that Arbuckle's shack was out there still—that the Deputies hadn't yet burned it like they had his father's. Arbuckle had been there not even one week before. Perhaps he had left something that could help her—food, an oil lamp. But even if he hadn't, she'd take what was left. The shadow of his memory, his scent clinging to the walls. The soft silence of his ghost.

Just then, a grosbeak called, and a flock took flight. There was the rush of wings and a cry high and long. Lady Mae jumped to her feet. She spun around and searched in between the birch limbs, but there was no one there. Not yet. The residents were likely setting out again in hopes of finding her exhausted body face down in the earth. There was nowhere to hide, and so she threw her belongings back into her satchel and began to walk.

Sometime around midday, the hot winds stirred again. The canopy swayed above, dappled sunlight fell onto the ground by Lady Mae's feet. Though she was mostly shaded, she was sweltering and faint; her hand trembled when she held it up to her face. She'd foraged along the way—berries, some chicory, the heads of dandelion. It wasn't enough; if she didn't eat more in the next few hours she wouldn't be able to go on. She counted her steps as she went. One was her mother and two, Arbuckle and three, the Deputy. There was four who was Edith and five, Ruby and six, the brothers who attacked her so long ago. Seven eight nine ten, all faceless but there just the same. They followed her, a bundle of missing limbs and whispers that whipped against her ears. There was a pulsing and a cry, and she realized it was her own heart against her breast, her own voice calling out.

In the late afternoon, the land leveled and the trees thinned. The sun shone down through the canopy, a bright stream that flowed from sky to forest floor. Lady Mae walked on, stumbling and delirious. Up ahead was the tree line, just past it a small structure. She felt a yanking at her heart, a pull down deep in her belly. It was his shack—she was sure of it—and so she stepped forward, her eyes fixed on the shelter she would soon have. If they'd left it alone, maybe part of him might still be there. But even if they hadn't, he'd still be in there somewhere, buried deep down under stone.

Something moved to the right of the structure. It was a streak of black, perhaps a small bear. She had yet to encounter one, yet they were common this high up; she needed those traps. But then there was more movement, and she heard a man call out. She dropped to a crouch and crept along the leaves until she was behind a tree trunk she thought big enough to conceal her. She listened.

There was shouting, the slamming of a door. In the distance, horses danced. The Deputies had beat her there. That shack was the only proof that he had been—his own house burned, his body no doubt taken and torn apart. She had nothing of Arbuckle—no letter or book, no photograph.

She remained shouldered up to the birch and quieted her breath. The Deputies were too far away; though she heard their voices, she could not make out what they said. There was the low tenor of one, the high response of another, and others still. She'd done exactly what they'd wanted, played right into it. If they heard her, or saw a limb poke out from behind the bark, they'd be on her like wolves. And so she stilled herself and wondered what it was to even live if living was nothing more than one loss piled on top of the other until it smothered her. Maybe she should flutter her hand, put it out there where the Deputies could see. They would act fast, no doubt. Maybe it wouldn't even hurt, and all that time she spent thinking of what it might feel like to lose something, well, maybe it was nothing at all. Maybe the loss wasn't the thing itself—the finger or toe or hand—maybe the loss was the emptiness. What could have been. She looked at her own hands. The emptiness was there, right underneath the flesh.

Found your way in me didn't you, Arbuckle?

You was always in me, my love.

There was a whistle in the distance, the cracking of a whip, and the sloshing of hooves in mud. Lady Mae watched as the men and animals burst through the tree line farther south, the tall hats of the Deputies tucked under their arms so as to not get knocked off by the low hanging branches. They weaved in and out of the trees fast, the Deputies kicking their heels into the animals' sides. The horses cried out and reared, but they obeyed. Lady Mae stayed where she was until the last galloping faded away and the sky once again began to darken. When several hours had passed without another sound, she stepped out from behind the birch and began to walk the last few meters toward the structure beyond the trees.

Lady Mae found herself standing in front of a wooden shack not unlike those in the settlement. Arbuckle had built it with his own hands and for that, she fell to her knees inches from the first step. Placing her palms on the wood still warm from the afternoon sun, she pushed herself up one two three steps, dragging her feet behind her until her entire body was on the porch. The grooves and notches left by a hammer—and by Arbuckle's hand—held her body as she lay there, her eyes closed, the call of the wild his voice in her heart.

18

When Lady Mae opened her eyes, the sky was black. She had lain on the porch for the afternoon, or maybe it was the next night or the night after. Her clothes were dry in any case, and only the dark earth and the stars above surrounded her. She felt her way around and found her satchel. Then she crawled toward the door, which was wide open as if someone were expecting a visitor. She slid her hands up the frame splintered no doubt by a Deputy's axe. They had come for her. But the rain had slowed her, and for that she was thankful. Had her feet hit dry earth, had she run faster, they might have found her. If they had, she'd be dead like her mother. No trial, no scaffold, no atonements. They'd never let her go, and it was only a matter of time before they descended once again upon Arbuckle's tiny shack up in the mountains.

The moment she walked through the doorway she smelled Arbuckle and nearly collapsed at the threshold.

It tumbled toward her: the woosh of grief, the sharp bite of an agony so deep and fresh it was as though she'd been cut in half. Maybe she was. Maybe her mother was half and Arbuckle the other and now there was nothing. After all, what was left now? Lady Mae was there, in the same space Arbuckle had been only days before. And instead of having him by her side as they'd planned, she stood there alone, the gulf of loneliness wide and deep.

She felt around for a lamp; next to it were the matches. Taking one, she struck it on the wall and held it to the wick, let it burn down near her fingertips. The room brightened, and as the shadows flickered against the walls, the light fell onto the floor, onto books thrown open by searching hands. Volumes littered the planks, leaned onto each other as if someone had come along and stood them upright with unsteady hands. She looked more closely; the cot was torn apart, a shelf hung half off a wall. As her eyes adjusted, she saw also a broom, one shoe, the glass of a lamp. The Deputies had destroyed what was left of Arbuckle. Of course they had. While she slept in the sumac, while she'd been staggering through the forest. Maybe that day was not the first time the Deputies had been in his shack. Maybe the moment Arbuckle had stepped out to return to Lady Mae, they'd descended on it like vultures, tearing at it as they had her mother, trying to dig out the thing they wanted. Had they wanted his life, too, or only to make Lady Mae suffer as she took twenty of his parts? Either way, they would have known that one begot the other.

She lifted the lamp and gingerly stepped deeper into the shack. The first thing she did was walk over to the cupboards to search for food. She found oats, old bread, a jar of berries. She opened the jar, took a piece of the bread, and ate quickly, hungrily, the sweetness of the berries overwhelming and the crust of the bread cutting through her gums. The pain distracted her, and she was glad for it. She wanted to hurt as Arbuckle had. If she did, she could keep him close, the weight in her heart her anchor. She'd stay tethered, even if she could not stay in his shack among his things.

Lady Mae took up the lamp and turned around to more closely examine the one-room shack. She walked over to where the books lay on the floor and picked each one up. She flipped through the pages, turned them on their sides, and shook them as if a secret message were there. But nothing floated to the floor, and though she scrutinized the title of each, she could not figure if there was something there. If she had more time, maybe—but every item she touched delivered to her a sickening pain. She faltered, stumbled across the wooden planks wanting only to be near Arbuckle again, to drink in the smell of him. There, up against the back wall, was the broken cot, the mattress on the floor. Lady Mae went to it and eased herself down.

Her bones cracked as she did, her feet thankful for the absence of weight. She was tired. She hurt. She lay back on the mattress. So grief had her again, all the way up the mountain in a shack built by Arbuckle's hands, her body upon his bed.

Lady Mae rolled over onto her back and stared up at the ceiling. What was she going to do? She hadn't thought beyond finding Arbuckle's shack. She hadn't thought of anything beyond being close to him once again, his spirit next to her. And now that she was there, how would she leave? Where would she go? Even if she went over the ridge and past the valley beyond—what then? Settlement Six was out there, but she did not know the way. And even if she made it— would there not also be Deputies waiting for her on the edges, their torches raised high in the sky? Lady Mae suddenly realized that the only reason Arbuckle's shack was still standing was because the Deputies wanted it that way. They wanted to trap her, draw her to the one place they knew she'd go. And she had done just that. A fear rippled in her chest; it was only a matter of time. She could have days, hours, maybe just minutes, but the Deputies would make their way through the forest and find her. If she wanted to live, she had to leave.

She pushed herself up, and as she did felt something hard through the mattress. She thought it was a book, but when she pulled the mattress back, she saw nothing. She felt again. Yes, it was there, something, inside of the mattress. She stood, took the scissors from her kit and cut into the mattress. It was filled with hay and cotton and feathers, but as she reached in she felt something else. Paper. The rough ends of twine. She put her hand around it and pulled it out.

Letters. It was a stack of letters, maybe three inches thick, held together by string. She flipped through them; they were from her. Arbuckle had kept them all and had, for some reason, hidden them deep inside his mattress. As Lady Mae looked around the room, she saw other things—clothes hanging from pegs on the wall, reading glasses on the desk. He had left many belongings there in his shack, and suddenly it was clear: he had not intended on staying in the settlement. What he had wanted, what he had said, had been true; he had come for Lady Mae.

Why couldn't you have tried before, Arbuckle?
You weren't ready yet, my love.

She unwrapped the twine and took an envelope from the stack. Opening it carefully, gently, as if the paper itself were her own skin, she unfolded the letter to reveal words written by her own hand. It was dated three years before, and she read it, the only sound the beating of her own heart.

Arbuckle,
I hope this letter finds you in good spirits. Your last letter had me worried. And when I didn't get

a book—well, I about went up in the hills myself to find you. I came home Saturday though and it was there. Set right at my door. I saw it and thought now that Upheavals in Moral Development is going to take a long spell to read. But would you know that I finished it in under a week. Things been slow here. Guess everyone's too hot to do much other than what they have to. I reckon it's cooler up where you are. I like to think about you up there. Sometimes when I can't sleep, I picture you watching me, keeping lookout like you gone and done so many times. Makes me feel better, I guess. Safe. This shack ain't never been the same since.

Lady Mae lowered her shaking hands and put the letter on her lap. The tears fell heavily onto the creased paper. She watched the ink spread, turning the white space gray. She didn't remember writing that letter, or that specific book, but it mattered not; they were all the same. Volumes of beliefs, all of which amounted to the same thing. Forgiveness. Empathy. Redemption. Her hands, which held the letter tightly; they had not forgiven. They had taken the life of a Deputy, and for that, she felt a piercing dread. The Deputies would certainly come for her now. But that wasn't all—she had done the thing Arbuckle had refused to, the thing he felt so deeply in his heart was wrong. She had killed. She dropped the letter onto her lap and collapsed into her own hands, the weight of her grief choking and fierce.

Her breath broke, and she tried to calm herself. She did not wish to live, but she did not wish to die by their hands, and so she stood quickly and, opening her satchel, went over to the cupboards and emptied the oats and three tins into the leather bag. It wasn't much—a day, two maybe, but it was something at least. Then she went back to the mattress, picked up the letters, took a shirt off the wall, stuffed them into her satchel, and slung the bag over her shoulder. She grabbed the oil lamp and the matches. Maybe she would stumble upon a hiding place, a space unknown to even Arbuckle. Perhaps there she would sit upon the ground, push her arms through Arbuckle's shirt, and wait.

Next to the back door were traps, but they were large and heavy. She lifted one, the metal cold and rusty to the touch. If she took it, she'd have to carry it. And how long could she do that? How long did she expect to stay up there above the settlement? She'd go up, find a place to hide, and come back for the traps when it was light out. Until then she would walk, one foot in front of the other, the remnants of her life small enough to fit inside her satchel.

19

There was a path in the middle of the farthest tree line. The lamplight bounced as she walked, but it was enough for her to follow where the trees broke. The ground was rocky but clear, and as long as she went slowly, she could reach the ridge by sunrise. She'd escaped their torches and chains, and had come away with her life. To turn back would be certain death, and while she did not know what lay on the other side of the mountain, she was willing to take the chance. Arbuckle had said there was a whole world out there. But Lady Mae did not care for any world that did not have Arbuckle in it, and so while it would only take a few more days to be up and over the ridge, she did not wish to. To leave was to leave her mother. It was to leave him.

What you want me to do, Arbuckle?
What you been doing your entire life, my love.

She walked quickly at first. Arbuckle must've cleared

the path. How long had he stayed in his shack until he struck out to see what was on the other side of the mountain? How many times had his own feet walked upon the same soil? The air, damp and hot, clung to her.

There was a snap beneath her foot and a piercing of leather and flesh. She cried out and fell to the ground. The lamp crashed and broke, the flame extinguished. In the pitch black, she tore at her leg and foot and felt the trap's teeth stuck in her just above the ankle. She saw nothing but sparks, heard nothing but the deafening silence of the forest. She rubbed her fingers together, felt the gliding warmth of her own blood; she could not tell how deeply she'd been cut, but did it matter? Her hands traced the trap until she found the release. She pried the trap apart, the long teeth rusty no doubt, and threw it off the path.

She had to stop the bleeding but had no tourniquet. She opened her satchel, searched around the tin cans, the ends of her dress, until her hands fell upon Arbuckle's shirt. Lifting it out, she felt her way past the buttons and pocket to the sleeves. There in the pitch black of night she wrapped his shirt around her calf and tied the sleeves together as tight as she could, which was not tight at all. If the blood slowed, she could make it until morning. But the wound was deep. She'd need to clean it, cover the gaping punctures with cloth she did not have. There was no stream nearby, no small lake to take from. All she could do was wait until light, and so she sat there in the darkness, the depth of the night dancing before her eyes.

She woke with the sun. She had slept fitfully, had dreamed of Arbuckle. He'd been standing in the square, suitcase in hand. Lady Mae called to him, but he could not hear her. The clock tower struck, and he stepped toward the courthouse. She called again and again, but he did not turn around. She tried to run to him, but her legs were heavy with mud, and each time she picked a foot up, it was like fire on skin. She stumbled, her hands waving, but it was no use. Arbuckle disappeared into the courthouse, and she was alone once again.

As she sat up, she did so gingerly as each movement brought with it nauseating pain. She'd never been injured this badly before—not even when Edith threw the stone at her head. Arbuckle's shirt was damp and dark; she had stopped the bleeding, but the gashes in her boot were large. She needed to get her boot off, her stocking, too. She untied the boot—took the laces all the way out—and slowly slid it off her foot. With each inch, with each pull, it felt like someone dragging a knife over her flesh. She bit her lip and breathed in once. Then she yanked the boot off her foot.

It was worse than she'd thought. The laced boot had actually helped; with it off, the air hit open skin. Her stomach turned, her mouth watered. She had worn her heaviest stockings; the wool was shredded and stuck to the blood, crusted and brown. She slowly peeled the yarn from the wound so as to not open it up again, but it was of no use. Before the stocking was all the way off, she'd begun to bleed again. It was a slow trickle, but still. With her finger, she tried to feel how deep the wound was, but she stopped at her first knuckle, turned her head, and vomited.

When the sick subsided, she put her hands on the ground and tried to push herself up. The pressure on her foot was unbearable, and she fell to the ground and squeezed her fingers into her palms until her nails nearly pierced through. Even if she could walk, what then? The trap had been metal, the rust ample. Even if she made it to the ridgeline, she'd die of the poison that was already in her. If she were in the settlement, if she had her tools, she'd go to the depot and take the bottom of her leg herself. There she'd be able to clean it and cauterize the stump. She'd have grain alcohol, a leather belt to bite down on.

Now I'll go the same as you, Arbuckle.

Ain't going to let you, my love.

If she waited long enough, the poison that was surely inside of her would kill her. After all, what would it be to live now? She'd thought the grief would kill her when her mother died, but Arbuckle had been there. And when she didn't have him any longer, not in the flesh at least, she'd had his letters. The letters—she felt down to the bottom of her satchel and removed the small stack, still held together with twine.

As the sun strode across the sky, she read them. One by one, she carefully opened each envelope and unfolded the paper slowly. Sometimes they were short, sometimes pages long, but there in her words she saw that justice had been in her always. But what good was it to her now? It had saved no one, barely even herself. It was too late, and she would die in the path carved by Arbuckle's hands. The earth would hold her until she was no more, and as she disappeared into the dirt, the clay, the loam, she would be near him once again. They'd both tried to save the other from harm, and in turn had inflicted a finality upon themselves. At least she'd read the letters—all of them—before she gave into it.

She counted the letters. There were nine left. Each had her name written in the corner and had been sealed by her own hand. She took one, opened the envelope and took out the paper inside, but as she did another piece of paper fell to her lap. Expecting to see perhaps a drawing she might have made for Arbuckle, or a page she had torn from a book that he had sent her, she put the letter to her side and unfolded the extra paper. There, on the yellow, creased sheet was her mother's handwriting, perfectly formed and looped from one side of the page to the other. Her heart slipped and tumbled its way down. Her eyes rushed, frantically trying to understand what she held in her hands.

Dearest Arbuckle,

I reckon what I'm about to say ain't going to be what you want to hear. But you been coming around now for years, and I think on you as one of my own. I am glad that you found in my daughter and me a place of comfort. A home. But even though we think you family, you ain't family. You got a family. Well, a pa at least. And I know that he treats you something terrible and for that I am more sorry than there are words for. And I ain't in no place to make excuses for that man, because you ain't wrong. He's awful to everyone, including me. But he's your pa, and that hatred that you feel in your heart ain't going to get you nowhere. It's forgiveness, Arbuckle. I don't mean you need to go and forgive your pa for all he's done. It ain't him that deserves forgiveness. But you do. Don't you know I see you brooding? Don't you know I see you hating who you are? I'm here to tell you you got every right to hate that man. You got every right to want to be far away from him. You don't let that go, well, it'll eat you alive. Find peace, boy, and know in your heart of hearts you do the best you can.

She watched the ink spread from her tears, little pools of black dotting the page. The letter had no date. Her mother must've slipped it in the envelope without Lady Mae knowing. How long had her mother thought of forgiveness? How long had she butchered with the desire to absolve not only her patients, but herself? Had she forgiven herself for letting that little boy go? For knowing what that meant? Maybe that was the thing: her mother had done what she needed to in order to right her own way in the world. She left it with a clear conscience; she'd stayed alive until Lady Mae could go on without her. She'd birthed her and loved her and protected her. Arbuckle had protected her, too—from her own loneliness and unrest. And here she was dying all alone on the mountainside, the words of her mother and lover spilling into her lap. They'd say *go and do what you need* and *it'll be alright in the end.*

She put the letters back, stacked the envelopes neatly, and tied the twine around them. She held them close to her heart, her head bowed. Once the poison set in—and she still had time as the wound was not yet black by the edges—she would not be able to walk. If she could take her leg before then, she might live. And if she lived, maybe Deputy Iverson—what would she do if she had the chance? Her mother had been right. Arbuckle, too; she should forgive, but what then? Let him rot underneath the courthouse?

She grabbed her boot, took a deep breath, and slid it back onto her foot. Then she took the laces and pulled and pulled until her fingers and palms turned white. Knotting the laces, she stood, and put her foot flat on the ground. She lurched forward and bit her tongue, sucked in air through narrow lips.

What will my hands still do, Arbuckle?

What they need to, my love.

20

When Lady Mae's feet met level ground, it was still dark enough to conceal her shape behind the asters and switch grass that bent in the soft breeze. She squatted down upon the earth, which was dry and hard, slowing her breath until her ears cleared. Then she listened. There was nothing but the call of a hawk far off in the distance and her own boots in the dust. She could see through the dried stems and seedpods the back of her childhood shack. There it stood—still stood—and though she wanted to tear through the brush and run up the steps, she could not bring herself to move. Either Arbuckle was there or he was not there, and she wanted only to remember his boyish face, his soft beard, his gentle hands upon her shoulders. No, she would not go back even if it meant one last time, for it would swallow her up.

The bells rang. The clang of metal hung in the air. They were steady, one long ring after another. It was a call to assemble, an order for the residents to follow. She could see the crescent road through the asters and the narrow gangways between the shacks and watched as the residents came out of their shacks and stepped into view. There was Mr. and Mrs. Tarvis, Ruby, Edith's poor parents. They walked slowly, carefully. It was as though each step itself was an atonement, the robbing of flesh as payment for sin. But they could not help but do it. Lady Mae wanted to call out to them, say *I'm here*. But when she opened her mouth, there was only the feel of air in her mouth and taste of sick in her throat. She watched the residents as they appeared and disappeared between the shacks, their small bodies powerless and resigned. Lady Mae crawled to her hands and knees, still hidden behind the asters. The residents walked in the direction of the square, and so Lady Mae, who was nearly dead herself, followed in the brush. She'd be able to stay hidden, take the long way around to the depot. If the residents were all in the square, no one would see her slip in through the back. There, she'd take her leg.

When she reached the curve in the road where the clearing was, she stopped. Beyond the clearing was the scaffold, and a crowd had gathered below it. It took only a moment—the high of day, the bells, the slow shuffle of the residents' feet. It was Saturday, market day, and if she squinted and strained to see, she'd be able to make out a man or a woman or a child kneeling on the splintered wood, the chains of the Deputies shining in the sun. The wind picked up and carried with it the crying of an infant and the whip of a rope. The crying stopped, the bells rang still, and Lady Mae found herself walking slowly to the edge of the brush instead of toward the depot, dragging her injured foot behind her. Maybe she was delirious, the poison blanketing her brain. But it was as though Arbuckle's hand nudged her, said *you got to see* and *he's right there* and *you ain't dead yet.*

She did not try to conceal herself as she walked up to the back of the crowd; after all, what could they to do that had not already been done? But as she was nearly there, she stepped on a fallen branch no bigger than a child's arm. It snapped, and a little boy who was not one meter from Lady Mae turned his head. She put her finger to her lips, her eyes softening, pleading. The boy pointed at her first, then reached his other hand up to the man that stood next to him. He tugged at the man's sleeve, and the man's eyes followed the boy's outstretched arm.

When the man's eyes fell on Lady Mae, three things happened. The boy cried out *the butcher,* the man looked down, and one by one, the residents shifted their bodies toward Lady Mae. They turned their heads slowly, raised their own eyes to her. They heaved before her, their bodies pressed up against each other like bricks. She waited for the first shout; torturer, they'd cry. Get her, they'd chant. She waited for the rush of skin; would they grab at her scalp and pull her to the ground, pounding her flesh until it looked like the earth?

But then. Nothing happened. The man gently put his hand on the child's head and leaned down to his ear. He whispered something and the boy turned to Lady Mae and bowed his head. The woman next to him bowed her head, too, and then another. One by one the women and men—those that had lost pieces of their ancestry to Lady Mae and her mother, to her mother's mother—softened their eyes and held their hands out palms facing sky. The stillness was broken only by the Deputies, whose feet shuffled on the scaffold as they tried to corral the woman they had pinned. But the rest, the old and the young; they stood silent but hopeful.

Maybe the residents had seen the love between Arbuckle and Lady Mae, had felt it all the way deep in their bones. Maybe when they looked over at the other side of the bed come morning they'd thought of the two of them, the butcher and the only boy that loved her. All that her mother had talked about—what she said the residents spoke of when in the chair. Forgiveness, that maybe if everyone had a little more there wouldn't be need for any Deputies at all. They weren't going to hurt her, and she was done hurting them.

The Deputies scrambled around the woman on the scaffold and Deputy Iverson broke from the circle and grabbed a megaphone from the scaffold's floor. He stood, his belly hanging over his belt like pregnant swine. He had one hand behind him, his palm pressed up the bottom of his back. He brought the megaphone up to his lips, which he licked slowly, purposefully, as if the taste of her death was there on his tongue.

"But as for this enemy of Settlement Five," he bellowed as he pointed a finger toward the poor woman who hunched from the lashes. "Bring her here, for blasphemy is slaughter and slaughter is divine."

Those at the front of the crowd who had not seen Lady Mae still cheered. But the others, the ones who had regarded and nodded and parted and gently tucked their children aside—they said nothing. Lady Mae took one step forward, then two and three and the residents whispered her name, said *like your mama*, and suddenly she understood. Deputy Iverson, who heard the thinned cries, lowered his megaphone and put his hand to his brow. The other three Deputies that had been restraining the woman dragged her to the center of the platform and there they pushed her down, her weak body falling at the feet of Deputy Iverson.

"Any blasphemous resident shall surely be put to death," he yelled into the speaker. "They shall be broken and put in the earth; their blood shall be upon them."

His voice was long and low. Lady Mae walked slowly, dragging her leg behind her. She limped and winced, and as she did, each resident pressed softly upon her arms or shoulders, their stump-like limbs cradling her as she went. They were carrying her, passing her from one to the next carefully and with purpose. All the while Lady Mae kept her eyes on Deputy Iverson, caught the gleam of the megaphone, the four lines across his cheek. She heard the salvation and the whip of flickering orange against the early blue sky. And suddenly it was all there with her: the stones at her back, her gray, tangled web, the stain on the floor. The stick through her skull, the ashes in the wind.

Their eyes met. When Lady Mae saw Deputy Iverson's upturned mouth and the way he held his palm against his belly, she tried to listen. His lips made *get her* and *can't live*, but she did not hear it; instead she heard only the sound of a whisper, feet shuffling, boots in the dirt. The shape of a knife poked into her palm, handle first.

The other three Deputies dropped their chains but held their clubs and moved away from the woman on the scaffold. They advanced toward where Lady Mae was quickly, but Edith's father jumped up onto the scaffold, and he threw his body upon Deputy Daniels. Then Mr. Tarvis scrambled up and pried the club out of Deputy Griffin's hands and shoved him down onto the wooden beams. Deputy Parson took two steps back now that he was outnumbered, but there was nowhere for him to go and so he teetered on the edge of the scaffold above the cries of the crowd.

Lady Mae turned her head back toward Deputy Iverson. He dropped his megaphone, and it rolled off the scaffold and into the dust. He fumbled with his chain, but before he could loosen it from his belt, a woman ran behind Lady Mae, up the steps, and onto the scaffold. Ruby.

She lunged at the Deputy who, so surprised, stumbled first to the side and then lost his footing. He fell, and though he thrust out his arms, he could not break his fall. He landed with a thud. There was an instant snap and his leg stuck out at an angle from underneath him. Ruby scrambled behind him and grabbed his necktie, pulling it up behind his head.

"I got him, Lady Mae," Ruby huffed.

Deputy Iverson's feet kicked and his hands tore at his throat, but he could not get away. Lady Mae had dreamed easily of the *how*. But there she found herself and there was no needle, no iron through his skull. His face grew red then redder still. He kicked and tore at Ruby with his hands, but she grabbed them with one arm and pinned them to her side. Lady Mae stared into the Deputy's eyes, which bulged and begged, and she did not look away.

Ain't gonna let him live, Arbuckle.

Forgive your own self, my love.

"What do you want me to do?" Ruby called.

"Don't let go," Lady Mae said as she took one then two steps, wincing, her foot fire until she was nose to nose with Deputy Iverson. Ruby pressed all of her weight down onto the man, hoisted him up nearly off the scaffold. He cried out, but Lady Mae heard only the guttural longing for pity, a last attempt to save himself.

Lady Mae took her knife, the knife some resident had passed her, and knelt before the Deputy, his mouth open, his throat seizing and choking. If she let him, he'd suffocate out there on the scaffold in front of all the residents. Already they shouted, stomped their feet in the dust once again. Their roars filled Lady Mae's ears like water, and she held on to the wave. Felt it deep in her bones like she had with Edith, that time on the telephone, on her back porch steps. It was a fury dark and pure.

"You took my mama."

On her knees she whispered it, bent her body so that her lips were near his ear. She said it slowly, her voice pausing between each word. She did not have to push hard to pierce the flesh; it gave easily like the sandy bottom of a river. She pulled the knife back out and watched as the cut remained clean for a moment. Then the blood bubbled up and ran down his neck, breaking off and branching away.

"Arbuckle, too."

She spoke louder, a rush of wind in his ears, her voice steady. Her left hand held his right ear at the lobe, and behind it she pushed the blade into his skin. His feet kicked, his body spasmed. He thrashed at her hands, but Ruby leaned over and grabbed his fingers, bent them back until he cried out. Bloody cricks became rivers, and the white of his collar turned dark.

"My life. Took my life from me."

She unstuck the blade from his skin quickly and without effort brought the blade just underneath his jawbone. She slid it into the Deputy, and moved the blade across. She made another pass and then another, spilling from his throat a reminder of what she'd lost. What had been stolen from her. And Deputy Iverson, who bled the same as any man, seized and shook before falling still in the bright light of the morning.

21

When Lady Mae woke, she was in the depot leaning back in the chair. She felt the hard leather beneath her, smelled the antiseptic in the hot, sticky air. She heard the shuffling of feet and clearing of throats. As her eyes focused, she saw that Ruby stood to her right, to her left Edith's father. They each held one of Lady Mae's hands, worry on their faces. She understood before she saw: her leg, dead and poisoning her body, was gone.

"Don't try to move there, Lady Mae," Ruby said. "We had to go and wake you up. We did what we could, but you ought to examine it yourself to make sure you'll heal."

Ruby squeezed Lady Mae's hand quickly and nervously, wincing at each press of the palm. Even still, she held on to Lady Mae who leaned into the touch. Her leg was fire and her heart scorched, but she was alive. And Ruby, the only one to ever say something kind about her mother, had been the one to save her.

"I don't understand—how—" Lady Mae took her hand from Ruby's and lifted the sheet up to peer underneath. Beneath her knee was nothing, the empty space full of sparks on invisible skin. She felt the need to wiggle her toes, point her foot forward, and stretch her shin. She tried to sit up and swing her feet—her foot—over the edge of the chair, but Edith's father pressed her softly back.

"You ought to know you've got to recover a bit."

"But how did you? How'd you know—"

"Well I can't rightly speak for all them residents," he said, "but Ruby and I figured we'd heard about atonements so much, nearly learned how to do them ourselves. Grown up knowing about which veins to avoid, how fast someone can bleed out. Almost like we'd been doing them our whole lives. Reckoned we ought least give it a go. Thought we lost you there up on the scaffold. Glad to see we didn't."

Of course. They were born and raised thinking about their turn in the chair, for in the end, nearly all ended up there. Did they gather around the kitchen table late at night, tell their wives and husbands and daughters and sons of how deep the first cut was? Did they pay attention, past the pain and delirium, watching as Lady Mae, her mother, her grandmother, and great-grandmother had clamped and burned the ends of veins into one tangled mass?

You thought you knew too, Arbuckle.
Just cut too deep is all, my love.

Ruby's hand moved down the length of Lady Mae's arm, and Lady Mae saw the four fingers wrapped in cloth, fingertips swollen, the heel of her wrist scraped and bruised.

"But the Deputies—" Lady Mae said.

"Ain't none left," Ruby said. "And seeing how there ain't no one that'll tell anyone, we're going to aim to keep it that way."

"But others could come—they could kill us."

"Maybe," said Edith's father. "But there's more of us than they'll ever be of them. Stands to figure that what happened to those on the scaffold would likely happen to any sent our way."

"It's okay, Lady Mae," said Ruby softly at her side. "Ain't nothing going to get you now."

In the weeks that followed, the residents showed Lady Mae many kindnesses. Ruby insisted that she recover in her care, and so she and Edith's father had carried Lady Mae down the dusty, crescent road to Ruby's shack and laid her on an old cot. As they went, residents had come out onto their porches, stepped into the road. They took their hats off and gently tilted their heads in her direction. Gone were the narrowed eyes, the aversion that balanced on their shoulders. She did not fully believe that the hatred had disappeared, but she hoped it was so.

Edith's father, who had long done woodcraft, came one day with a prosthetic for Lady Mae. It was rare that such a thing was done; for although life was more difficult with fewer hands and feet, it was a permanent reminder of one's atonement and part of the punishment.

When the old man handed her the delicately carved wooden leg, Lady Mae held it in her shaking hands. There on the bottom, just like she'd etched in her own shack so many years before, were a dark L and M, branded into the oak with irons. The sides of the leg were ornate with swirls of honeysuckle. The oak itself was pale but sturdy. It could take her up the hills and back onto the mountain. She sat there cradling the wooden leg until night fell trying to figure what to do. The residents would have her if she wanted, but would she ever really be free if she stayed? Everywhere she went, she'd see her mother, Arbuckle. The depot, even if it were old and run down and empty. The cannery. Where Arbuckle's shack once was. The burn pile. The square. No—she needed to get away. She would go back up the mountain as she had planned, to Arbuckle's shack where she could be near him forever. And though the residents had begged her not to, said *you got a place now* and *nothing left up there*, she would spend the rest of her days with Arbuckle's ghost.

Three months after she killed Deputy Iverson, Lady Mae packed her satchel and struck out down the crescent road. It was early, and there were none about. She limped and hobbled like the other residents now, but she did not mind. As long as the earth was dry, she could move freely even if slowly. Her bag was full and heavy, and Ruby had promised to bring her supplies once a month. They did not wish her to go, but understood.

Before making her way to the settlement's edge where the switch grass met the hard, dry earth, though, she had needed to see for herself. When Lady Mae arrived at her own shack for the last time, she hesitated at the rocky, overgrown path that led to her porch. From where she stood, she could see the eaves were charred black; the Deputies had been there, their torches scarring the ceiling. When they entered her shack and found no one there but Arbuckle's lifeless body, what did they do? When they opened the back door to find the Deputy lying face down in the mud, did they cry out? Did it matter that one of their own was dead? Or did they only care that it had been done by Lady Mae's own hands, their desire to punish her greater than their loss?

She walked up to the porch and opened the door, stepping into the living room. Although it was early morning, she was met with darkness and the unmistakable scent of rotten flesh. As her eyes adjusted, she expected to see her shack torn apart as Arbuckle's had been. But everything was as she had left it. They had not gone through her things to find evidence of betrayal, of blasphemy. They did not need it, for they never intended on letting her live. She understood. She had been just a pawn, just like all the other residents, used by the Deputies to get what they wanted.

You wouldn't let nothing ever happen to me, Arbuckle.

Only thing I was willing was my life for yours, my love.

In the stillness of the room, she walked toward the kitchen. Arbuckle's body, now mostly just a pile of bones, was where she had left it, slumped up against the wall behind the table. His head still leaned up against the wall, and she buckled and crouched down in front of him. She took the bones of what was his left hand and curled her fingers around them. They were dry and hard, and she wept. There was time now. No one would come for her, so she sat on the floor opposite Arbuckle and, hands entwined, spoke to him.

"I know you might be in there still, Arbuckle. Maybe you can hear me, but even if you can't, know that you were right. All them words, all them years you talking about forgiveness. I understand—found the letter from my mama. She was right, you know. You were always so hard on yourself, and I know you aimed to be better than your pa. Wish you would've known that you were since the day you were born. All that talk about forgiveness. Weren't about nobody else, were it? Was about what's in here." She tapped her chest with one hand. "Were about being able to wake up day in and day out and know you've done right by yourself. That's what tore at you, weren't it? You always trying to live for someone else. For something else. But that's what they did, ain't it? Made it so our lives weren't never our own. We ain't had no choice how to live. Only choice we had was how to feel. My mama was right—but you know that. Always was, I suppose. Living by her own truth killed her. Living by yours killed you. Nearly killed me, too. But we did it, didn't we? Did the right thing in the end, I mean."

She took the bones of his hand, put them into her bag, and stood. It was nearly dark outside, but she could see enough to walk into the living room and gently lift her great-grandmother's quilt from the sofa. She hugged it close, breathed in the smell of it, of her mother, of her home she once had. She carefully draped it over one arm, and with her free hand lifted the glass lamp by the door. Pulling out the wick, she turned it over and poured out the kerosene onto the sofa. Then she picked up a match, struck it on the wall, and watched it catch. As it burned down the wooden stick she thought of all that she lost, and she had lost so very much. She'd found something, too, though. Love. Acceptance. Forgiveness. All the things she'd wished for her whole life were there now, right in front of her. She tossed the match onto the sofa and for just a moment, watched the flames dance and grow. Then she opened the door, felt the hot wind upon her flesh, and walked out of her shack.

ACKNOWLEDGMENTS

I'd like to thank the many people in my life who gave me love, support, and guidance during the years in which I worked on this book. To my family for making sure I had the time and space to write and for loving me endlessly. To Bill Lovaas, your spirit and love means everything to me. To my Dewey Lounge crew—Jolene McIlwain, Jan Elman Stout, Dave Barnette, Jean-Marie Saporito; writer friends are the best friends. To my colleagues—Peter Kahn, Erika Eckart, Bernie Heidkamp, and Aaron Podolner—thank you for reading and championing my work. To my teacher Lee Martin at VCFA for pushing me to stick with the story even when I doubted myself. To my #PitchWars mentor Carolyn Topdjian for recognizing promise in my first draft and guiding me to exactly where I needed to go. To my agent, James McGowan, for working tirelessly to ensure that this book found the perfect home. And to my editor at Titan Books, Sophie Robinson, for her keen eye and spectacular vision.

ABOUT THE AUTHOR

Laura Kat Young is a writer and teacher living in Chicago with her family. Her works blend genre and seek to explore a deeper understanding of human behavior. The 2019–2021 Writer-in-Residence at the Ernest Hemingway Foundation, her works have appeared in *The Blood Pudding*, *Shoreline of Infinity*, *The Lindenwood Review*, and others. *The Butcher* is her debut novel.

www.laurakatyoung.com
@writerlylaura

For more fantastic fiction, author events,
exclusive excerpts, competitions, limited editions and more

VISIT OUR WEBSITE
titanbooks.com

LIKE US ON FACEBOOK
facebook.com/titanbooks

FOLLOW US ON TWITTER AND INSTAGRAM
@TitanBooks

EMAIL US
readerfeedback@titanemail.com